P
Josie Marcus,

D0546231

Murder

"Without a doubt, the combination of love, humor, and wedded bliss truly distinguishes *Murder Is a Piece of Cake* as one of Viets's very best." —Fresh Fiction

"A well-written, well-plotted mystery with several good suspects ... and a sharp, determined amateur detective who is very clever when it comes to ferreting out information." —The Mystery Reader

Death on a Platter

"With her quirky characters and unexpected plots twists, [Viets] combines the perfect list of ingredients to whip up a cozy treat.... *Death on a Platter* serves up her most hilarious mixture of mystery, love, and adventure to date." —Fresh Fiction

"Each of Viets's titles is top-notch." —AnnArbor.com

"Engaging." —*Publishers Weekly*

An Uplifting Murder

"Entertaining.... As always, Viets creates a heroine replete with wit, intelligence, and a sense of humor and entwines her in complicated plot strands."

—*Mystery Scene*

"Viets designs a flashy murder with just the right amounts of sparkle and shine." —Fresh Fiction

The Fashion Hound Murders

"Superb ... a wonderful cozy read." —Gumshoe

continued ...

"Elaine Viets does it again! ... *The Fashion Hound Murders* is a hilarious story ... [and] a fun-filled adventure. ... Pick this book up if you are looking for a lighthearted read with great shopping tips!"

—The Romance Readers Connection

Murder with All the Trimmings

"Viets milks much holiday humor in her novel, pulling out all the wonderfully garish stops."

—*Pittsburgh Tribune-Review*

"Elaine Viets writes exciting amateur sleuth mysteries filled with believable characters; the recurring cast, starting with Josie, adds a sense of friendship that in turn embellishes the feeling of realism."

—*Midwest Book Review*

Accessory to Murder

"Elaine Viets knows how to orchestrate a flawless mystery with just the right blend of humor, intrigue, and hot romance. If you are looking to complete your wardrobe for the fall, you just found the most essential piece."

—Fresh Fiction

"The writing and plot are superb ... no wasted words, scenes, or characters. Everything advances the plot, builds the characters, or keeps things moving. It's what her many fans have learned to expect." —Cozy Library

High Heels Are Murder

"*High Heels Are Murder* takes Josie into the wicked world of murder, mayhem, and toe cleavage. ... Viets spans the female psyche with panache and wit."

—*South Florida Sun-Sentinel*

"Viets has written one of the funniest amateur sleuth mysteries to come along in ages. Her protagonist is a thoroughly likable person, a great mother, daughter, and friend. ... The strength and the freshness of the tale lie in the characters." —*Midwest Book Review*

Dying in Style

"Finally, a protagonist we can relate to."
— *Riverfront Times* (St. Louis, MO)

"Laugh-out-loud humor adds to the brisk action."
— *South Florida Sun-Sentinel*

Praise for
The Dead-End Job Mystery Series

"Clever.... [The] real satisfaction is in observing the club members at their worst."
— Marilyn Stasio, *The New York Times*

"Wickedly funny." — *The Miami Herald*

"A stubborn and intelligent heroine, a wonderful South Florida setting, and a cast of more-or-less lethal bimbos ... I loved this book."
— #1 *New York Times* bestselling author Charlaine Harris

"Hair-raising.... Viets keeps the action popping until the cliff-hanger ending." — *Publishers Weekly*

"Hilarious." — *Kirkus Reviews*

"A fast-paced story and nonstop wisecracks.... Elaine Viets knows how to turn minimum wage into maximum hilarity."
— Nancy Martin, author of *Little Black Book of Murder*

"Elaine Viets reaches the right equilibrium with well-placed humor and lively plotting."
— *South Florida Sun-Sentinel*

"A quick summer read for fans of humorous mysteries with clever premises." — *Library Journal*

Also by Elaine Viets

Josie Marcus, Mystery Shopper Series

Dying in Style
High Heels Are Murder
Accessory to Murder
Murder with All the Trimmings
The Fashion Hound Murders
An Uplifting Murder
Death on a Platter
Murder Is a Piece of Cake

Dead-End Job Mystery Series

Shop till You Drop
Murder Between the Covers
Dying to Call You
Just Murdered
Murder Unleashed
Murder with Reservations
Clubbed to Death
Killer Cuts
Half-Price Homicide
Pumped for Murder
Final Sail
Board Stiff

Viets, Elaine, 1950-
Fixing to die /
[2013]
33305230458568
wo   03/21/14

FIXING TO DIE

JOSIE MARCUS, MYSTERY SHOPPER

Elaine Viets

AN OBSIDIAN MYSTERY

OBSIDIAN
Published by the Penguin Group
Penguin Group (USA) LLC, 375 Hudson Street,
New York, New York 10014

USA | Canada | UK | Ireland | Australia | New Zealand | India | South Africa | China
penguin.com
A Penguin Random House Company

First published by Obsidian, an imprint of New American Library,
a division of Penguin Group (USA) LLC

First Printing, November 2013

Copyright © Elaine Viets, 2013

Penguin supports copyright. Copyright fuels creativity, encourages diverse voices,
promotes free speech, and creates a vibrant culture. Thank you for buying an
authorized edition of this book and for complying with copyright laws by not
reproducing, scanning, or distributing any part of it in any form without permission. You are supporting writers and allowing Penguin to continue to publish
books for every reader.

OBSIDIAN and logo are trademarks of Penguin Group (USA) LLC.

ISBN 978-0-451-24098-9

Printed in the United States of America
10 9 8 7 6 5 4 3 2 1

PUBLISHER'S NOTE
This is a work of fiction. Names, characters, places, and incidents either are the
product of the author's imagination or are used fictitiously, and any resemblance
to actual persons, living or dead, business establishments, events, or locales is
entirely coincidental.

If you purchased this book without a cover you should be aware that this book
is stolen property. It was reported as "unsold and destroyed" to the publisher and
neither the author nor the publisher has received any payment for this "stripped
book."

For my Grandma Frances Vierling, who made unforget-table memories on her Magic Chef stove.

Acknowledgments

For Josie Marcus and me, cooking is a mystery. Good cooking, that is.

I can scramble an egg and boil water, but even that water-boiling claim is iffy. I burned boil-in-the-bag beans when I was distracted by the Internet.

I never thought I'd say the words "good-looking" and "kitchen," until I found Carrie Welch's renovated kitchen on the Retro Renovation blog. There's a version of it on the cover. You'll read more about how Carrie's kitchen became Josie's in the Shopping Tips section.

I needed lots of help for this book, but any mistakes are mine. Three people — Carrie Welch, the kitchen renovator, Pam Kueber of Retro Renovation, and Greg Wiley, publisher of *R3 Saint Louis* magazine — are discussed in detail in the Shopping Tips section. Thank you all.

Former kitchen designer Karen Maslowski guided me through the kitchen appliance wilderness. Josie and I believe the answer to "What type of stove do you have?" is "Four burners and an oven."

Jeanne Rolwing is not really a kitchen contractor, but a generous woman and the highest bidder at the silent auction for St. Henry Catholic School in Charleston, Missouri.

Laura Hyzy, the new veterinarian at Dr. Ted Scottsmeyer's clinic, is named in honor of the late Laura Hyzy. Her friends Liz Mellett, Lenore Boehm, and Jack and Judy Cater made a generous donation to the Malice Domestic convention charity auction to have her name in this novel. Laura, a 2009 Malice Fan Guest of Honor, loved traditional mysteries.

"Laura was short, not thin, and not a natural blonde," Liz wrote, "so we were hoping that perhaps her character could be tall(er), slender and a natural blonde." She is, and I'm proud to have her in *Fixing to Die*. I hope Laura will be in future books. Franklin, her fictional father, may also have a role.

Dr. Ted Scottsmeyer graduated from the Mizzou veterinary school, so I naturally asked Mizzou for help with veterinary questions. Thank you, Dr. Ronald K. Cott, DVM Associate Dean for Student/Alumni Affairs and Director of Development for the College of Veterinary Medicine.

Special thanks to C. Anne Eckersley of Chadwick Cavalier King Charles Spaniels. She is a Breeder of Merit—a major honor—and an international dog show judge. http://www.ChadwickSpaniels.com

Maryann Schnoor really does have a cocker spaniel named Marley who carries beer cans halfway home during their walks. They live in Fort Lauderdale.

Thank you Liz Aton, Valerie Cannata, Kay Gordy, Jack Klobnak, Bob Levine, Molly Portman, Janet Smith, and Anne Watts.

IT whiz Alan Portman patiently explained how Amelia and Emma cracked the case of the mean girls' photos. Thank you, Alan, for making your explanation so simple even I understood it.

I don't have to watch my language. MarySue Carl's second-period biology class at Arroyo High School in El Monte, California, does that for me. Go, Blue Pride! The students gave me the freshest slang, and reminded me that nobody says "fresh" anymore. As Josie says, keeping up with teen talk is like learning a new language. Every week.

Coke collectors are fanatics, but they are also extremely helpful. Thank you, Heather Seitsinger, vice president of the Gateway to the West Chapter of the Coca-Cola Collectors Club, and thanks to longtime collector Terry Buchheit of Perryville, Missouri.

Special thanks to Detective R. C. White, Fort Lauderdale Police Department (retired), and to the law enforcement men and women who answered my questions on police procedure. Some police and medical sources have to remain nameless, but I'm grateful for their help. Thanks to Rachelle L'Ecuyer, Community Development Director for the City of Maplewood. Amelia's cat is based on my striped writing partner, Harry, who snores by my monitor while I write. He never dipped a paw into a paint can, but one of my other cats did, and tracked black enamel across a beige carpet.

Jane's dog, Stuart Little, is a real shih tzu. His owner, Bill Litchtenberger of Palm City, Florida, made a generous donation to the Humane Society of the Treasure Coast auction to see Stuart's name in my novels. Harry and Stuart's photos are on my Web site at www.elaine viets.com.

I'm lucky to have Sandra Harding as my editor at New American Library and her tough but thorough critiques. I appreciate the efforts of the never flustered assistant Elizabeth Bistrow, the hardworking publicist Kayleigh Clark, and the New American Library copy editor and production staff.

For my long-suffering agent, David Hendin, thank you for your good advice.

Many booksellers help keep this series alive. I wish I could thank them all.

Thank you to the librarians at the Broward County Library, the St. Louis Public Library and the St. Louis County Library. Librarians are the original search engines. As Neil Gaiman said, "Google can bring you back a hundred thousand answers; a librarian can bring you back the right one."

Last, but never least, thank you to my husband, Don Crinklaw. You are my first reader and critic, and I always rely on your advice. Except I'm not putting more blood and bodies in this book. Josie's not that kind of girl.

You can reach me at eviets@aol.com. Enjoy Josie's adventure.

Chapter 1

"Wait till you see the living room," the real estate agent said. "It's amazing."

So far, Josie Marcus thought, the only amazing thing about this house was the paint color: gray. Not a soft, sophisticated gray. Damp basement gray. Concrete gray.

Sally Redding Rutherford, the real estate agent, called the grim gray entrance hall "cozy." Josie had looked at enough homes to translate real estate lingo. "Cozy" meant coffin-sized. There was barely room for her and Sally in the entrance. Josie felt like she was stuck in an upright burial vault.

Sally struggled to turn this dismal introduction into a sales plus. "Gray is chic again."

"It's like being trapped in a permanent rainy day," Josie said.

"Don't let that color fool you," Sally said. "The right paint and a nice mirror will transform this entrance into a real showcase."

Sally was small, blond, and muscular with a perpetually perky smile. Josie thought she must have been a cheerleader for a hopeless high school team, the way she relentlessly cheered one loser after another. Sally had shown her so many dogs, Josie felt like she was at the Humane Society.

The agent's footsteps echoed in the empty house. "Now here's the living room." Josie heard the flourish in Sally's voice.

That room was gray, too—from the floor to the fog-colored ceiling.

"Well?" Sally asked.

"Uh, the floor's gray concrete," Josie said.

"That's right," Sally said proudly. "Concrete flooring is stylish, smart, and tough. You'll only have to wax it every six to nine months, depending on the level of traffic."

"It's just my husband, my twelve-year-old daughter, a Lab, and two cats," Josie said.

"Excellent. Pet claws won't scratch the surface," Sally said. "And look at that fireplace!"

It was gray slate with steel fireplace tools—a shovel, a brush, and a poker.

"You won't find a feature like that in a—"

If Sally says "starter house" one more time, I'm going to brain her with that poker, Josie thought. She's said it six times since we parked in the driveway.

"—starter house," Sally finished.

Josie's fingers twitched. The poker was in reach. A jury of house hunters would never convict her.

Instead, she got a grip on herself. What's wrong with you? she asked herself. Sally is a hardworking divorcée. You were single long enough to know it's a tough world.

"The dining room is taupe," Sally said.

More gray, Josie thought. But she saw bright spots of red in the chandelier, the only color so far in the house, except for Sally's pink pantsuit.

"The owner wants to take the chandelier," Sally said. "It's Southwest style and he had it custom-made."

Josie fought back a giggle. The spiky wrought-iron

chandelier was trimmed with polished cow horns and long red plastic peppers. She wished Ted was there to see the chandelier. Or her best friend, Alyce.

"It's amazing," Josie said, truthfully. "But I don't think this is the house for us."

"But the seller is motivated," Sally said.

That means "desperate," Josie thought.

"And it's in Maplewood. You said you wanted a starter house in Maplewood."

That was the eighth time she said "starter house."

"Sally, you're doing a good job," Josie said. "But I've seen six houses so far today and I don't love any of them. I've been scouting houses every day for three weeks and I haven't seen one I thought Ted would want to see, much less live in."

"Josie, honey, you've given me so many restrictions," Sally said. "You don't want to buy a foreclosure."

"This is our first house," Josie said. "I don't want someone else's misery."

"You insist that the house be in either Maplewood or nearby Rock Road Village," Sally said. "St. Louis County is huge—more than five hundred square miles, Josie. That leaves out so many good locations. There are darling, affordable houses in Manchester, Ballwin, and Crestwood. Your daughter, Amelia, goes to a private school, so you don't have to worry about finding a house in a good school district."

"Ted spends long hours at his veterinary clinic in Rock Road Village," Josie said. "I don't want to add a commute to his already long day. When he's on call for after-hours emergencies, he has to be at the clinic in minutes."

"I understand," Sally said. "You're doing what any good wife would do, trying to find the perfect home for your family. Are you sure you don't want to see the kitchen? Or the master bath? It has a sunken tub." She said this as if she was offering Josie a tempting treat.

"No, let's call it a day," Josie said, and managed a lop-sided smile. "Take me back to my car, please."

"I will," Sally said. "But promise me you'll think about some of those properties I showed you. What about that cute fixer-upper? It's convenient to transportation, like you wanted."

"It needed a gut rehab," Josie said, "and was located between a highway ramp and the railroad tracks."

"Trains sound so romantic," Sally said.

"Not coming through the living room," Josie said. "When that freight train roared by, the plates rattled in the kitchen."

Sally locked the charcoal front door and put the key back in the lockbox. The late afternoon was pleasantly warm for early January. Sally unlocked her silver Chevy Impala and Josie sank gratefully into the passenger seat.

Why do I feel so exhausted? she wondered. All I did was look at houses.

The real estate agent started her car and revved up her sales pitch. "What about that sweet split-level with the country kitchen?" she asked. "The one we saw yesterday?"

"Ten minutes in that kitchen and I had nightmares that I was pursued by ducks with yellow ribbons around their necks," Josie said.

"It's just wallpaper. You can make those ducks go away," Sally said, flapping her fingers.

"Not from my mind," Josie said.

"You said the executive home near Brentwood Boulevard was gorgeous," Sally said.

"It was," Josie said. "It was also too big and too expensive."

"What was wrong with the charming rambler with the green shutters?" Sally asked. "It had a big sunny lot."

"Sunny! So's the Sahara," Josie said. "Nothing grew in that yard, not even grass."

"You're overlooking the—" Sally said.

Potential, Josie thought, bracing herself. Sally's going to say "potential." I hate that term even more than "starter house."

"—potential," Sally finished, predictably. "Josie, honey, you look worn-out."

"You've got that right," Josie said.

"Why don't you take off a day or two? Talk over what you've seen with that hunky new husband of yours. Take him on a few virtual house tours online. Then kick back and spend some quality time with him. How long have you been married?"

"Forty-four days," Josie said.

"Oh, that's so sweet," Sally said. "You're still counting the days. Think about what we've seen, Josie, then discuss it with Dr. Ted and Amelia. Buying a house is a family decision. You've been working too hard. You need some distance."

"That's for sure," Josie said.

Sally sailed smoothly onto Manchester Road toward her real estate office in Rock Road Village. Rush-hour traffic clogged the lanes, and lines of cars were backed up at the lights.

"Meanwhile, I'll try to come up with more fresh listings for you," she said.

"Good idea," Josie said. "You're right. I need a break."

Sally pulled into the parking lot at her office, a white clapboard building with green awnings and topiary trees beside the red door.

"House hunting is hard work," Sally said. "People don't understand how difficult it can be. Or how tiring."

"I don't know why I'm so tired," Josie said. "You did all the driving."

"Looking for a house is a very emotional experience," Sally said. "That alone will tire you out. But don't you worry. I'll find you the perfect house." She parked her Chevy next to Josie's car.

"Thanks for your time, Sally," Josie said. "I'll think about what you said."

"You do that," she said, and smiled. It was 5:10, and the sky was the same color as the home they'd just toured. Sally got out, shook Josie's hand, then headed toward her office.

Josie saw the agent's blond hair and trimly tailored suit swallowed by the red door and waved good-bye.

Josie didn't realize this was the last time she'd ever see Sally Rutherford.

Chapter 2

Josie stood on tiptoe to reach the pasta sauce in the kitchen cabinet. Her fingers couldn't quite touch the jar. She grabbed a slotted spoon from the rack to nudge it toward her. The jar fell into her hands, narrowly missing the pot of boiling pasta.

Good catch, she thought, then looked around. Glad Amelia isn't here to see that stunt, after all the lectures I've given her about kitchen safety.

Josie and Amelia had moved into Ted's rented house right after the honeymoon, but this was still his kitchen. The sleek granite counters and high-tech appliances were a major reason why Ted had signed the lease on the house. The house itself was comfortable, but the owner had upgraded the kitchen to professional quality. A few of their wedding presents were on the granite countertops, including Ted's red stand mixer. The spices, boxes, bottles, and cans were still arranged for his convenience.

My six-foot husband forgets I'm six inches shorter than he is, Josie thought.

She savored that possessive phrase "my husband." She'd never expected to marry, certainly not a catch like Ted. She knew a thirty-two-year-old single mom with a tween daughter was unlikely marriage material.

No point in rearranging the kitchen today, she decided, as she chopped up fat, fragrant basil leaves from the plants growing in Ted's window. We'll be moving out of here in a few months. If I can find us a new house. She kept busy, trying not to brood about her discouraging day with Sally the real estate agent.

Josie checked the bow tie pasta. Most of the water had boiled away and the pot sported a brittle starch skin. She poked the skin with a fork and sniffed the pasta. Didn't smell burned.

Whew, she thought. I can still serve it. They'll never know.

Josie drained the pasta and dumped it into a casserole dish. It made an odd rubbery plop. The bow ties were stuck together and she separated them with a fork. This didn't look like Ted's pasta, or Amelia's.

Ted usually does the cooking, with Amelia as his eager apprentice. But tonight I'll surprise them. Ted might be too tired to cook. Business is growing at the St. Louis Mobo-Pet Clinic. Ted and his partner, Dr. Chris, have more work than they can handle. Even after they hired Laura Hyzy, a new graduate from the University of Missouri Vet School, the three doctors are still overworked. I'm glad his practice is thriving, but he needs to rest after a hard day of dealing with sick and sometimes surly animals.

Josie added the bottled marinara sauce and mixed it with half a package of shredded mozzarella. The sauce was thick and the floppy pasta uncooperative and leathery on the tips. She looked at it closer, but it definitely wasn't burned.

She wasn't going to ask Amelia for her advice. She was in her bedroom, doing something complicated on her laptop. Last time Josie had checked, Harry, Amelia's striped tabby, was curled next to her.

Josie mixed in the freshly chopped basil. That personalized the bottled sauce, taking it to another level. Amelia's cooking and computer skills have outstripped mine, Josie thought, and that's a good thing. Right now she wants to be a vet like Ted, but she's only twelve. I think she has the talent to be a chef or an IT expert—and that's not just motherly pride. I've eaten enough of her meals to recognize her flair for cooking. And she gets A's in the school math and science programs.

Josie put the lid on the casserole and slid it into the oven to bake.

I don't want Amelia to make the same mistake I did: get pregnant and drop out of college. I don't regret having my daughter, but she doesn't have to be a mystery shopper like me. My career—if I can call it that—promises low pay and long slogs through malls.

Josie heard Ted's tangerine '68 Mustang roar into the driveway. Harry raced for the kitchen door to greet Ted, Amelia following behind.

They heard Ted talking to his black Lab. "Come on, Festus," he said. "It's dinnertime. Something smells good."

"Ted! Festus!" Amelia wrapped her arms around Ted when he entered the door. He hugged her, then gave Josie a warm kiss. She could feel the winter chill on his coat.

"You're cold," she said.

"It's not bad for mid-January," he said.

Festus slurped his water while Amelia poured him more dry food, then scratched his soft, dark ears.

"Did Amelia make dinner?" Ted asked.

"No, I whipped up pasta," Josie said. "It should be ready in ten minutes."

"That's nice," Ted said, hanging his jacket on a hook by the door. Josie heard the forced enthusiasm.

"I'll make a salad," Amelia said.

"I'll do the garlic bread," Ted said.

Ted and Amelia worked with the swift, silent movements of professional disaster relief workers. Josie set the table, feeling slightly hurt. Was her cooking that bad?

Fifteen minutes later, the three filled their salad plates. Then Josie spooned generous helpings of pasta onto her sophisticated brown-and-gold bridal china.

"Great salad, Amelia," Ted said. "I like the artichoke hearts and pimentos."

"The garlic bread is crisp and buttery," Josie said. "How's your pasta?"

Ted chewed thoughtfully. "Interesting texture."

"Did you let the water boil out, Mom?" Amelia asked. "It's a bit crunchy."

"Not all the water," Josie said. "The pasta that stuck out of the water got a little leathery on the ends, but I thought the pasta was okay because it wasn't burned. At least we have your spice cake for dessert."

Ted reached over and squeezed her hand. "Thank you for making dinner, Josie. That was thoughtful. How's the house hunt going?"

"It's not," Josie said, and tried not to sigh. "I looked at six more houses. They were either too small, too expensive, or too noisy. The last one had an entry hall the size of a phone booth. The whole place was painted gray and the floors were concrete. It was like being in a giant basement. Amelia, is that you crunching your dinner? It sounds like you're eating shredded wheat."

"I can't help it, Mom," Amelia said.

"You shouldn't eat that," Josie said, removing her daughter's plate. "Let's order pizza."

"Better yet, why don't I make omelets?" Ted said. He stuck his head in the fridge and took inventory. "We've got plenty of eggs, ham, cheese, onions, and green peppers. How do Western omelets sound?"

"Better than crunchy pasta," Josie said. "Quieter, too. We already have the salad and garlic bread."

Josie cleared their plates and scraped her pasta into the disposal, then reset the table.

"Tell me more about the house hunt," Ted said as he

broke almost a dozen eggs in a bowl and beat them with a whisk. Amelia chopped the ingredients on the counter beside him.

"Sally says I'm giving her too many restrictions. She thinks we should consider buying a foreclosure," Josie said, "but you know how I feel about taking on someone else's bad luck."

"I wouldn't want a foreclosed house, either," Ted said. "I've read there can be legal problems."

"Then we're in trouble," Josie said. "Sally says we've looked at every available house in Maplewood, Richmond Heights, and Rock Road Village. Any farther away, and you'll have a long commute. And your lease is up soon."

"Good," he said. "I'm glad you haven't found a house yet. You've been working so hard with Sally, I wasn't sure how to bring up this subject. My partner, Chris, may have a house we can buy. She and her son and the twins live near the clinic, but she inherited a second house from her aunt Gertrude. Aunt Trudy's house is a mile from the clinic in Rock Road Village. Chris says she doesn't want to move. She's rented it for the last five years, but that isn't working out, either."

"Not all renters are as thoughtful as you," Josie said.

"The last renter was her sister," Ted said. "She lived in it eighteen months. One day she took off. Just packed up and left. Didn't even say good-bye. Just sent an e-mail."

"Not very sisterly," Josie said.

"Her name is Rain. I gather she's kind of a flake," Ted said.

"Rain?" Amelia said. "That name's even worse than Oakley. She says girlie names like mine are stupid. I call her Annie just to piss her off."

"Amelia!" Josie said. "We don't use that language. You tick her off or make her angry."

"Whatever," Amelia said, and went back to chopping

ham into cubes. The cheese and onion were already in neat mounds.

Josie tried to change the subject. "Do you think naming a baby girl Rain guarantees she'll be offbeat? Christine is so levelheaded."

"I think it has more to do with the parents," Ted said. "Her sister Susan is two years older than Chris. Chris is in the middle, five years older than Rain. She says her mom and dad went through a hippie phase before they switched back to their old nine-to-five selves.

"Chris's second house has been empty for six months now, ever since Rain left. Chris is worried it will be vandalized if it stays empty. She can't find a reliable renter. She wants to sell it. It's got some problems, but she'll sell it to us as is."

"What kind of house?" Amelia said, slicing a thick red pepper. "Ready to go, Ted."

"So's the omelet pan," he said.

Ted sautéed the ingredients, scraped them onto a plate, then poured the eggs into the big pan. "I want you to keep an open mind," he said. "All I'm telling you for now is the house has three bedrooms, a finished basement, and it's seventy-six years old." He added the sautéed ingredients to the bubbling eggs, then folded the omelet.

"Sweet," Amelia said. "A historic house. Grandma's sixty-six. She's almost as historic."

The finished omelet, dotted with confetti bits of red pepper and green onion, oozed warm cheese. Ted sliced it into three servings and put them on plates.

"Amelia, I doubt your grandmother would like being called historic," Josie said, "even by you." She tasted a forkful of omelet. "Um. This is perfect. Thank you both for rescuing dinner."

"I don't think the house is historic," Ted said. "Just old. Chris knows the details."

"When can we look at it?" Josie asked.

"Can we go tonight? I've finished my homework," Amelia said.

Ted checked the kitchen clock. "It's six thirty," he said. "I'll call Chris now. I told her we might see it tonight. Why don't we meet her there at seven? We'll have to look at the house in the dark."

"What's new about that?" Josie said. "I've been in the dark the whole time."

Chapter 3

The full moon was a glowing pearl set off by a black velvet sky, softly silvering the four brick homes that circled Fresno Court. Each had a wide, well-tended lawn of thick winter brown zoysia, framed by dark evergreens and graceful trees. Lights in the windows added a welcoming warmth.

"I love the arched wooden doors with the wrought-iron hinges," Josie said. "What do they call that rough-looking stone over the doors and on the chimneys?"

"Rusticated," Ted said. "These homes have beautiful craftsmanship."

"They're wicked," Amelia said. "Ella could live here."

"Who's Ella?" Ted asked.

"*Ella Enchanted* is a fairy tale based on Cinderella," Josie said. "A crazy fairy puts a spell on Ella so she has to obey any order, no matter how stupid. It's popular with the tween crowd, who have to obey stupid orders from parents."

"Mom," Amelia said, drawing out the word. "It's more than that."

I'm too rough on my daughter, Josie thought. "You're right," she said. "Ella is smart, adventurous, and thinks for herself."

"Just don't confuse *Ella Enchanted* with *Enchanted*

Ella," Amelia said. "It's way better, even though the names are almost alike."

"I'm already confused," Ted said. "But I agree Fresno Court is a fairy-tale street."

"That looks like Chris's SUV in that driveway," Josie said.

"Then we're here," Ted said.

Chris marched down the sidewalk with long, sure strides. Ted's clinic partner wore a tailored blue blouse and jeans. About forty, Chris was thin and angular with short, neat brown hair that showed off her elegant cheekbones.

Her son, Todd, was Amelia's age. His face seemed soft and unformed under a thatch of thick black hair. Todd already towered over his mother, and tripped over his feet on the sidewalk. Josie thought he'd grow into a tall, strong man once he got through this awkward stage.

Josie heard dogs yapping, probably from the yard on the east side, hidden by a privacy fence and an eight-foot tree with a graceful fan of bare branches. "Is that a redbud?" she asked.

"It is. Wait till you see it blooming in the spring," Chris said. "It's like a purple cloud. That two-story tree on the other side of the house is a white dogwood."

"Dogwood and redbud," Josie said. "My favorite flowering trees."

Chris hugged Ted, Josie, and Amelia. Todd hung back behind his mother.

Amelia greeted him shyly but stayed with Ted and Josie.

"Glad you could make it tonight," Chris said.

"Where are the twins?" Ted asked.

"With their church group," Chris said. "It's just Todd and me tonight. You can't see much by the streetlights, but we spent hours getting this lawn back in shape. I'm afraid my sister Rain didn't do much yard work."

"Ted said your sister is a bit of a free spirit," Josie said.

"That's a nice way of saying she has lots of boyfriends and can't hold a job," Chris said. "Rain is the original Miss What, Me Worry? She makes Alfred E. Neuman look like a nine-to-fiver."

"Well, he is a MAD man," Josie said.

Chris switched back to sales mode. "In the spring, you'll have daffodils, tulips, and iris. The backyard has more spring flowers."

"I like the mellow orange-gold brick," Josie said. "Most older St. Louis homes are redbrick."

"The house was just tuck-pointed, including the chimney," Chris said. "A boring but necessary detail if you're buying. Come on inside."

Ted, Josie and Amelia trooped up the flagstone steps after Chris and Todd.

"What style is this?" Josie asked. "It's definitely not a ranch or a rambler."

"It's a Tudor Revival cottage," Chris said. "Very popular in the twenties and thirties. If it were any bigger, it would have half-timbering."

"So we're looking at a distant ancestor of a McMansion," Ted said.

Josie stood in the doorway, pleasantly surprised by the nearly empty interior. The woodwork and floors were a warm, satiny brown, and there were pretty details like art glass windows.

"The house has central air," Chris said, "and the furnace is only four years old. Neither one is on tonight."

Their footsteps echoed on the bare polished floor. "Gorgeous wood," Josie said. "Did you have to refinish the floors?"

"Just buffed and waxed them," Chris said. "Aunt Trudy, bless her, covered these floors with thick carpets. After my sister moved out, Todd and I pulled up the old carpets and saw these floors. Solid elm. The woodwork is maple."

"Why is there a wooden box on the wall?" Amelia asked.

"That's an indoor mailbox so the letters don't fall on the floor when they go through the mail slot," Chris said.

The house smelled pleasantly of fresh paint and floor wax, overlaid with fragrant eucalyptus in a basket by the fireplace.

"The fireplace works. I painted it white," Chris said. "Todd here helped me paint all the rooms and clear out the junk. I don't know what I'd do without him."

Todd studied his feet while the tips of his ears turned red.

"I rented the house furnished, but after Rain took off, Todd helped me haul Aunt Trudy's worn-out furniture to a thrift store. I did keep the mission-style dining set."

"I like it," Josie said. "And that big window overlooking the side yard."

Chris wrinkled her nose. "Betty, my next-door neighbor, lives on that side and raises show dogs—Jack Russell terriers. I put up a privacy fence and planted evergreens to deaden the sound, but those dogs bark at everything, even leaves."

"I'm used to barking dogs," Ted said.

"I barely hear them," Josie said.

Amelia was studying the rose-shaped art glass window in the front door.

"Cordelia, the neighbor on the other side, is a college professor," Chris said. "You couldn't ask for a quieter neighbor. The master bedroom overlooks her yard. Let's go upstairs for a look."

Josie could see a flash of the kitchen, but Chris steered them firmly up the stairs. Must be saving the worst for last, Josie thought.

The master bedroom was painted a fresh light blue. Warm red-brown woodwork framed the double-gable window.

"Wait till you see this in daylight," Chris said, "when the sun pours through that window. That's the master bath through that door."

"It's new!" Josie said. "And it has a Jacuzzi."

"Not that new," Chris said. "Aunt Trudy updated it ten years ago. I don't want this house to hurt our friendship—or my partnership with Ted—so I'm pointing out all the flaws I know about. This fall, both neighbors complained about a bad smell, so I had the plumbing checked. The plumber said the pipes were fine—no blockages or leaks in the stack pipe or the main line to the sewer. He thought maybe some large animal, like a deer or a big dog, died in the hedge around the back fence. I never found any trace and the smell went away."

"It's okay, Chris," Ted said. "Old houses, like old people, have plumbing problems. Let's see the other rooms."

The hallway was lit by graceful wall sconces with amber shades. "Those are nineteen thirties Virden lights," Chris said. "By some miracle, Rain's drunken boyfriend didn't break them."

Josie thought Todd made a small noise that sounded like a protest.

The hall was so narrow they walked single file to inspect the other two bedrooms. Both were small, with sloping walls, tiny windows, and more polished wood. The room closest to Betty, the show dog breeder's house, had a purple bathroom.

"Purple! That's so sick!" Amelia said.

"That's a good thing," Josie interpreted.

"I know," Chris said. "Todd speaks the same language."

"I love the slanted walls," Amelia said. "Can I have this room, please?"

"If we buy it, you've got dibs," Josie said. "And before you ask, you can paint your bedroom purple."

"Yes!" Amelia high-fived her mother.

"But we haven't decided anything," Josie said.

"And the tour isn't over," Chris said. "The kitchen may be a deal breaker. Be careful on those stairs. That polished wood is slippery. Turn right, and you'll see the ugly pink-and-black bathroom Aunt Trudy and Uncle Ben installed in the fifties."

She flipped on the bathroom light.

"I kind of like it," Ted said. "My grandparents had one like it."

"It glows pink," Amelia said.

"The kitchen is another fifties special," Chris said. "It needs serious work."

Even Josie, who'd fallen in love with the house, thought the kitchen was awful. The cabinets were either dingy white or grimy aqua, and two doors were loose. The oven's bottom drawer hung sideways. The black-and-white tile floor was chipped and cracked. The tile in front of the sink was worn down to the concrete. A dining nook held a bench seat with a fresh turquoise cushion and three white molded fiberglass chairs.

"I like it," Amelia said. "This is an amazing midcentury modern kitchen. Do you know how much a decorator would charge for this?"

The adults stared at her. "How do you know about midcentury modern design?" Josie said. "You weren't even alive in the fifties. Neither was I."

"From Jace at school," Amelia said. "Her mother paid some big-deal decorator to put in a midcentury modern kitchen. The whole house is torn up and Jace spends every lunch period showing us photos on her phone. All she talks about is how much it costs. Those chairs look like Eero Saarinen tulip chairs, or at least copies. He designed the St. Louis Arch. Her mom bought a real Saarinen dinette set for five thousand dollars."

Josie looked at Amelia as if aliens had abducted her. "You know all this?" she asked.

"I can't get away from it. I'm tired of Jace bragging, but we can have something supersick. If we buy the house, that is," she added.

"Amelia has a point," Ted said.

"I know about 'aqua boomerang laminate' and 'back-splash,'" she said. "I can tell you why stainless steel edging is better than aluminum. If we make this kitchen aqua and put in a checkerboard tile floor, we'll have the best kitchen ever. For once, I'll have something better than everyone else at school."

Amelia's passionate plea hurt Josie's heart. Her daughter was a scholarship student at the Barrington School for Boys and Girls, a private school for the richest kids in St. Louis. Thanks to Josie's job as a mystery shopper, she could find fashionable tween clothes on sale, so Amelia was as stylish as the other students. But their Maplewood flat was no millionaire's mansion, nor did Josie drive a sleek Beemer like so many mothers.

"We'll discuss kitchen pros and cons at a family meeting when we're home," Josie said.

"Why don't I show you the backyard?" Chris said, and herded them toward the kitchen door. She couldn't open it fully. The door hit a sagging gazebo built too close to the house.

"That gazebo was a gift from Rain's latest boyfriend," Chris said. "He built it without asking my permission. Rain liked doing her yoga out here. She was dating Harley, a Coke addict."

"He used drugs?" Ted asked.

Chris laughed. "That's Coke with a capital *C*, as in Coca-Cola. Harley's rich, hunky, and a rabid collector of Coke memorabilia. Old Coke signs, trays, and ads are extremely collectible. Harley did a lot of repairs on this house, most of them badly. This gazebo is a sample of his work. It's too close to the house and doesn't have a proper foundation. You may want to move it."

Ted pulled on a weathered wooden handrail and it came loose. "We could also tear it down," he said.

Josie liked that "we." She thought Ted liked the house as much as she did.

"Good idea," Chris said. "It's coming apart. I had to nail down some boards on the deck and steps. The gazebo is technically in Rock Road Village. The city line runs right through the kitchen, but it's mostly in Maplewood."

"Good," Josie said. "I don't want to leave my favorite city if we buy. Is the tour over?"

"Almost," Chris said. "Just the basement and the laundry room."

They trooped down a stairway paneled in mellow knotty pine and followed Chris through a door on the left. There was nothing special about the concrete laundry room, except its generous built-in shelves. "My uncle built those," she said. "Not Harley the Hopeless Handyman. The washer-dryer goes with the house. The gas furnace and water heater are in the utility room next door."

The rest of the basement was L-shaped and paneled in knotty pine. The long section was furnished with a fat brown recliner, a comfortable-looking leather sofa, a black coffee table, and a stylish black-and-brown rug.

"A man cave," Ted said. "I'll put a TV and a CD player down here. That short section will make a good office."

"You can have this furniture, too," Chris said. "I don't want the movers cussing me when they haul that recliner up those stairs."

Ted kicked back in the recliner. The three women sank into the sofa and Todd slouched against the knotty pine wall.

"Are you sure your sister won't come back and want to live here again?" Ted asked.

"Positive," Chris said. "She didn't have a lease. Rain just took off and nobody's heard from her since. She drifts from one family member to another. She showed up on my doorstep with no warning, carrying a suitcase and a yoga mat. This place wasn't rented, so Rain moved in."

Todd shifted uncomfortably from foot to foot, and his cheeks reddened under his newborn, scraggly beard. Josie wondered if Todd was uneasy about his mother criticizing Rain.

"She got a job at the Peace Co-op and Farmers Market on Manchester," Chris said. "At first, she kept up the property and paid the rent. She dated Donny, the beer can collector."

"People collect beer cans?" Ted asked.

"Donny is serious. He belongs to the Beer Can Collectors of America, an international organization founded here in St. Louis. He has more than a thousand cans in his rec room. After a few months, Rain realized Donny was emptying way too many noncollectible beer cans. They had a fight and he hit her when he was drunk. Rain dropped him. I was glad. Next, she took up with Harley, the Coke collector and DIY guy."

"Two collectors?" Josie said.

"Rain collected people," Chris said. "But I wasn't collecting rent anymore. I should have seen the warning signs: A month before she took off, she quit her job, stopped paying rent, and let trash pile up in the yard. I hoped she'd move in with Harley and I wouldn't have to evict my own sister."

"Was she still seeing him when she left town?" Josie asked.

"No, they broke up two days before she left. Rain damaged a valuable Coca-Cola calendar and didn't tell him. When Harley discovered it, he was furious. He stormed over here. She was out in the gazebo and they had a fight so loud Betty called the police.

"Betty called me and complained about the fight and said the place was going to seed. I'd had enough. I marched over to talk to Rain. She didn't answer her door. When I saw her doing her damned yoga in the gazebo while the place was a wreck, I lost it.

"The next morning, I got an e-mail from Rain. I'll never forget it. 'I've broken up with Harley,' she said. 'I need to get away from your negative energy.' My negative energy! When she didn't have the energy to pick up the trash."

Josie watched Chris try to master her anger. After a pause, she took a deep breath and said, "Rain said she was going to an ashram in California. 'I need to' "—Chris made air quotes—" 'transform my thought process and uncover my deepest capacities within the context of an active modern life. I'll contact you when I get my head together.' Typical Rain—no thank-you, no forwarding address or phone number. I'm relieved she's gone. We all are."

Todd looked up. "I—," he said, his voice a croak. "I kinda like Aunt Rain. She talked about world peace and saving the animals and greedy corporations."

Josie liked that Todd defended his aunt, even though she suspected Rain was annoying.

"I'm glad you still like your aunt even after you cleaned up her mess, Todd," Chris said. "Sorry, everyone. I didn't mean to rant. Ted and Josie, I hope you'll buy the house. It's for sale as is."

Chris named a price that was fifty thousand dollars cheaper than Ted and Josie had expected. Josie's eyebrows shot up. Ted said, "Why so generous? That's way below market price."

"Because I don't know what kind of DIY land mines Harley left," she said. "You've seen that wreck of a gazebo." She handed Ted a folder. "These are a year's worth of utility, tax, and insurance bills. I'm going to list the house next week, so I'd appreciate an answer in seven days."

"We may have an answer for you sooner," Ted said. "Why don't you and Todd go upstairs so we can have a family meeting?"

Once they were gone, Josie perched on the arm of the recliner, next to Ted. They studied the bills while Amelia watched anxiously.

"So, what do you think?" Ted asked.

"I love it," Amelia said. "Can we keep the kitchen?"

"Me, too," Josie said. "The house is the right size for us, and seems in good shape. The bills aren't bad, except for the gas, and we can handle that. The price is better than I expected. If there are repair problems, we'll have enough in our budget to fix them and still renovate the kitchen."

"I like the kitchen's midcentury look," Ted said. "We'll keep it."

"Yay!" Amelia said. "When do we move in?"

"Not till after the kitchen renovation," Ted said. "I want it done right, according to EPA standards. Jeanne Rolwing, a clinic client, is a kitchen contractor who specializes in old houses. I hear she's good."

"Let's do it," Josie said, hugging Ted. "Welcome to your fairy tale, Amelia. Let's give Chris the good news."

Josie felt like she was floating up the stairs, she was so happy. Chris met them at the top.

"Well?" she asked.

"I still have one more question," Ted said. "This house is way too cheap. Are you sure you won't regret this deal?"

"Absolutely not," Chris said. "I know Harley's left some unpleasant surprise."

"We'll take it," Ted said. "We've been warned."

Chapter 4

April 2013

"You're right, Amelia," Josie said. "We do have a fairy-tale house. Someone waved a magic wand and made all the red tape disappear. It's only April and the house is ours."

Amelia, Ted, and Josie were crammed into Ted's vintage Mustang on the way to Fresno Court, wearing their oldest clothes. Josie thought Ted looked especially handsome in his worn jeans and blue work shirt.

"We were lucky," Ted said. "We needed a fairly small loan and Christine was a motivated seller."

Josie winced. "Ouch," she said. "I hoped I'd never have to hear 'motivated seller' again."

"It was meant to be," Amelia said. Josie noticed her daughter's T-shirt was a shade too tight for her budding figure. This was its last wearing, she decided.

"What am I doing today?" Amelia asked.

"Helping me when I meet with Jeanne Rolwing, the kitchen contractor. You're my cooking expert."

"Wicked," Amelia said.

"I'm working with the Quick Micks to tear down the gazebo," Ted said. "They're two Irish brothers who have a light hauling company."

"Clinic clients?" Josie guessed.

"Michael has a brindle pit bull named O'Hara," Ted said. "Gentlest dog you'll ever meet. The brothers gave me the name of a good contractor to build our deck. You don't mind me taking over like this, do you?"

"Mind?" Josie said. "It's the best part of being married."

"Really?" Ted said, raising an eyebrow.

Josie realized her daughter was in the car. She blushed and said, "I've had to make all the decisions for so long, it's good to share them. I hope it won't be too hot for you guys working outside."

"It's a sunny seventy," he said. "Perfect for gazebo wrecking."

Two pickup trucks were parked in the circle at Fresno Court. The black one with ROLWING CONSTRUCTION painted on the side was nearly new but already getting the dents and dings of a working truck.

A red-haired woman was talking to two men leaning against a battered red Quick Micks Light Hauling pickup. Both looked like they could bench-press the truck.

"That's Patrick with the dark hair and handlebar mustache," Ted said.

"He looks like Wyatt Earp in the movie," Amelia said.

"The redhead is Michael," Ted said. "I mean, the guy with red hair. Jeanne is the other redhead."

Jeanne was a short, fit woman in overalls and a black ball cap. She and Michael were scratching a brown dog with a white face. "I told Michael it was okay to bring O'Hara."

Ted hauled a cooler filled with water and soda out of the trunk, and threw his work gloves on the lid.

After introductions, everyone headed for the backyard. The Quick Micks drove their truck around to the alley entrance with the wide gate. Ted held the gate for them and they drove their faded truck into the yard.

The three men discussed how to attack the gazebo while O'Hara shamelessly begged for ear scratches. "We should tear out those bushes Chris planted near the steps first," Ted said. "They're dying."

Josie unlocked the back door and it hit the gazebo. "We can't open this door all the way," she told the kitchen contractor. "That's one reason why we're tearing it down."

"Good," Jeanne said. "That will make my job easier."

Josie liked her no-nonsense attitude. Jeanne was in her late twenties, but her air of authority made her seem older. She could barely squeeze through the door, loaded down with a tool belt and a clipboard.

Jeanne stood in the middle of the kitchen, hands on hips, taking in the dilapidated room. "Wow," she said.

Was the contractor admiring the kitchen? Or overwhelmed by the work? Josie couldn't tell.

"We want to keep the midcentury look," she prompted.

"Good. You've got a fabulous retro kitchen and breakfast nook here," Jeanne said. "It needs work, though."

She reached down and pulled a loose chunk of tile off the floor. "You're lucky," she said. "This isn't asbestos. We'd have a heck of a problem disposing of that. It's going to take a crew two days to scrape up this old tile."

Jeanne studied the grease-spattered aqua paneling. "That paint's probably lead-based. Are you going to be living here while the work's going on?"

"No, we won't move in until you finish," Josie said.

"That will speed things up. I can strip off the paint with a low-temperature heat gun, and then hand-scrape it. The aqua tile on the splashboard is good. We can keep it," Jeanne said.

"I like that," Josie said. "Okay by you, Amelia?" Amelia nodded agreement.

"I can fix the loose doors, but the other retro cabinets

may be a problem. This counter is supposed to extend out, but it's broken. We might find one on eBay or in an antiques store."

"I can look online," Amelia said. "Just tell me what you need. And the counter edging can be aluminum instead of the more expensive stainless steel."

"Say, you know your stuff," Jeanne said. "What about these appliances?"

"The fridge is good," Josie said. "We'll need to look for a new stove and a dishwasher."

"What kind of stove?" Jeanne asked.

"Black," Josie said. "White would look good, too. Or aqua, if we can find it."

"Not what color," the contractor said. "What kind?"

Josie felt like a C-student trying to guess the answer to a test question. "Four burners and an oven?" she asked.

"I mean, gas or electric?" Jeanne said.

Josie looked at Amelia. "What do you think? You and Ted do the cooking."

"Gas stoves are the best," Amelia said. "We'd like to find a six-burner, but we'll settle for four. I'd really like a cooktop and a separate oven."

Josie noticed—again—that Amelia was as tall as she was. It felt odd when Jeanne addressed her daughter as the competent one.

Get used to it, she thought. You need Amelia's help and she knows more than you do about kitchens.

"This old stove is electric," Jeanne said. She opened the oven door and examined the inside with a flashlight. "I can fix that loose stove drawer and use this one until you find the gas stove you want."

"Deal," Josie said.

Jeanne sized the stove with a yellow tape measure. "This is thirty-six inches wide," she said. "Unless you want to reconfigure the counters, you'll have to stick with a four-burner. Do you have the budget for a cooktop and an oven? That's six or seven thousand dollars."

"Way too expensive," Josie said.

"We can look for a used stove online," Amelia said.

The contractor talked about suppliers, shipping, electrical work, insulation, and plumbing until Josie's head hurt, but Amelia seemed to enjoy it. Josie had to fight to keep her mind from wandering.

She could hear Ted and the Quick Micks tearing down the gazebo, section by section. Power saws shrieked and hammers thudded. The dry wood screeched and moaned like a living thing as the gazebo was ripped apart. Josie hoped Ted's heavy work gloves were thick enough that he wouldn't hurt his hands.

Suddenly the wrecking crew was so loud they drowned out Jeanne's latest question. The three women stopped to listen.

"Easy, now, easy," Michael said. "That whole section is coming apart. Don't hit the house, Pat. Careful there, Ted."

"Got it," Pat said. There was a rending screech, a thump, and a clunk as the section joined the rest of the ruined gazebo in the truck.

"That's it for the walls," Ted said.

"Man, I don't know who built this thing, but they did one sorry-ass job," Michael said.

"Makes it easier for us," Pat said. "We got that ratty canopy off in no time. All that's left is to pull up the steps and the deck."

"Okay," Michael said. "Let's finish this last bit and we're out of here."

Jeanne worked to make herself heard over the hammering, thudding, and ripping. "I'm going to close off the entrance that leads to the rest of the house," she said, "and seal it with plastic and masking tape, but you'll still have plaster dust all over everything."

"That's what I expected," Josie said. "How long will this job take?"

"I'd say two to three months," Jeanne said. Josie mentally added another two months and figured they'd be moved in by the end of the summer.

"This packet has my proof of insurance and licensing," Jeanne said. "Here's the cost and a payment schedule. You and your husband can take the contract to a lawyer. I'd like a check for the first payment when you sign it."

"Fair enough," Josie said.

In the yard, she could hear more ripping and tearing, followed by the thunk of wood. "The steps have left the building," Pat joked. "Just the deck now. It's shifted and fallen down where the steps were."

More cracking noises, then a dragging sound. "One, two, three, lift," Michael said. "That's it! That's it! It's all in the truck."

A crash, then a thunderous silence.

"What the hell?" Pat said. "If I didn't know better, I'd say that was a grave under those steps. Michael, what's your dog doing? He's digging like crazy."

"O'Hara!" Michael said. "Stop it. Stop it right now. Stay! Sit! What's wrong with you?"

"Oh my Lord, what's that awful smell?" Patrick asked. "I'm going to be sick."

The three women ran to the back door. Josie got outside first, and saw Michael trying to drag his dog away from the spot where the steps used to be. O'Hara snapped and growled at his master.

"I don't know what's got into him," Michael said.

"He's dug up something," Ted said. Holding his glove over his nose, he moved in closer. "Now he's tearing up a trash bag. Easy, boy, easy. Let me see what you have there."

O'Hara sat down and wagged his whiplike tail. Ted bent closer, then backed away. Josie glimpsed a messy tangle of long hair.

"Oh God. No, no, no," Ted said. "It's a woman."

Chapter 5

"Keep Amelia inside," Ted said. "Don't let her see this."

"I'll take care of her," Jeanne called out, her face gray as plaster dust. The contractor didn't have to see what Mike's dog had dug up. The sickly-sweet scent and shocked faces told the story.

"I'm not a baby," Amelia said. She tried to push her way outside, but Jeanne stopped her.

"I know that," she said. "I need your advice. You and Ted are going to use this kitchen the most. See that broken counter? Do you want it to extend out again, or keep it flush with the cabinets?"

"The extra work space would be nice," Amelia said as she and the contractor examined the truncated counter.

Josie silently blessed Jeanne for her tact as she shut the back door. She moved carefully toward Ted, as if the yard would cave in under her. No wonder she felt unsteady. Her new life had been torn apart by a curious dog.

She clung to Ted for comfort, but missed his familiar smell of coffee and cinnamon. The odor from the hidden grave had overwhelmed the yard like a conquering army.

"I'm so sorry, baby," he said, kissing her forehead. "Mike called nine-one-one and I called Chris."

"Why call your partner?" Josie asked.

Ted glanced over at Michael, slumped on the truck bumper, his face as pale as a boiled egg under his fiery hair, and lowered his voice. "I really hope I'm wrong," he said. "I never met Chris's sister, but I think the dead person may be Rain. I saw a peace sign around its—I mean, her—neck."

"Poor Chris," Josie said.

"Poor Rain," Ted said. "When Mike's dog ripped open that trash bag, I saw a tangle of long blond hair."

"Me, too," Josie said.

"There was a shirt, all stained and dirty, but I think it had a peace dove on it."

Doesn't mean that's Rain, Josie wanted to say, but she knew better. This wasn't an offbeat neighborhood.

Michael had shut O'Hara in the truck's cab. Now he and his brother scratched and petted the dog through the open window. O'Hara whimpered. The Jack Russells next door howled and yipped frantically, their small bodies thudding against the privacy fence.

Josie winced at a loud *crack!* as the dogs threw themselves at the fence. "I hope the wood holds," she said.

"Quiet!" a woman's high-pitched voice commanded. "What's wrong with you animals? Settle down."

The thudding stopped, but not the howling.

"That must be Betty," Josie said. "I should introduce myself, but what a way to meet our neighbor."

Now howling sirens added to the Jack Russells' racket. "The police," Josie said. "I'll bring them back here."

A chill wind sprang up, and dark clouds smothered the sunshine. The changeable St. Louis spring day was turning cold. Josie shivered.

"We'll go together," Ted said. "You look shaky."

Together, Josie thought. She loved being married. He took her hand.

A Rock Road Village police car screeched into the driveway and a uniformed officer jumped out. His nameplate read DIMON. His pink balding head was crowned with a wreath of gray hair.

Josie thought Officer Dimon was somewhere past fifty. The buttons straining across his massive belly said he'd lost the battle of the bulge. Josie wondered why he was still a uniform cop at his age.

"You call nine-one-one?" he asked.

"I did," Ted said. He introduced himself and Josie, then said, "My wife and I just bought this house. We were tearing down an old gazebo when the hauling company's dog found it. I mean her. I think it's a her. It's hard to tell. The body's in the backyard."

Ted led the way to the backyard. Halfway down the walkway, the stench slapped them in the nose.

"Jeezzuz!" Officer Dimon said, and gagged. "No need for an ambulance. This is definitely a coroner case." He covered his face with a not too clean handkerchief. After a hasty inspection of the grave, he radioed a carefully coded message into his shoulder mic, then said, "You can come around front until Detective Stevenski arrives."

"Can we leave?" Patrick asked. Chalk white under his outdoor tan, the muscleman looked like he might throw up. Even his dapper handlebar mustache drooped. "She's been dead a long time. We didn't have anything to do with it."

"That's for the detective to decide," Dimon said. "But you don't have to wait here in this stink. Bring your dog and come out front."

Michael attached a leash to his pit bull and the two shaken brothers raced down the walkway. Ted, Josie, and Officer Dimon followed almost as fast. They reassembled on the front lawn under the dogwood tree, taking deep lungfuls of fresh air.

"Is Detective Gray still on the Rock Road force?" Ted asked.

"Naw," Officer Dimon said. "He retired after that

screwup when he arrested some rich lady from Boca for murder. Her husband threatened to sue and Gray bailed."

Josie nearly choked. The rich lady from Boca was her mother-in-law, Lenore Scottsmeyer Hall.

"He's lucky he got out with his pension," Officer Dimon said. "That wasn't his first mistake, either."

Both Ted and Josie had had unhappy encounters with Detective Gray. Josie was glad he was gone. Now she knew why the indiscreet Dimon was still a patrol officer on a small force.

"Did you know him?" he asked.

"My partner and I have a vet clinic in Rock Road Village," Ted said.

Dimon nodded, as if Ted had answered his question. Not too sharp, Josie decided, or he would have remembered Ted Scottsmeyer's mother was the rich lady from Boca. The story had gotten enough press.

A plain black Dodge Charger slammed behind the police car, and a woman in a navy pantsuit climbed out. She was short, stocky, and self-important. Josie felt her hackles go up before the woman even opened her mouth.

"Detective Stevie Wonder," Officer Dimon said, and grinned.

Her glare should have melted his badge. The grin disappeared.

She turned her back on Dimon and said, "Detective Noelle Stevenski, Crimes Against Persons, Rock Road Village Police. You found a body?"

"Rock Road Village?" Josie said. "We're in Maplewood."

"You're on the border," Detective Stevenski said. "We caught the case. I don't have time to stand around and trade cocktail party chitchat. I asked if you found a body. Take me there."

"We found her in the backyard," Ted said, "when we were tearing down the old gazebo."

"Why are those clowns with the pit bull loitering on the lawn?" she asked.

"That's Patrick and Michael of Quick Micks Light Hauling," Ted said. "Their dog found the body. Officer Dimon told them to wait there until you showed up."

The detective turned on Dimon. "And you didn't separate them? Sweet suffering saints, Dimon, if you weren't retiring I'd fire you. Haven't you learned anything after all these years on the force?"

"I—," he said.

She cut him off. "Don't bother."

"You two." She pointed at Ted and Josie. "You live in that house?"

"We just bought it," Ted said. "We haven't moved in yet. My wife's twelve-year-old daughter and our contractor are in the kitchen."

"Dimon," the detective said. "Get those two inside and put them in separate rooms. Don't let them talk to each other, though it's probably too late now."

Ted tried to smile at the detective. "This is my wife, Josie Marcus," he said. "I'm Ted Scottsmeyer."

"Scottsmeyer. Scottsmeyer," Detective Stevenski said. "Why is that name familiar? I know—you're the vet who was involved with that nutcase bride. Detective Gray arrested some rich bitch for killing her and she had him by the short and curlies. Ended his career."

Ted's voice was ice. "My mother is Lenore Scottsmeyer Hall. She was wrongly arrested by Detective Gray," he said. "She was innocent. Gray is lucky she and my stepfather didn't sue. They can still sue."

"Doubt it," Stevenski said briskly. "The paperwork is all signed. Now, for the third time, where's the body?"

"Back through here," Ted said. He took Josie's hand and they started down the walkway. "We found the body about noon. Actually, the hauling company's dog found the body. It was buried under the gazebo."

Ted wasn't moving fast enough for Detective Stevenski. She rudely brushed past him and charged down the walkway, then stopped.

"Whoo!" she said. "Smells like you got yourself a real stinker."

Ted and Josie were too shocked to answer. Stevenski lit up a cigar. "Smoke helps with the smell," she said, surrounding herself with a thick, odiferous cloud.

Josie thought the cigar smelled almost as bad as the decomposing body.

"Who'd you buy this place from?" the detective asked.

"My partner at the clinic, Dr. Christine Dillon Cormac."

"How long did she live here?"

"She didn't," Ted said. "Dr. Cormac inherited the house from the original owner, her aunt Trudy, and rented it for about five years. The last renter was her sister Rain."

"Rain?" Puff. Puff. "What the hell kind of name is that? Sounds like some kind of hippie."

"I think she was," Ted said. "But I never met her. She took off about six months ago. Chris couldn't find another reliable renter and she sold the house to us."

"Where'd the hippie sister go?" Detective Stevenski asked.

"I don't know," Ted said. "Dr. Cormac said she was kind of a free spirit."

"Slept around a lot, huh? Those hippie types got no morals. Screw anything that moves."

Ted and Josie stayed silent.

"I'm going in for a closer look," she said. "You two stay back."

Ted and Josie stepped back against the fence on Cordelia's side. "Looks like a dead hippie," the detective said. "Long hair, peace sign necklace, peace dove shirt. Don't think she's been here since 1968. I'm no expert, but judging by the decomp, I'd say she's been here maybe six or eight months. Hard to judge, though. We had a hot, dry fall. No rain. Except for this puddle of Rain here." Her laugh was coarse and ugly. She puffed more smoke.

"You think this is the hippie sister?" she asked.

"I never met Rain," Ted said.

"But your partner wanted her sister out of here?"

"I don't know," Ted said. "She never discussed it with me."

More shrieking tires, a slamming door, and the sound of running feet through the walkway. The footsteps stopped abruptly halfway down, where the awful odor started, and Josie heard someone being sick. Then Christine appeared at the entrance to the backyard, her face as green as her clinic scrubs.

Josie didn't recognize Ted's cool and calm partner. Chris's short hair shot up in crazy spikes, and her eyes were as wild as her hair.

"Where is she?" Chris said, her voice high and tight with fear. "Where's my sister?"

She ran toward the open grave. Ted caught her in his arms and tried to hold her back. "No, Chris," he said. "We don't know if it's Rain. Let the medical examiner identify the body."

Chris gathered all her strength and pushed Ted away, then ran to the edge of the grave and looked down. She gave an anguished cry, then fell to her knees and ripped her top. Her howl set off the dogs next door, and they joined in, a mournful canine chorus.

"Rain!" she screamed. "No! I gave you that shirt for your birthday. You can't be dead! I didn't mean to get mad at you. This is all my fault."

Chapter 6

"Why didn't you report your sister missing, Ms. Cormac?" Detective Stevenski asked.

"Because she wasn't missing," Chris said. "Rain is a free spirit. She doesn't stay too long in one place."

The detective had ordered Officer Dimon to show everyone into a different room, "then march your sorry ass up and down those stairs and make sure they stay there and don't talk to one another."

Dimon put Patrick in the kitchen, Jeanne in the living room, and Michael wound up in the basement rec room with the dog. Amelia was sent to her future bedroom, where Josie could hear the snap of Jeanne's measuring tape. Amelia must have borrowed it to measure her windows for curtains.

Ted paced in the middle bedroom like a caged cat. Dimon showed Josie to the empty master bedroom. She sat on the polished floor by the heating vent, where she heard Detective Stevenski questioning Chris. The detective had set up her command post in the dining room, directly under Josie.

The stairs creaked under Dimon's weight. He was following Stevenski's orders, making sure nobody talked, puffing when he reached the top step. So far, he hadn't noticed Josie eavesdropping.

Judging by her wobbly voice, Josie thought Chris was still shaken. Sometimes she had trouble talking. The detective pushed until Josie was afraid Chris would snap. Maybe that's what Stevenski wanted.

"You were saying your hippie sister was a homeless drifter," the detective said.

"I didn't say that," Chris said. Josie heard a spark of anger; then Chris carefully stamped it out. "Rain doesn't want to settle down. When she tires of a location, she moves on."

She's still talking as if her sister is alive, Josie thought.

"Did you contact anyone in your family to find out where your sister was?"

"There's just my older sister, and Susan and Rain weren't getting along. I won't call one sister to bash another."

"So where did Rain live before she moved in here?" the detective asked.

"With our widowed mother for two years in Tucson," Chris said. "When Mom died of cancer, Rain inherited a little money."

"How much?" Stevenski asked.

"Ten thousand dollars," Chris said. "All three sisters got the same amount. Mom's mortgage was underwater and she had a lot of medical debts. There wasn't much money."

"Ten thousand sounds like a lot to me," the detective said. "What did Rain do with her inheritance?"

"I don't know," Chris said.

"She have a bank account?"

"She paid her rent with checks from Rock Road Mutual," Chris said.

"What about a credit card?"

"I never saw her use one," Chris said.

"So your sister inherited a nice chunk of change and then what?"

"After Mom's estate was settled and her house sold," Chris said, "Rain moved in with Susan until her husband complained that she sponged off them. Then Rain showed up on my doorstep about eighteen months ago."

"And sponged off you," the detective said.

"No, she had a job at a co-op and paid rent."

"And never skipped a single payment?" Stevenski asked.

"A couple," Chris said. "Right before she moved out—"

"Died," the detective said. "Maybe her death was an accident. Maybe she got herself murdered. She sure as hell didn't crawl into that hole by herself and throw dirt over her face."

Chris gasped.

"Somebody wanted to cover up the fact that she was dead. So don't tell me she moved out. Now, did she ever skip a rent payment?" the detective shouted, and slapped the dining table.

Josie jumped.

"She paid on time until the last month," Chris said, her voice shaky with tears. "Then she quit her job, stopped paying rent, and didn't take care of the property."

"And you wanted her out of this house," the detective said.

"No, I wanted her to pay rent and cut the grass."

"Did you fight about this?"

"We had a disagreement," Chris said. "A sisterly squabble."

"And how soon after this squabble did she take off?"

"The next day," Chris said.

"Did she stop by your office and say, 'Sis, I'm hitting the road'? Did she call you?"

"No, she sent an e-mail," Chris said. "She was going to an ashram in California."

"Do you still have it?" the detective asked.

"It's somewhere in my old e-mail."

"Did your sister ever correspond by e-mail before?"

"Yes," Chris said. "Especially if she thought I was angry with her."

"Did she have a cell phone?"

"Yes, in an earth-friendly bamboo case."

"Did you find it when you cleaned up the house?" Stevenski asked.

"No," Chris said. "She took it with her."

"Tell me about this gazebo. When did you build it?"

"I didn't," Chris said. "Harley, her boyfriend, built it."

"Harley like the motorcycle?"

"His name is Harley Scranton. He did a lot of work on this house, most of it shoddy. My sister liked to do yoga in his gazebo."

"Was she still dating this Harley when she disappeared?"

"They broke up shortly before she left, after a fight."

Josie struggled to keep quiet. She wanted to shout, Ask her where Harley lives, what he does for a living, why they fought, and what they fought about, Detective. Find out about her other boyfriend, the drunken beer can collector.

But Detective Stevenski wasn't interested in Harley or Rain's other boyfriends. Josie wondered if she'd already made up her mind that Chris had killed her sister, either accidentally or on purpose.

"About this gazebo," Detective Stevenski said. "Did you do any work on it?"

"After she . . . after my sister wasn't living in the house anymore, I noticed the gazebo steps were loose. I nailed the boards down and put in some bushes."

"Did anyone see the loose boards before you nailed them down?" the detective asked. "A real estate agent or another handyman?"

"I didn't list the house," Chris said. "I sold it privately to my partner, Dr. Scottsmeyer."

"So nobody else saw those loose boards?"

"Maybe a neighbor," Chris said, her voice trailing off into a question.

"Why didn't you hire a handyman to fix the boards?"

"Because I didn't have the money."

"You're a successful doctor. Your clinic lot is packed with cars." Stevenski made Chris's success into an accusation.

"I'm a divorced mother of three, still paying off my vet school student loans," Chris said. "Ted and I took out more loans to remodel the clinic. Our practice is doing well, but we both have debts.

"My son helped me move out the old furniture, paint the house, and get the yard in shape. I fixed the gazebo stairs, but I didn't do much else because I wasn't sure I wanted to keep it. When Ted and Josie bought the house, the first thing they tore down was the gazebo."

"Smart of you to sell the house to someone you trusted," the detective said. "Too bad he tore that gazebo down in front of witnesses and had to call the police."

"What!" Chris said. "You think I killed my sister?"

"Hey, when there's a murder, we always suspect the family," the detective said. "If you think siblings don't kill one another, open your Bible and read Cain and Abel again."

"I didn't kill my sister," Chris said.

"Maybe you didn't mean to," Detective Stevenski said, her voice suddenly soft with sympathy. "Maybe it was an accident. I'm sure a hippie-dippie type like Rain would drive anyone to murder. You're working fifteen, sixteen hours a day at the clinic, trying to pay your bills, and this so-called free spirit is freeloading, chanting 'Om' in a gazebo while you're dealing with cantankerous cats."

"No! It's not like that," Chris said. "I love my job. I love my sister."

"But you picked up a loose board or something and whacked her. You couldn't take her self-righteous attitude anymore."

"No!"

"Yes!" Stevenson said. "It's not too late to confess. I can get you a deal."

"I didn't kill my sister," Chris said. "And that's that. I'm not saying another word."

Ask for a lawyer, Chris, Josie wanted to shout, but the vet simply shut down and shut up. Detective Stevenski made her sign a statement, then told her not to leave town, just like in the movies.

"Where am I going with three kids?" Chris asked.

Ted was called next. He said they tore down the gazebo to put in a deck. He'd never met Rain and Chris didn't talk about her family, except her children. He didn't notice the boards on the stairs. He signed a statement and was escorted back upstairs to wait for Josie and Amelia.

Jeanne said she was in the kitchen with Amelia and didn't see anything. The contractor said she kept Amelia busy so she wouldn't see the body in the yard. She'd barely glanced at the gazebo. Jeanne said she'd never met Rain and only knew Christine and Ted from the clinic. Jeanne signed a statement and left.

First Michael and then Patrick were questioned. Their answers were similar to Jeanne's. No, they'd never met Rain, but they knew Ted and Christine from the clinic, where Michael took his dog.

"Was there anything to suggest the gazebo stairs had been loose as Christine Cormac said?" the detective asked them. "Did you notice any extreme cupping? See any rusted nails or deck screw holes?"

"I just tore it apart," Michael said. "I didn't pay special attention to the stairs."

"The whole thing was a wreck," Patrick said. "We busted it up and tossed it in the truck. It was a cheap prefab model and came apart pretty easy."

The brothers' interviews were so similar Josie stood up, stretched, and stared out the bedroom window, watching the crime scene crew swarming over the backyard. They looked like a sinister army in their khaki uniforms.

The yapping Jack Russells were even crazier with more strangers in the yard. Betty gave up trying to shush them. Next, Josie heard a rumbling, squeaking sound, and a petite brunette trundled a serving cart over to Josie's wide alley gate. The cart was loaded with a huge coffee thermos, foam cups, sugar, a milk jug, and a platter of cookies.

Betty had a constant, restless energy and a shrill voice. No wonder she raises Jack Russells, Josie thought.

"Excuse me. Excuse me," her neighbor trilled. "I'm Betty from next door. Would anyone like some hot coffee and chocolate chip cookies?"

The crime scene workers ran to the alley, filled the coffee cups, and stuffed themselves with cookies.

"I won't come in and disturb your crime scene," Betty said. "I thought you could use a treat. Your work is so important, but how do you stand that terrible smell?"

"You get used to it," said a fortyish man, reaching for another cookie.

"Is the dead person the hippie girl who used to live here?" Betty asked.

"The body hasn't been identified," a young woman said, warming her latex-gloved hands with her cup of hot coffee.

"But could it be her?" Betty asked. "If it is, I might have important information for the police. About how she died, I mean."

"We can't say, ma'am," another cookie scarfer said. "But the detective is interviewing people inside."

They were still eating cookies when Josie heard Patrick ask Detective Stevenski, "Can we go now?"

"After you find those gazebo stairs in your truck," the detective said, "so we can photograph them."

From the window, Josie watched Michael and his brother rummage through the wreckage in the truck. She heard slow footsteps on the stairs, heavy breathing, then a pause to recover.

"Amelia Marcus," Officer Dimon called.

"I'm going with my daughter," Josie said. "She's underage and must have a parent present." She would not let her daughter talk to the abrasive detective alone.

She put her arms around Amelia's shoulders. Dimon shrugged and let her walk downstairs with her daughter.

In the dining room, the detective glared at Josie. Before she could say anything, Josie said, "I can be with Amelia, or we can wait for my lawyer, and it will take him a long time to get here on a Saturday."

Stevenski quickly realized Amelia hadn't seen anything and sent her back upstairs.

The detective spent more time grilling Josie. She repeated why they wanted the deck torn down, said she didn't notice anything except it was a wreck, and she was inside when the body was discovered. Finally the detective tired of torturing Josie.

Dimon was escorting her upstairs when she heard a loud knock on the front door.

"Get that, Dimon," Detective Stevenski said. "Tell the media all statements come through the department's community relations office."

Instead of a reporter, Josie heard the sharp voice of her neighbor. "I'm Betty Ann Goffman," she said, stepping past the befuddled police officer. "I live next door and I have important information."

Betty was soon seated at the dining table. Josie ran up to the bedroom furnace duct and listened.

"Is that body in the backyard Christine Cormac's sister Rain?" Betty asked.

"The sister has tentatively identified the person, yes," the detective said.

"Then I feel it's my duty to tell you this," Betty said. "Christine had a bad argument with her sister and ordered her to leave. They were in the gazebo. I couldn't help hearing them. It was very . . . personal."

"How?" Stevenski asked.

"Christine was angry because her sister had quit paying rent and wouldn't keep the yard nice. I can tell you, the place was a mess. Trash all over."

"Yeah, yeah, we know that," the detective said.

"That's when the fight turned ugly. Rain shouted that Christine hated her because she'd, uh, had an affair with her husband. 'Ex-husband, thanks to you, slut,' Christine said. I won't repeat the other word she used, but she said Rain had sex with her husband in their bed. 'Now I'm supporting three kids on my own. He's late with his child support and you're not paying rent. I need money and I need it now.'

"Rain said, 'Monogamy is a patriarchal tool used to control women. The Goddess'—her word—'supports open relationships, but you chose the male slavery of marriage. I choose to be free.' Christine told her to pack up and get out."

"Then what?" the detective asked.

"It got very quiet," Betty said. "Christine drove off. The lights were off in the house. I didn't see Rain leave, but I never saw her again.

"After that, Christine and her son, Todd, worked weekends, hauling away old furniture, lamps, and clothes."

"Clothes?" the detective said. "What kind of clothes?"

"I couldn't see," Betty said. "They painted, too, cleaned up the yard, and she planted some bushes around the gazebo steps. Don't get me wrong, I'm grateful the yard looks good again."

"You never saw the sister after the fight?" the detective asked.

"Christine said Rain went to an ashram. I never knew Christine to lie. She's a good person. Oh, I forgot something.

"Two days after the fight, Christine woke me up hammering on the gazebo stairs. She said they were loose, but I never saw anything wrong."

Chapter 7

Media and flies. A dead body attracts both. Josie was horrified to see the swarm of TV vans parked outside her home.

"How do we get out of here, Ted?" she asked.

"I've asked Officer Dimon to escort us to the car," he said. "He's moving his car and Detective Stevenski's so we can get out of the driveway. Then he'll get us."

"Amelia, put your jacket over your face when we go out," Josie said.

"I'm not doing a perp walk, Mom," she said.

"I'm worried the kids at school will give you a hard time," Josie said.

Amelia shrugged. "So? I'm the token 'diversity' student, remember? I got a scholarship because they think I live in the city. That's diversity for Barrington."

My daughter is definitely learning at that school, Josie thought. But are these the right lessons?

"Most kids don't understand Maplewood is really an old suburb of St. Louis," Amelia said. "Anyway, they think murder is normal in the city. Some moms fly to Paris more often than they drive downtown."

Officer Dimon knocked at the door. "Make sure you take your things," he said. "This house is a crime scene until Detective Stevenski releases it. And don't ask me when. It could be two days if you're lucky, a week or more if you're not. We're going to your car now. Keep your heads down. You can do what you want, but it's better if you don't talk to those bloodsuckers. They'll twist your words."

Ted put his arms around Josie and Amelia. Dimon went ahead, cutting through the mob, and they raced for the car, reporters pelting them with questions: "Who died?" "Who killed her?" "Was it murder?" "Did you know the victim?" "Dr. Scottsmeyer, do you think your partner is guilty?"

Silence seemed to encourage the pack. Ted opened the car doors, and Josie and Amelia flung themselves inside. They'd barely buckled their seat belts when he threw the Mustang into reverse and peeled out of the driveway.

"Whoa, Ted," Amelia said. "You nearly ran over that reporter."

"He deserved it," Ted said, speeding toward their rented home. "He asked me, 'How does it feel to find a dead body in your yard?'"

"It feels awful," Josie said. She tried to hold back the tears, but couldn't. They were home already.

"Nobody followed us," Amelia said.

"Good," Ted said, taking Josie into his arms and kissing her forehead. "It's okay," he whispered. "Please don't cry. Let's go inside."

In the kitchen, they were greeted by a wagging, wriggling welter of warm fur. They stopped to pet Harry, Ted's cat, Marmalade, and Festus, his dog. The animals had blended nicely into a pack. Josie felt better after a pet distraction.

"Can we order pizza?" Amelia asked.

"Tonight is definitely a pizza night," Ted said.

Josie nodded. "You make the call, Amelia. A large

pepperoni and mushroom for Ted and me and whatever you want."

"Awesome!" Amelia said.

After she placed the pizza order, Amelia scratched Harry, Marmalade, and Festus. "We're having a scratch-a-thon," she said. "I can do both cats with one hand and Festus with the other."

"Amelia doesn't seem upset," Ted said.

"I hope it doesn't hit her later," Josie said. "I need to call Mom. I don't want her to see it on TV."

Josie's mother was nearly as upset as her daughter. "Oh no," she said. "Not your lovely house. Josie, I can hold off renting your old flat. You all can move back here."

"Thanks, Mom, but Ted's landlord has extended his lease till September first. We'll be fine. In a few days we'll be able to start the work on the new house. We'll be moved in by the time Ted's lease is up."

"And living in a crime scene?" Jane asked.

"Not exactly. The body was in the backyard under the gazebo," Josie said. "That's gone, Mom, and we'll build a deck over it. You need to rent that flat and get some income. We'll be by tomorrow to help you paint it."

"Pizza's here," Amelia called.

"Gotta go, Mom," Josie said. "Love you."

The pizza-loving pets were banished to Amelia's bedroom. Harry had a bad habit of poking mushrooms with his paw, Marmalade liked to lick the sauce, and Festus had once gobbled Ted's leftover pizza.

Josie put plates and stacks of paper napkins on the table, and everyone sat down. "Grease, calories, carbs, and cholesterol," Ted said. "My favorite food groups."

"I'm starved," Amelia said. "I missed lunch."

Josie was surprised she was hungry, too. The pizzas disappeared while they talked.

"I don't want to ruin your meal," Josie said. "But do we want to keep the new house?"

"Why not?" Amelia said. "It's amazing. If we lived in England or someplace where houses are hundreds of years old, lots of people die in them. Anyway, like you told Grandma, the lady didn't die in the house."

"We don't think," Josie said.

"You're putting a deck on top of where she was found," Amelia said, "so we won't even see it."

"Ted, you actually saw the body," Josie said. "Can you erase that sight from your mind?"

"No," he said carefully. "But I can learn to forget it. I see sad and terrible things every day at the clinic, but I still love animals and enjoy working with them. What about you, Josie? Can you live there?"

"I hope once the deck is up, I won't be reminded of Rain's death. I still love our house."

"Me, too," Amelia said.

"It's not like we have another house to move into," Ted said. "We didn't like anything the real estate agent showed us, and you've looked at every available house in the area.

"Besides, we can't sell now. You saw that horde of reporters. Our house is big news. The whole city will know there was a dead body in the backyard. We'd have to sell at a big loss."

"Let's give it a year," Josie said. "If we find out we can't live in it, we can sell it. By then the ruckus will have died down."

"Agreed," Ted said.

"Yay!" Amelia said. "We get to keep the house. It's almost six o'clock. Can I turn on the TV? I want to see if our house made the news."

By the time they were settled on Ted's bachelor black leather sofa, the news was on. That's when they made the second awful discovery of the day: their house was the lead local story.

A reporter in a bad toupee intoned, "A newlywed couple got a chilling housewarming . . ."

Ted switched to Channel Seven and Honey Butcher, a blonde with bloodred lipstick and straight hair, said, "The decomposed body of a woman was discovered in the backyard of this Maplewood home."

"That's our house!" Josie said.

"Our redbud tree looks good," Amelia said, but Josie was too heartsick to admire it.

"The body is believed to be the sister of the previous owner, Christine Cormac," the reporter said, "a partner in this Rock Road veterinary clinic."

The St. Louis Mobo-Pet Clinic flashed on the screen. The camera zeroed in on the clinic's blue van, with the cartoon picture of the dog, cat, and bird.

Ted groaned. "This will kill us," he said.

"You have a loyal following," Josie said, hoping her fear didn't show.

"Christine Cormac had this to say to reporters at the scene," the lipsticked blonde said. The video showed a wild-eyed Chris pushing her way through the horde of reporters, shrieking, "Leave me the hell alone, you (bleeping bleep bleeps)."

"Poor Chris," Josie said.

"The home's current owners refused to comment," the bloody-lipped blonde said.

"That's us!" Amelia said. "Except you can't see anything of me but the top of my hair."

Josie was stunned to see Officer Dimon pushing through the screaming crowd while Ted, Josie, and Amelia struggled to get to the Mustang. Ted clung heroically to his family in the roiling sea of reporters. Once they were inside the car, the camera focused on Ted nearly clipping a reporter as he roared out of the driveway.

"Hey!" the reporter shouted. "Did you see that? He nearly ran over my feet!"

"A Rock Road Village police spokesperson would not comment on the cause of death or how long the victim had been buried in the backyard," the blonde said. "Fortunately we have this exclusive interview with a public-spirited neighbor, Mrs. Betty Ann Goffman."

Betty was sitting on a plush ice blue living room couch, petting a bright-eyed Jack Russell on her lap.

"Christine was nice, but never very friendly," Betty said. "She was busy with her career and of course she has three children. Very well-behaved children, I should say. You don't see children that polite these days.

"Her sister Rain lived here for about a year and a half, but we didn't have much in common. She was a hippie. You can probably tell that by her name. Rain was a bit trusting when it came to men, and sometimes there were arguments. Two were so loud I was forced to call the police. I felt bad about that, but it was for her protection, and mine. We're both single women."

"Were those the only fights?" Honey Butcher asked.

"Uh . . ." Betty hesitated.

"The public has a right to know," Honey said.

"Well, there was one more," Betty said. "I didn't call the police. I wouldn't call it a fight, exactly, but Christine and her sister had discussion in the backyard gazebo."

"What kind of discussion?" Honey asked.

"It was a bit heated," Betty said.

"What was it about?" Honey refused to back off.

"I can't repeat the words Christine used, not on television, but she ordered her sister to leave. I never saw Rain again."

"And when was this heated argument?" Honey asked.

Betty looked around wildly, as if she wanted to escape.

"Mrs. Goffman, when was this discussion?" Honey demanded, a prosecutor hammering an uncooperative witness.

"Six months ago," Betty said.

"And the workmen tore down that same gazebo today and found a body under it," Honey said. "The very same gazebo where Christine Cormac fought with her sister. Isn't that true, Mrs. Goffman?"

"Yes, but—," Betty said.

"And the dead person is Ms. Cormac's sister Rain Dillon," Honey said.

"That bitch!" Amelia said.

"Amelia!" Josie said.

"I was talking about the dog, Mom," Amelia said, wide-eyed and fake innocent.

"The dog is a male," Ted said, trying to hide a grin.

"That's not official, is it?" Betty asked. "I haven't heard the police say the body is Rain."

"I have two sources to confirm it," Honey said. She looked the camera right in the lens. "You heard it here first, folks."

Betty stroked her terrier's ears as she talked to the reporter.

"Do you take your dogs to Christine's veterinary clinic?" Honey asked.

"No," Betty said.

"Because you don't want to expose your doggies to a veterinarian who uses bad language and has a violent temper?"

"That's not the reason," Betty said, but Honey talked right over her. "I have a little Chihuahua," the reporter said. "My doggies are like my children and we can't have our children exposed to bad language."

"That b-"—Josie fought her own urge to use the b-word—"bad woman."

Betty finally managed to say, "I take my dogs to a vet who specializes in show dogs. I raise Jack Russells, you know. I still have two young ones for sale. Both blue-ribbon winners."

"She's turning this into a commercial," Josie said.

"Sounds like she's trying to turn the subject away from Chris," Ted said. "That reporter really has it in for my partner."

"And who's this little guy?" Honey asked playfully.

"This is Belmont's Jack Dandy," Betty said. "A purebred AKC-registered Parson Russell terrier. That's what the AKC calls this type of Jack Russell. He's not for sale. He's the future Westminster Dog Show Best in Show champion."

Even Josie had to admit the dog was handsome. "His brown ears look like the tips of a button-down shirt collar," she said.

"Those are button ears," Ted said. "Ears are an important part of a show dog's appearance. Fine chest, too. Jack Dandy has the makings of a champ, all right."

The phone on the lamp table rang and Ted reached for it. "Chris," he said. "How are you? I'm so sorry about your sister. What a horrible way to find out about your loss."

A pause, while Ted listened. "Yes, I saw how they ripped you up on television. And I watched that b—" He glanced at Amelia. "—bad woman try to twist Betty's words. Of course I don't believe you killed your sister.

"Look, Chris, I know you're innocent, but I think that detective has it in for you. You need to hire Renzo Fischer. He's the best criminal defense attorney in St. Louis."

Another pause while he listened.

"Is he expensive? Yes, but he's the best."

"Tell her we can lend her some of the money from our renovation fund," Josie whispered.

Ted nodded, then said, "Chris, we'll lend you the money. Josie just suggested it."

Another pause.

Ted said. "Chris, I know a lawyer is major money, but

right now you can't *not* afford to hire him. Okay, I understand. But I still think it's a mistake. You're going to need a lawyer sooner or later. Protect yourself and make it sooner."

Chapter 8

"Josie? You feel like working? I've got a new job."

Harry, her boss at Suttin Services, called at nine on a Monday morning with a new mystery shopping assignment.

Good, Josie thought. I can use the work for the remodeling—if we ever get our home back. She pictured Harry at his desk, then wished she hadn't. Harry lived up to his name, or grew into it. If he'd been that hairy as a baby, he would have been a chimp. Mother Nature had given him luxuriant hair from his knuckles to his nose, then cruelly made his head follicle free.

"You bet," Josie said. "Bring it on."

"You're sure you can work, after finding that dead body at your new house?" he asked. "I saw the story on TV."

"Thanks," she said, surprised by Harry's sudden sensitivity. "That was a shock. I was meeting with the kitchen contractor, and Ted was tearing down the gazebo with a work crew when they discovered that poor woman."

"Musta stunk like hell, huh?"

So much for sensitivity, Josie thought. "You have an assignment?"

"Yeah. Funny you should mention kitchen contractors," Harry said. "You know how these midcentury kitchens are getting to be big deals now? All the yuppies want the same junk my mom tore outta her place years ago. Contractors are making big bucks on this stiff. I need you to mystery-shop a contractor who wants to join the AKC."

"The American Kennel Club?" Josie asked.

"No," Harry said. "The American Kitchen Contractors. Big-deal national organization. This local guy wants to be a member, but the AKC isn't sure. They're too cheap to hire a private detective to investigate him, but they think a mystery shopper could go undercover, like James Bond, you know?"

Josie Marcus, suburban spy, she thought.

"Why aren't they sure about him?" Josie asked.

"They've heard some rumors he doesn't follow the EPA procedures and other stuff he's advertising on his Web site. I'll fax you the questions. I got more work, too. I want you to mystery-shop a store that sells recycled cabinets and stuff—a green hardware store. They have midcentury fixtures sometimes."

Josie tried to hide her excitement. If Harry knew she wanted this assignment, he was perverse enough to take it away.

"I could do that," she said, hoping she got the right balance between indifference and disinterest. "You sound different this morning. Usually you call during breakfast."

Most conversations with Harry were punctuated by hearty slurps and crunches. Her boss was a fearless foodie, eating deadly dishes that gave cardiologists heart attacks.

"Already had breakfast," he said. "The Carnival Diner had deep-fried Twinkies with powdered sugar. Kinda like them things you get in New Orleans, whad'ya call them, benyets."

"Beignets?" Josie said, pronouncing the name correctly.

"That's what I said. Twinkies are a versatile food," Harry said. "The diner has Twinkie dogs for lunch, hot dogs wrapped in bacon and served on a deep-fried Twinkie."

Recycling the breakfast leftovers, Josie thought.

"Now, there's a meal. Dinner and dessert at the same time." Harry smacked his lips.

"Amazing," Josie said.

She'd barely put the phone down before her mother-in-law, Lenore Scottsmeyer Hall, called from her Boca Raton mansion. Josie could tell it was Lenore by the frost on her phone.

"Josie, dear, you and Ted didn't tell me about the problem at your house," she said. "I had to see it on national TV."

Uh-oh, Josie thought. She and Ted had hoped Rain's death would stay a local story.

"We didn't want to worry you," Josie said.

"We offered to lend you the money for a new home, but Ted wouldn't hear of it."

My husband doesn't want to be under your thumb, Josie thought. It's one more reason why I admire him.

"My son seems to prefer used goods," Lenore said.

Ouch. This wasn't the first time Ted's mother has let me know her son could have married better.

Josie didn't want a battle with Lenore. She tried to remember the tips from that article "Ten Ways to Bond with Your Mother-in-Law." The first tip said, "Ask to see pictures of her early life." Forget it. Lenore didn't want anyone to know how old she was. Tip two was also out — cooking a meal together. Lenore's housekeeper did the cooking.

"Speak her language," the article suggested, and gave a heartwarming example of a bride who learned Spanish to chat with her mother-in-law. I can say "nasolabial fold," "tear trough," and "rhytidectomy," Josie thought, but I doubt we'll bond. Lenore has had more face-lifts than Joan Rivers. Fortunately her plastic surgeon husband is skilled with the knife.

"Make her part of your life and bridge the difference with photos," the article said. Josie decided that tip was safe.

"Did you get the photos I e-mailed you?" she asked.

"Yes. Little what's her name—"

"Amelia," Josie said through gritted teeth.

"Is growing like a weed. But, Josie, dear, is it healthy to have so many animals in the house? It seems so Third World."

"Harry, Festus, and Marmalade are part of the family," Josie said.

"Exactly," Lenore said. "Well, I didn't call to gloat about your house. I'm not one to say 'I told you so,' but I am sorry you and Ted didn't take my advice. Good-bye."

Josie wasted several minutes fuming, but didn't dare complain to Ted. She called her own mother for comfort.

"Thank you again, Josie," Jane said. "You three did wonderful work yesterday on the downstairs flat. I can't believe all the rooms are painted. I got up early this morning and waxed the floors. The flat is ready to rent. I'm putting the ads in the neighborhood papers and a sign in the window."

"You should get a good price, Mom," Josie said. "More than I was paying."

"The extra money will be nice, but I loved having you live in this house," Jane said. "You're welcome back anytime. You know that."

Talking to her mother soothed Josie's wounded feelings. She tried to remind herself that she and Jane didn't always get along so well. Jane had had harsh words for her daughter when she was pregnant with Amelia and unmarried. Josie had dropped out of college in her senior year to become a mystery shopper.

Jane was furious when Josie refused to marry Nate, Amelia's father, but Josie had discovered her Canadian lover was a drug dealer about the time she'd learned she was pregnant. She'd refused to tell Nate. She wasn't dragging her baby into the dark, dangerous world of drug dealing.

Once Jane saw her newborn granddaughter, Josie was forgiven. Sort of. She and baby Amelia moved into Jane's empty downstairs flat. To please her mother, Josie went along with Jane's lie that Nate was a pilot killed in the Mideast.

Jane didn't want her church lady friends to know her daughter had a child out of wedlock—and the baby's father was in a Canadian prison for drug trafficking.

That lie was exposed when Nate was pardoned and showed up on Josie's doorstep drunk. His demands to marry Josie were cut short when he died suddenly. Two good things came out of that reunion: Amelia met her father and now had a loving grandfather in Canada.

Jane was thrilled when her stubborn daughter married Dr. Ted. Maybe my story has a happy ending after all, Josie thought, but she still couldn't shrug off her mother-in-law's hurtful words.

She heard the fax line ring in her office, then churn out her new assignment. Ted had divided his office in two with bookcases, giving Josie the best space and the only view.

Harry's fax said she had to mystery-shop ReHab and interview Travis Ray Porter, a contractor with an office in Mehlville.

Might as well get Travis Ray over with, Josie thought, and called him.

Mehlville was a southern suburb, but not that far south. Travis Ray had a Deep South accent.

"I can see you before noon, darlin'," he said. "I'm on Lindbergh just south of I-55, in the strip mall with the big American flag."

Travis Ray's office was no advertisement for his work, Josie thought. The parking lot was potholed, his sign was sun-faded, and the glass door was streaked with mud. Josie knocked on the locked door and a bear-sized German shepherd threw itself at the door, snapping and snarling. His paws left more mud streaks.

"T-Rex!" a man commanded. "T-Rex! Stop that! Now!"

The man who swaggered to the door was cowboy lean, with a tool belt slung low on his hips and a Skoal chewing tobacco ball cap. He grabbed the big dog by the collar and unlocked the door.

"I'm Travis Ray Porter," he drawled. "You're the lady who called about the kitchen? No need to look so scared. Ol' T-Rex won't hurt you. He just likes to hear himself bark. Sit, T-Rex."

Josie was relieved when the dog crawled under the contractor's dusty desk. She sat in a comfortable leather chair and Travis Ray took the handsome executive chair behind the desk. Josie could barely see him over the yellowing pile of papers, catalogues, and invoices, some stamped OVERDUE.

"Now, what can I do you for?" he said, laughing at his old joke.

"My husband and I would like to remodel our kitchen," she said, following her mystery shopper script. "We have a big eat-in kitchen from the seventies, and it needs serious updating—new tile, windows, plumbing, paint, and more. We'd like a kitchen island, too."

"Sounds good," he said. "What kind of budget do you have in mind?"

"Ten thousand is our limit," Josie said. "How many kitchens have you remodeled?"

"A bunch," he said. "All over town."

Wrong answer, Josie thought. You're supposed to show me a list.

"Do you have references?" Josie asked.

He rooted through the pile of paperwork and said, "I do. They're in here somewhere. I'll find them for you and send them later."

Wrong again. "Your Web site says you remove paint and asbestos according to EPA guidelines," Josie said.

"Well, I put that there to keep the tree huggers off my back," he said. "I can do it the EPA way, but I'll be honest with you, that's gonna cost you more. All that environmental crap is nothing but government interference. I mean, what's the environment ever done for me?" He laughed loudly.

Three strikes, Travis, Josie thought, but I'll ask you the last two questions and leave.

"Who will handle the permits?" Josie asked.

"You can take care of those," he said. "A cute lady like yourself can get anything you want out of the boys at city hall. They'll just wrap me in red tape."

"What type of insurance do you have?"

"BlueCross BlueShield," he said, and grinned. "Now, don't go worrying your pretty head about that kind of thing. I've got all the right stuff to do the job. I even have a contract if you'd like to sign now. I prefer all payments in cash, with half up front."

"I'd have to show it to my husband first," Josie said.

"Of course, darling, that's what a good wife does," he said. "Let me tell you about my special wives' discount. I'll put one price on the contract, but give you ten percent back if you're nice to me. If we're talking ten thousand dollars, I'll give you a thousand dollars cash. We'll have a little fun, your old man will never know, and you'll have some play money for yourself."

"That's an interesting offer," Josie said. "I'd like to think about it."

"You do that, darling," he said. "And think about all my satisfied customers."

Chapter 9

"Campbell Witherspoon!"

"Kendall Dickenson!"

"Kennedy Duckworth!"

One by one, Miss Apple, the head of school, called the names and the students ran out to their waiting cars at the Barrington School for Boys and Girls.

Barrington students did not rudely race out of school, Josie thought. These future lawyers, doctors, and CEOs were announced, after Miss Apple recognized their approved designated drivers. That was her title, head of school. Ordinary schools have principals. Rich ones have headmasters, or heads of school. Josie wondered if "headmistress" sounded too racy for Barrington.

"Palmer Lindell!"

"Jace Parkington!"

"Emerson Middleton!"

Rich kids have such gender-neutral names, Miss Apple could be announcing law firms. Josie had to actually see the students to know if they were boys or girls. The first group was boys. The next trio was girls.

Barrington's redbrick campus was a restrained Georgian style suitable for the scions of old money, or new money hoping to be old. The cars waiting to pick them up were mostly black and quietly pricy: Mercedes, Beemers, Lexus, an occasional Jaguar, driven by women well off enough to be stay-at-home mothers. The beat-up older models belonged to housekeepers, nannies, and Josie.

She wondered if Travis Ray, the creepy contractor, would have propositioned the wealthy Barrington mothers. No, she decided, but he'd definitely hit on the help. Travis Ray was a predator and Josie didn't regret destroying him in her mystery-shopping report. She felt good saving other ordinary women from that slime. Josie's job—her career, if you wanted to give it that dignified name—was representing American shoppers, the invisible women often dissed and dismissed by the stores they supported. Josie had nicknamed them Mrs. Minivan, and her mission was to make sure these women got good treatment.

"Everett Chadwin!"

"Bailey Marie Novak!"

"Amelia Marcus!"

At last. Josie's daughter hurried across the sunlit grass, brown hair blowing in the spring breeze, shoulders hunched. Josie frowned. That wasn't like Amelia. Was she trying to hide her new womanly figure?

"Hi, Mom!" she said, and plopped down on the passenger side, clutching her backpack to her chest.

"Hi, sweetie." Josie no longer kissed her girl hello. At this age, public parent smooching triggered major embarrassment. "Why don't you throw that in the backseat so you can be comfortable?"

"Can't. I've got this gross stain on my blouse," Amelia said, in the tone reserved for tween tragedies. "I don't want anyone else to see it. Think you can get it out?"

She moved the backpack enough so Josie could see the greasy red splotch on her white blouse.

"Pasta?" Josie guessed.

"Pizza," Amelia said. "Oakley hit my arm. She said it was an accident."

"Was it?" Josie asked.

Amelia shrugged. "Whatever. I had to go around like this all afternoon. I don't want more kids to see it."

They drove in silence for the rest of the trip home, while Amelia texted Emma, the friend she'd seen all day in school. How did she make her thumbs move so fast? What did they talk about? Josie wondered. She and her best friend, Sue Brandt, had talked for hours when they were Amelia's age. Josie didn't remember a word, but those conversations had been vitally important at the time.

Amelia didn't say another word until they were at the house. "Will Ted be home at six thirty tonight?"

"He should be," Josie said.

"Thought I'd start the marinade for salmon in Thai sauce," Amelia said. "We bought salmon steaks yesterday."

"Yum," Josie said. "You fix the fish and I'll make the salad."

If it wasn't for that body in the backyard of our new house, my life would be perfect, she thought. Hunky husband, a daughter who's doing well in school and likes to cook, and no crises with Mom.

"I can probably make it myself, even if Ted's late," Amelia said. "It's pretty easy."

"For you," Josie said. "My fish would make Mrs. Paul hang up her apron."

"It's not frozen fish, Mom," Amelia said, and rolled her eyes.

The eye roll was Amelia's new, annoying habit. Distancing yourself from your mother is a natural part of growing up, Josie reminded herself. So why do I have this unnatural urge to shake my daughter until her teeth rattle?

Harry was waiting for Amelia at the kitchen door. She hoisted her striped cat onto her shoulder and went to her bedroom to text and do her homework. Josie knew most of the time would be spent texting, but Amelia was good about her homework.

Ted called about four o'clock. "Detective Stevenski was by this afternoon, Josie," he said. "Our house will be released as a crime scene tomorrow."

"That's good news," Josie said. "Why do you sound so worried?"

"Because she's still hounding Chris," he said. "I'll tell you about it when I get home tonight."

Josie hung up, her stomach twisting into a knot. That boneheaded detective could ruin their clinic. Ted needed his partner to keep it running. Even with Laura, the new vet, there was still too much work.

Chris and Josie weren't gal pals, but Josie had come to know her well during the hectic wedding time. Chris had graciously ignored Lenore's jabs that Ted's best man was a woman. She'd reacted with dignity when Ted's brother, a childish practical joker, had planted an ice cube with a plastic fly in her water glass at the rehearsal dinner. Chris was practical, organized, and kind. Josie hoped Ted's partner could handle this pressure.

Rather than brood, she called her best friend, Alyce Bohannon, and gave her the good news about the house.

"I can't wait for my tour," Alyce said. "I haven't seen it yet."

"Come by tomorrow morning," Josie said.

"How do you feel about it after the . . . problem?" Alyce asked, too tactful to say "dead woman." Josie's friend lived in Wood Winds, a genteel subdivision where the only dead things in yards were plants, and the lawn service quickly removed them.

"You mean Rain's body?" Josie said. "The new deck will cover the site soon. As long as I can't see it, I won't

think about it. After you see the house, want to go
mystery-shopping? It's in the city."

Going into St. Louis was Alyce's walk on the wild
side. Her husband, Jake, was a corporate lawyer. His income was enough for a McMansion in the burbs and the
freedom of a nanny for their three-year-old son, Jason.
Mystery-shopping trips to exotic city neighborhoods
provided small, safe doses of excitement.

They agreed to meet at the new house after Josie
dropped off Amelia at school the next morning.

Josie called the kitchen contractor next, and Jeanne
wanted to meet with her about eleven. She was glad Alyce would be there. She'd need her friend's help with the
contractor.

At six o'clock, Amelia came out, carrying the sauce-
stained blouse. Josie worked on the stain while her
daughter started dinner, chopping and organizing the ingredients.

"I like the smell of that lemongrass," Josie said. No
response.

"Where's the rice vinegar?" Amelia said, studying the
bottles in the cabinet. "Ted always puts things up so
high."

Amelia mixed the ingredients in a saucepan. Soon the
kitchen was scented with the sharp smell of vinegar.
Then she started the jasmine rice while Josie made a
salad. Josie liked working side by side with her daughter.

At least one of those bonding tips was right, she
thought. Cooking was a good way to spend quality time
with Amelia without talking, and her daughter had less
to say to her each day.

Six thirty passed. Josie eyed the clock anxiously and
set the table to distract herself. Ten minutes later, Josie
heard Ted's car pull up. Harry ran to the kitchen door to
greet Ted, Festus, and Marmalade. The Lab and the or-

ange tabby cat worked at the clinic as blood donors but lived with Ted.

Harry and Marmalade sniffed each other politely while Festus wagged his tail. All three stopped for an after-work slurp at their water bowls while Ted poured out their dinner.

"Ted, you look tired," Josie said, smoothing his rumpled hair. She kissed him, enjoying his slightly scratchy beard, and caught his end-of-the-day smell—coffee and dog hair. "Rough day with the animals?" she asked.

"Good day at work," he said. "Some of my favorites were in. I am worried about Chris, though. I'll tell you later, after dinner."

When Amelia isn't around, Josie thought. This must be serious. Her stomach tightened a bit more. She didn't like waiting.

Ted sniffed the air and changed the subject. "What smells so good?"

"Salmon with Thai sauce. Made it myself," Amelia said, her pride obvious. "The fish is about done. Time to slather on the sauce."

"You wash up, Ted," Josie said. "Dinner will be on the table when you're finished."

Ted and Josie gave Amelia's salmon the extravagant praise it deserved.

"Whatever," Amelia said, but Josie thought this was an enthusiastic "Whatever." She was learning the incredible range of emotion those eight letters could convey in tween talk, from disgust to delight.

"Which favorite was in today?" Josie asked.

"Marley," Ted said. "He belongs to Maryann Schnoor. Marley's a cocker spaniel, but he's really a retriever. Each morning on his walk, Marley has to find a beer can, or the walk's not finished. They may search for half an hour. Marley carries his beer can halfway home, then drops it. Maryann has to pick it up and carry it the rest of the way. The walk is not complete without that ritual."

"What happens if Marley can't find a beer can?" Amelia asked.

"He'll settle for a soda or iced tea can," Ted said, "but he drops that halfway, too. If Maryann can't find a trash can, she has to walk through the neighborhood at seven a.m. carrying a beer can. She hopes the neighbors don't think she's a drunk."

Amelia giggled.

"The only thing Marley won't touch is an energy drink can," Ted said.

"I won't touch them, either," Amelia said.

Ted looked at the empty plates. "Fabulous dinner, Amelia. Josie, I think we should do the dishes and let the chef have the night off."

"No dishes! That's legit!" She shot out of her chair toward her room, followed by her animal entourage.

Josie scraped the plates and brought them to the sink. Ted rinsed and loaded them in the dishwasher. The running water covered their voices.

"What's wrong with Chris?" Josie asked, handing him their plates and silverware.

"The medical examiner found Chris's sterling silver earring with the body," he said, rinsing the saucepan. "Detective Stevenski demanded to know if it was hers. I went to my office and listened. You can hear everything through those thin walls. I didn't like the detective's tone."

"Maybe it wasn't Chris's earring," Josie said.

"She said it was," Ted said, loading the plates. "That wasn't great detecting by Stevenski. The earring is a veterinary caduceus, a snake winding around a staff with a V over it. Chris said her sister gave it to her as a graduation present and she lost it six or eight months ago."

"I don't think I've ever seen Chris wear earrings except at our wedding," Josie said.

"She rarely wears them to work," Ted said. "Stevenski asked her again about the fight with Rain. Chris insisted they argued because her sister wasn't paying rent or keeping up the property. She denied that Rain had had an affair with Chris's ex-husband."

"Again?" Josie asked. "Didn't you tell Chris what I heard at our house? Betty, the dog show neighbor, said the fight was about Rain having sex with Chris's husband."

"Of course," Ted said "Chris says it's her word against Betty's."

"But that detective wants to believe Betty," Josie said. She wiped down the kitchen table, then the stove.

"I can't make Chris see that," Ted said. "She's being stubborn and it's dangerous. Except for the fight, Chris was straight with the detective. She admitted planting new shrubs around the gazebo and said the stairs were coming loose and she hammered the boards back into place.

"The detective asked what kind of work Chris had done after her sister left. Chris said she and her son had hauled her aunt's furniture to the charity resale shop. She decided that people who couldn't afford their own furniture wouldn't be reliable renters,

"Chris said Rain took all her belongings with her. The detective accused Chris of lying about that, too. She showed her the charity shop receipt, which said Chris donated 'two bags of women's clothing.' "

"The receipt didn't say what kind of clothes?" Josie asked.

"No," Ted said. "Chris said she gave away some suits, but there's no proof.

"After the detective left, I begged Chris to get Renzo Fischer again. I'm worried, Josie. Chris has three children. What happens to them if she's jailed?

"Chris said the kids were three good reasons why she

can't afford a lawyer. She won't hear of us lending her the money, either. She says she's telling the truth and that's enough."

"What did you say?" Josie asked, over the growl of the garbage disposal.

"That the truth won't set her free." Ted scrubbed the kitchen counter. "Not when a detective wants to twist it."

He wrung out the dishcloth and hung it up to dry.

Chapter 10

The warm yellow spring day was the perfect showcase for Josie's home on Fresno Court, and Alyce poured on the praise.

"What a glorious garden, Josie," she said. "Those yellow daffodils really set off the bluebells."

"You should have seen them with the yellow crime scene tape," Josie said.

She'd spent half an hour that morning removing the last traces of the police presence and the media horde, but the hole where the gazebo once stood was unmistakably a grave. Josie couldn't wait until the new deck covered it.

"Oh, honey, I'm sorry," Alyce said. "You can't tell anything happened. Really."

"You can't," Josie said, "but I can. Look how those reporters trampled the flowers along the driveway." She pointed to the crushed tulip bed.

"They broke a branch off the redbud tree, too. At least the police chased them off the lawn before they did more damage."

Alyce hugged her friend. "Let's go inside," she said, "and see your house. I brought us lemon cream-cheese cupcakes and coffee in case your stove isn't working." She handed Josie a wicker picnic basket.

Alyce looked like a spring earth goddess with her generous build, pale skin, and silky blond hair. If earth goddesses wore lavender pantsuits.

"My favorite," Josie said.

"But I've never made them before," Alyce said.

"Everything you make is my favorite," Josie said.

Alyce was a master cook and full-time mom who didn't have Josie's money worries. The two friends had hit it off when they'd volunteered for the same civic committee several years ago.

Inside the house, Alyce oohed and aahed over the architectural details—the well-polished woodwork, working fireplace, and art glass windows. Josie glowed with pride. Her old flat had been homey, but a bit run-down.

Alyce's flow of praise dried up at the kitchen door. The harsh morning light revealed all the flaws from the broken tile to the aging appliances. "Uh, this has great potential," she said.

Josie didn't flinch when her friend used that overworked real estate term.

"Amelia wants to keep the midcentury look," Josie said. "It's being rehabbed. The contractor is coming at eleven."

"'Rehabbed'?" Alyce looked blank for a moment, then said, "Oh. Right. I'm such an outsider. I forgot that St. Louisans say 'rehab' instead of 'renovate.' It sounds like your kitchen went on a bender."

"I'm going on a bender if we aren't moved in here by fall," Josie said. "Let's have some coffee."

Alyce had prepared her treat with her usual flair. The wicker basket was packed with hand-painted china in velvet holders, sterling silver, linen napkins, two dozen cupcakes, and a silver coffee thermos.

"Elegant," Josie said, after they'd set the dining room table. They settled in for a talk until they were interrupted by the doorbell. "It's too early for the kitchen contractor," Josie said. "I'll see who it is."

Josie found a tall, thin man with a noble nose and thick gray hair wearing a navy uniform with DAVE on the pocket. "I'm here to install your window shades," he said.

Josie said, "But I didn't order—"

"I did," Alyce said. "Happy housewarming. These shades are for all your windows facing the backyard. Fortunately Dave knows this neighborhood."

"I've installed shades in just about every house around here," he said. "I made an educated guess on the window sizes, and if the shades don't fit, I'll take them back to the shop and adjust them. Where do you want me to start?"

"Uh—" Josie was so surprised she couldn't remember which windows faced the backyard. "The master bedroom upstairs and the adjoining bath. Then the kitchen."

"Let me get my tools out of my truck." Dave ran briskly down the stairs.

"Thank you, Alyce," Josie said. "But the kitchen shades will be ruined when we remodel."

"Maybe not," Alyce said. "If they are, the shades are recyclable. By the time the kitchen is finished, your deck will be going up, covering any reminder of poor Rain. See if you like the shade colors."

Dave was back with his toolbox and the new shades. He unrolled a creamy beige fabric one.

"These are honeycomb shades for the bedroom," Dave said. "The 'cells' are lined with black so the morning sun won't wake you."

"The white kitchen shades don't have that lining," Alyce said.

"Perfect," Josie said. "You've saved me hours of work."

"If you ladies will excuse me, I'll start mine," Dave said. "Up those stairs to the master bedroom?"

"Right. The blue room," Josie said. Dave turned down coffee and cupcakes. She heard an occasional thump and metallic screech while Dave worked overhead.

"Okay if we start mystery-shopping after I meet with Jeanne the kitchen contractor?" Josie asked. "I may need you to translate."

"The nanny stays till four," Alyce said. "I'm yours till then. Where's our assignment?"

Josie liked that "our." Alyce wasn't paid to mystery-shop with Josie, though she was a big help. "ReHab, the green hardware store run by that organization that helps low-income people build homes," she said. "In midtown St. Louis."

"Cool," Alyce said. "I've wanted to go there." Women in Alyce's suburban enclave did not go into the city alone.

Josie's cell phone rang and she saw Ted was calling. "I have to take this," she said, excusing herself.

"Josie, Rain's body has been released after the autopsy," Ted said. "Chris is planning a funeral for the day after tomorrow. Rain wanted a green burial, so Chris is having her cremated. Will you go?"

"Of course," Josie said. "Did the autopsy show what killed her?"

"An overdose of an animal tranquilizer, acepromazine," Ted said. "It's sort of like Thorazine for humans, but stronger. Rain was probably unconscious when she died. Chris feels a little better knowing that. When Chris saw that peace sign necklace, she was afraid Rain had been strangled."

"Strange what gives us comfort," Josie said. "How's Chris holding up?"

"So-so," Ted said. "Detective Stevenski was here this morning again, wanting to know if Chris had access to acepromazine. Of course she does. All vets do." He dropped his voice. "She still insists she didn't argue with Rain about having sex with Rodney, her ex-husband."

Dave carried the white shades into the kitchen and started working on the double window over the sink. The electric screwdriver shrieked.

"What's that noise?" Ted asked.

"The shade installer. Alyce bought us a housewarming present—new shades to cover the windows facing the backyard."

"She really is a friend," Ted said.

"Any luck getting Chris to see a lawyer?" Josie asked.

"No. Maybe her sister can talk some sense into her. Susan's flying in for the funeral."

"I hope so," Josie said. "It sounds like that detective wants to throw her in jail."

Wild yapping interrupted their conversation. "Oops, a pup got loose in the waiting room and he's charging down the hall," Ted said. "Gotta help round him up."

Josie barely had time to tell Alyce about Ted's call when Dave said, "All finished. Perfect fit. Do I know these houses or what?"

Now the bright daylight in the kitchen was filtered through the pure white shade. The dreadful grave was hidden.

"That's so much better," Josie said. She was showing Dave out when Jeanne the kitchen contractor arrived, carrying a ladder.

"I'll take this in the back to the kitchen," she said. Josie was relieved that she didn't mention the gazebo grave.

Jeanne had brought her own coffee, but she did take a cupcake. Between bites, she fired questions at Josie.

"About these old cabinets," she said. "Some are wood." She tapped four doors near the stove. "Some are metal." She pointed to two sets on either side of the window.

"And this metal cabinet by the door is hopeless." She kicked it and it gave a hollow boom. "You need a new one. Alyce, these lemon cupcakes are a religious experience."

"Amen," Josie said. "Can I get new old cabinets? Used ones, I mean, that look like this one?"

"Sure," Jeanne said. "Some Web sites specialize in antique cabinets, and St. Louis has midcentury antiques stores. This is a good city for rehabbers."

"We're going to ReHab this afternoon," Josie said.

"If you find any cabinets, buy them," Jeanne said. "Good things don't last long there. I'll get you the measurements."

Jeanne whipped out her measuring tape, then wrote the cabinets' dimensions on a card for Josie.

"We can take my SUV," Alyce said. "There's room in the back if we find something."

Jeanne finished the last bite of cupcake, then asked, "What about the dings and scratches on the cabinets we're keeping? Do you want me to take them out? How pristine do you want this kitchen?"

"It's been around more than fifty years," Josie said. "We've got a dog, two cats, and two serious cooks. The kitchen should be useful but lived-in. Fresh paint, new appliances, new tile, definitely. A few dings won't hurt."

"Good. Do you want me to take out the soffit?" Jeanne asked.

"What's that?" Josie asked.

"The big wooden strip between the cabinets and the ceiling," Alyce said, and pointed to it.

"Right," Jeanne said. "Nice lights, by the way. Those are hand-painted aqua schoolhouse globes.

"Your steel sink and aqua tile splashboard are in good shape. Tomorrow, my crew starts taking up this old floor tile. I'll have the electrician check the wiring and get your stove working until you find a new one."

"I appreciate that," Josie said.

"I'm not fixing the stove for you," Jeanne said. "I want my coffee."

After Jeanne left, Josie and Alyce packed away the delicate dishes. "There's still a dozen and a half cupcakes left," Alyce said. "Take them home to Ted and Amelia."

Josie climbed into Alyce's comfortable Escalade for the short trip. ReHab was a plain brick cube on the Forest Park Parkway, a wide treelined boulevard. The store was near St. Louis University and the city's revitalized theater district.

While Alyce parked, Josie checked the questions on her mystery shopping evaluation sheet. She couldn't take it inside with her.

The sheet asked, "Were you greeted at the door? Did an employee try to build rapport and emotional connections with you? Are employees asking the right questions and ensuring that they match the right products to each customer's needs? Are employees correctly informing customers about your products, services, and/or policies?"

Inside, ReHab was strictly business, divided into sections for paint, hardware, doors, cabinets, plumbing fixtures, and more.

"It looks like a smaller, hipper Home Depot," Alyce said.

"That's the first time I've heard 'hip' and 'Home Depot' in the same sentence," Josie said.

A thin, ponytailed man in white overalls waved as they walked inside. "Hi, I'm Eric. You need anything, just call my name," he said. "We don't see too many women here. You've come at a good time. There's not a lot of floor personnel. This store is pretty much a labor of love. The pros show up early in the morning and the rehabbers in the late afternoon. Saturdays are a zoo.

"You know about us? We sell primarily recycled

building materials, with some new materials—usually donated by local companies—that are overstocks."

"We're looking for kitchen cabinets," Josie said.

"Follow me," Eric said.

Josie's shopping cart rumbled over the bare concrete
floor. They passed recycled molding, a compost tumbler,
and a solid wood entertainment center big enough to be
a room.

"Here we are." Eric gestured proudly at a bewildering
jumble. "Looking for a particular kind?"

"I need a metal two-door cabinet for a midcentury
kitchen," Josie said.

He shook his head. "No luck. These are mostly oak
and dark wood from the eighties and nineties. But don't
give up. Cabinets come in all the time. Anything else?"

"Paint," Josie said.

"This way," he said.

"I know where to come if I need Sheetrock," Alyce
said as they headed toward the paint aisle.

"This is remanufactured," Eric said. "That means recycled latex paint is reprocessed, and new resins and col-
orants are added. We also sell overstocks and donated
paint."

"Amelia could use this in her new room," Josie said.
"I'm looking for purple."

"No paint in that color today," he said.

Someone called Eric's name from the granite coun-
tertop section, and he waved good-bye. Josie filled her
cart with painting supplies—rollers, tape, sandpaper, and
brushes.

"So how did the store do?" Alyce whispered.

"Passed with flying colors," Josie said. "On the way
home, I'll tell you about the way-too-handy handyman."

In the checkout line, they watched a man try to bully
a young woman clerk with straight brown hair. He
slapped the handle of a cart loaded with a rolled-up rug.

"You want one twenty-five for this?" he said. "What about a hundred? Huh? You wanna sell it or not? Well?"

Yellow underarm rings decorated his grimy gray-white T-shirt. The lights cruelly revealed his balding dome.

"Sorry, sir," the clerk said. "I can't go any lower. It's a twelve-by-eighteen Oriental rug in good condition."

"Well, I'll think about," he said, and slammed out the door.

"May I see the rug?" Alyce asked.

Josie helped the clerk unroll it. "It's wool," she said.

"I like the blue-and-coral design," Alyce said. "No major stains or bald spots."

"Unlike the surly guy who tried to buy it," Josie said.

"It will look good in the guest room," Alyce said. "Credit card okay?"

Alyce was signing the charge slip when Mr. Surly returned. "I've changed my mind," he said. "I'll take it."

"Too late," the clerk said, and smiled sweetly. "It's been sold."

Chapter 11

"Welcome to Seiwa-en. That means 'the garden of pure, clear harmony and peace' in Japanese," said the melancholy young woman. Even her long pale brown hair seemed weighted with grief.

"I'm Melody, Rain Siobhan Dillon's friend and colleague from the Peace Co-op and Farmers Market. It is my sad duty to officiate at her memorial service at the Japanese Garden in the Missouri Botanical Garden."

Melody stood at a podium but did not have a mic. She wiped her tear-reddened eyes and continued in a wobbly voice, "I must honor my friend and try not to cry."

Josie was touched. Instead of funereal black, Melody wore a vibrant teal and bronze Navajo print skirt, but her grief seemed sincere.

"Tears honor her, too, Melody," said a tanned young man with an acoustic guitar. He was lean, with muscular calves. Josie wondered if he rode bikes. She guessed he also worked at the co-op. "Thank you, Kevin," Melody said. She couldn't hold back her tears any longer.

A woman in a peace dove T-shirt handed her a handkerchief, patted her back, then told the two dozen mourners, "My name is Chelsea. To avoid using tissues that kill trees, I have hankies for everyone. This is my gift to keep Rain's memory and her memorial service green."

Chelsea moved through the attendees, solemnly passing out clean cotton handkerchiefs as if they were Communion.

Most mourners looked like they were from the co-op: They wore Indian prints, peace shirts, or yoga pants. Almost everyone had long hair and many of the men had beards.

There were no chairs at the service. The mourners stood in raggle-taggle groups. Chris, the chief mourner, was a gaunt specter in black. Todd slouched next to his mother, in a black polo shirt and khaki pants, formal dress for twelve-year-olds. Chris's two younger daughters were absent. At school, Josie decided.

On Todd's other side was a shorter, stockier version of Chris, a brown-haired matron who looked uncomfortably warm in her heavy black wool suit. Josie guessed she was the oldest sister, Susan.

Josie saw Detective Stevenski and two uniformed officers hovering in the back. Next to them was a paunchy man with slicked-back hair and a shiny, ridiculously stylish suit. His skinny pants and round belly made him look like a spider in a silver tie. Josie remembered a saying of her mother's: "He's so sharp he'll cut himself."

Chris glanced back toward Mr. Slick. Josie felt her hot hate arc through the small group. It should have singed off Slick's hair. Was that Rodney, Chris's unfaithful ex? Why was he standing with the police?

Ted and Josie stood behind Chris. Josie thought her husband was the handsomest man there in his lightweight gray sport coat and blue shirt. He squeezed Josie's hand.

Melody took a deep breath and said, "This was one of Rain's favorite places. You can see why."

The Japanese Garden was heartbreakingly beautiful this morning, Josie thought. Pink cherry blossoms drooped by round-backed bridges. A stone Rankei lantern, which looked like a little curled-roof teahouse perched on a graceful curve, was reflected in a clear pool. Fat carp darted through the water. Even a young green leaf floating on the pond looked like a painting.

"Rain was with us in St. Louis for about a year and half," Melody said, "but she supported the Botanical Garden's sustainability and conservation efforts, and found harmony and peace whenever she visited.

"This Japanese Garden is a small version of the great world, with the earth, water, the sky, and nature. It's designed so that we see a different aspect of its beauty each time we encounter it.

"That's what Rain was like. She was a beautiful soul, and an old one. She is being cremated and returned to Mother Earth.

"I want to thank Christine for giving her sister a green cremation and memorial service," Melody said. "By avoiding a burial, our dear friend will not pollute Mother Earth, the way so many do. Americans use more than eight hundred thousand gallons of embalming fluid, waste a hundred thousand tons of steel on caskets, and one point six tons of concrete for burial vaults every year."

Enough with the green sermon, Josie thought. This is Rain's memorial.

"Now Christine will tell us her favorite memory of her sister."

Chris's face was ghost white, and her eyes were sunk deep in dark circles.

"Rain was my baby sister," she said. "When we were little, I admired her pink velvet hair bow. 'You can wear it when I'm not using it,' she said. 'What's mine is yours.'"

And what's yours is mine, Josie thought, at least when it came to Chris's husband.

"My sister and I parted on bad terms," Chris said. "I'll always regret my harsh words, but I also feel her love. I know she forgives me."

She left, shoulders bowed by regret and sorrow. Josie hoped Chris would forgive herself.

"We'd like the rest of you to come up to the podium with your memories of Rain," Melody said. "There's no microphone so that we do not waste electricity when we have the sun."

Many co-op friends spoke. "Rain loved life," Kevin said. "I will always remember her dancing in the Butterfly Garden."

"Rain was brave," said a woman with long, straight gray hair and peace symbol earrings. "She picketed to make major polluters understand how they were hurting Mother Earth. One man got so angry he shoved her into a parked car. She wore the purple bruise on her arm as a badge of honor."

A chill breeze rustled the cherry blossoms, and a snowfall of petals drifted across the pond.

A young man with long eyelashes and shining blond hair held up the program with Rain's photo, laughing amid the cherry blooms. "I'm Zander, and this is how I will always remember Rain," he said. "She looked smiling and delicate, but she was strong and determined."

Determined to get her own way? Josie wondered. Is that why she died?

"Thank you, Christine, for this green funeral and memorial," Zander said. "You thought of everything, even recycled paper for the program."

Josie examined the photo in her program. Rain was a radiant beauty, with full pink lips and gently curling hair. Her slightly large nose made her face more interesting. Josie hoped that pretty picture would replace the awful image the gazebo grave had burned in her mind.

Plop! Josie felt a drop of water on her nose. She looked up and saw dark clouds swallowing the dandelion yellow sun.

Todd shambled up to the podium next. "Rain was my

aunt," he began, his voice baritone deep. "She loved animals, and she loved the earth." His voice grew reedy as he talked and cracked once. One or two people bit back understanding smiles.

"She belonged to PETA and fought against animal cruelty. I will try to follow in her footsteps and defend the planet," Todd said, and fled the podium.

Plop! Another drop. Now Josie was sure it was going to rain. The sun was gone.

Chris hugged her son when he returned, but he shrugged her away. Embarrassed? Josie wondered. Or angry at his mother? Coldness gripped her heart. Todd didn't think his mother had killed Rain, did he?

Melody was back at the podium. "We'll end this service with Rain's favorite song," she said, "Pete Seeger's 'To My Old Brown Earth.' Kevin will play it for us. Please join hands in a circle while we sing."

The mourners formed a large, awkward circle.

Plop! Then two more drops. The crowd looked uneasy, but determined to finish the service. They tried to hold hands and read the lyrics at the same time. Josie thought that Seeger's song about his beloved "old brown earth" summed up Rain's wishes for a green service. The promise to give that old brown earth and old blue sky "these last few molecules of 'I' " were pure poetry.

The rain was falling faster now, and the mourners scrambled to leave. "There will be a reception at the Spink Pavilion," Melody shouted. "That's the redbrick building overlooking the lily pools. By the Climatron, the big domed greenhouse."

The shower was over as quickly as it started. The sun came out again and a rainbow lit the sky. Josie heard Chris say, "It feels like Rain is with us. She's smiling on her memorial."

"Yes, she is," Ted said, putting his arm around his partner. They walked toward the reception. "Melody did a fine job. You gave your sister a good send-off. How are you?"

Chris shrugged. "My sister's dead, my ex is here, and the cops are hounding me. I just want to hold together until I put Susan on the plane tomorrow."

Josie walked behind them, talking to Susan and Todd. "I'm glad you spoke about your aunt," Josie told Todd. "You gave us a real feel for what Rain was like."

"Whatever," Todd said, and blushed scarlet.

"I wish Chris had gotten a real preacher instead of that hippie," Susan said, her words acid-etched.

"Uh, Aunt Susan, I . . . I disagree," Todd said. His words poured out in a rush. "Aunt Rain didn't like organized religion. She thought the churches had forgotten their mission to help the poor and to love one another. And Melody was her good friend. She volunteered to lead the memorial service and Kevin didn't charge anything for his music."

"I can't imagine what Chris spent on this," Susan said.

"Mom said whatever the cost was, Aunt Rain was worth it," Todd said.

"I—" Susan said.

"Isn't that dogwood magnificent?" Josie said, deliberately interrupting. "Look, there's the awning of the Spink Pavilion. We're here."

Josie heard Kevin playing "Where Have All the Flowers Gone" and saw servers passing trays of appetizers under the awning. "Would you like a chicken skewer?" a fiftysomething woman asked Josie.

Josie took it, then a pita triangle with hummus, and a savory caponata on crostini. The salty taste of the olives blended nicely with the crunchy toast.

She found Ted by the bar, ordering a glass of wine. "There you are," he said. "Did you try those duck and goat-cheese wontons? Amelia would love this food. Want a drink?"

"Water is fine," Josie said. She gave Ted a kiss, then took her glass and said, "I'll go say hi to Chris."

Chris looked shockingly tired. "Thank you for coming," she said.

"It was a lovely memorial," Josie said. "You went out of your way to please Rain's friends with those amazing vegetarian appetizers."

"They're good people," Chris said, and managed a smile. It vanished when Detective Stevenski and the two uniformed officers stepped in front of Josie.

"Excuse us, Ms. Marcus," the detective said. "We need to talk to Ms. Cormac." She shoved Josie out of her way. Josie stumbled slightly, then stepped behind a potted palm to listen.

"Ms. Cormac, do you still say that your sister did not have an affair with your then husband, Rodney Xavier Cormac?"

"Yes," Chris said, and looked her right in the eye.

"That's not what we heard," Detective Stevenski said.

"If you mean my neighbor, Betty, she bends the truth," Chris said.

"We mean your husband, Rodney. Mr. Cormac told us he had an affair with Rain and that's why you two divorced."

Chris swayed as if she might collapse. "No," she said, her voice a whisper.

"Yes," Stevenski said. "You're the liar, not Betty."

"I didn't lie," Chris said, louder now. "Todd idolized his aunt Rain. I didn't want my son to know she'd had a sordid affair with his father. I wanted to protect my boy."

Josie noticed that Kevin's music had stopped. Now the guests were staring at Christine and the police. Todd pushed through the crowd toward his mother, followed by Susan.

"You also use the drug that killed your sister," Stevenski said.

"Every vet has acepromazine," Christine said. "It would be strange if I didn't."

"And your earring was found on your sister's body," she said.

"I—I can't explain the earring," Chris said. "I lost it. I don't know where or when."

"I do," Stevenski said. "You lost it when you murdered your sister—your temper and your earring. I also think you're unusually forgiving. You let the woman who had an affair with your husband live in your house."

"He's my ex-husband," Chris said, emphasizing the ex, "and she's my baby sister. I helped change her diapers. I took her for walks in her stroller. I decided that worthless piece of—that pointless man—wasn't coming between us. My sister made a mistake. But Rain wasn't his first affair. Rodney hopped from bed to bed and I'd had enough. If I was going to kill anyone, it would be him. He's useless and he's behind on his child support."

Please be quiet, Chris, Josie prayed. You're only making this worse.

"I'm glad you admit you're capable of homicide," Detective Stevenski said. "Christine Dillon Cormac, I am arresting you for the murder of Rain Siobhan Dillon."

"No," Chris said. "I didn't do it."

Ted stepped forward from the stunned-silent crowd. "This is wrong, Detective," he said. She ignored him.

"Chris," Ted said. "Do you want me to get you that lawyer?"

She nodded.

"Mom!" Todd said, his thick black hair falling in his eyes. "Mom, what's wrong?"

"I'm sorry, Todd, but your mother killed your aunt Rain," Detective Stevenski said. Her words hung in the heavy silence.

"What!" Todd said. "No! She wouldn't. She didn't. Mom, I knew about Aunt Rain and Dad. Everyone knows he's a hound. Aunt Rain was good with animals, but not smart about dudes."

"I'm sure this is a mistake, Todd," Susan said. "I'll take care of you and your sisters until it's straightened out."

"No, I will." Rodney the Slick was there, a bourbon glass in his hand. "He's my son. He's staying with me. All three of my children are."

"You don't care about us," Todd said. "You never come to our games or school stuff. Mom does that. You always make some excuse when it's your weekend because you're hungover or shacked up with some slut."

"Todd!" Christine said. "Don't talk like that."

Rodney clamped his hand on Todd's skinny arm.

"It's true," Todd said, struggling to get away from his father.

"You have to excuse my son," Rodney said smoothly. "He's a little emotional. I have the custody papers here, Detective. I assume Brook and Cam are at school, Todd?"

"You don't want us," Todd said. "You just don't want Mom to have us."

"I don't want my children to have an unfit mother," Rodney said. "Come along, son."

"Come along, Ms. Cormac," Detective Stevenski said.

Both prisoners were led away.

Chapter 12

"Bailey Marie Novak!

"Palmer Lindell!

"Emma Kleeban!

"Amelia Marcus!"

Miss Apple announced each student's name as if she were a future donor. But Josie had never seen Amelia— or any other Barrington students—run so fast to their rides. They looked like a pack of hounds had been turned loose after them. Sounded like it, too. Josie heard rabid barks, crazy yaps, and horror-movie howls.

What the heck? she wondered as Amelia threw open the front passenger door and dropped breathless into the seat. She didn't even take time to toss her backpack in the seat.

"Hurry, Mom. Let's get out of here," she said.

"What's wrong?" Josie asked.

"Nothing," Amelia said. "I just want to leave. Please." Her brown eyes were too big and the freckles stood out in her pale face. She was twisting the ends of her long blue scarf.

"Not till I know what's going on," Josie said.

"Please," Amelia begged. "Just go."

Josie threaded through the parked cars in the drive

while Amelia slouched down so she couldn't be seen through the window.

"Please tell me," Josie said, softly. "I want to help."

Amelia shook her head, then burst into tears as soon as they left the school. Josie pulled into a parking lot and stopped the car. "Amelia Marcus, we're not going any farther until you tell me what's wrong."

"I can't tell you," Amelia said, crying harder. "I have to show you. I need my laptop. We'll have to wait until we're home."

"This bookstore has Wi-Fi," Josie said.

"No, I don't want to see anyone from school," Amelia said. She sounded desperate.

Josie didn't want to go home. She was sure this involved Barrington. If so, she was heading right back to speak to the head of school. Josie did a quick mental inventory of nearby places with Wi-Fi and chose Kaldi's, a coffeehouse in DeMun, a handsome old redbrick neighborhood that was too urban for the Barrington crowd. They could be there in five minutes. Amelia always felt grown-up going to a coffeehouse. Coffee was a rare treat for her.

Josie found a parking spot near the Kaldi's black awning. They claimed a table in a dark corner. Both wanted frosted sugar cookies. Josie ordered an espresso and Amelia a caramel latte. The barista put a flower in Amelia's latte, and Josie tipped him extra for making her distraught daughter smile.

Amelia had her computer connected to the Internet by the time Josie carried over their coffee. She waited until her daughter was fortified with caffeine and sugar before she said, "Now show me what's wrong."

"It's this Facebook page," Amelia said, tears sliding down her cheeks. "I'm on it and so are my friends Bailey, Palmer, and Emma." Those tears felt like acid splashing on Josie's heart. Who had hurt her baby?

At first, Josie had trouble focusing on the page. Then she saw it and a slow anger burned through her. Someone had spent a lot of time creating this. "The Bitches of Barrington" page featured four tween girls, each photo in a doghouse frame.

Amelia was "Clumsy Bitch: Likes 2 wear her lunch," the text under her photo said. "This bitch has her own bones—in her backyard. Ha-ha."

Red-haired Palmer was "Rich Bitch: Her daddy's rich but can she buy cute clothes? NOT," it said.

Emma was "Fugly Bitch: Mirror, mirror on the wall, who's the fuggliest of them all?"

Emma with her light brown hair was effing ugly? Josie thought. No way. Someone was jealous. But Josie remembered her mother dismissing a hateful girl at her school with those words. Jane was right, but they didn't help.

Black-haired Bailey was "Fat Bitch: Her daddy's the biggest lawyer in Clayton and she has the biggest ass." That was just cruel.

Josie took a big gulp of coffee, hoping she'd calm down enough to say something helpful.

"Who did this, Amelia?"

"I don't know." More tears. "I think Zoe's the leader. She says 'fugly' a lot."

"I thought you two got along."

"We did, sort of," Amelia said. "Then she started hanging around with Jace and Oakley. It got worse around your wedding. She said you were getting married twelve years too late and you were a wench."

"What's wrong with being a 'wench'?" Josie asked. She thought it sounded Shakespearean, and pictured herself as a saucy actress in an Elizabethan drama.

"'Wench' means 'slut,' Mom," Amelia said, as if Josie didn't know anything. "I got mad and said they couldn't say that 'cause you were my mom, and then Zoe, Oakley, and Jace never stopped saying, 'Your mother is a wench.'"

They'd whisper it when I walked down the hall or in the cafeteria. They'd say things like 'My dad uses his wench a lot. In the garage' and act like it was a big joke, but I knew they were talking about you. They even wrote 'wench' on my locker, but I rubbed it off."

"And you didn't tell Miss Apple you were being bullied?" Josie asked.

"No," Amelia said. "I mean, they didn't hit me or anything."

"That's verbal abuse, Amelia. You shouldn't have to put up with this."

"I'm not a snitch," she said. "Anyway, it won't do any good. Miss Apple likes them."

"Finished with your latte?" Josie asked. "Pack up your laptop. We're going."

"Where?" Amelia asked. She sounded frightened.

"Back to school," Josie said. "I'm going to have a talk with Miss Apple."

"No, Mom, you can't," Amelia said. "You'll make it worse."

"I can and I will," Josie said. "Nobody bullies my daughter. This stops now. You can wait in the car, if you want."

Josie fumed all the way back to Barrington, while Amelia tried to distract her with questions: "How was the memorial service, Mom?"

"The service itself was beautiful, but then that detective arrested Chris at the reception and the police took her away in handcuffs." Josie waited at a red light, drumming her fingers on the steering wheel.

"That's so wrong," Amelia said.

"Yes, it is," Josie said. "And I'm going to do something about it. Chris is a good friend, a good vet, and a good mother. That detective didn't even bother to investigate. She just threw Chris in jail."

The light changed at last. "Ted and Chris's sister Susan are trying to hire Renzo Fischer, if they can. He's the best trial lawyer in the city."

"What will happen to Todd?" Amelia said.

"He and his sisters have to live with their father," Josie said.

"But Todd's dad always cancels on the weekends he's supposed to take them," Amelia said. "They don't even have a room in his apartment. Todd said the girls sleep on a daybed in his office and he gets the lumpy couch in the living room. Can't they stay with us?"

"They could," Josie said, "except his father has legal custody."

Barrington's spring green lawns were in sight now, darkened by long late-day shadows. Josie parked in the drive again. "That's Emma's car," Amelia said.

"I bet those other two cars belong to Bailey's and Palmer's parents," Josie said. "Do you want to wait here?"

"I'll come in," Amelia said.

Josie marched straight down the hall toward Miss Apple's office. In the waiting room, Josie saw a tight, angry group of two men and a woman. Three unhappy girls looked lost on a long brown leather couch. Josie could almost feel their hurt and vowed to get the mean girls. She knew Emma and recognized the other two as the victims of the infamous page. The girls greeted Amelia and she dragged a chair over to sit with them.

Emma's father, Sam, said, "Hi, Josie."

"I'm Josie Marcus," she said to the other two adults. "Amelia is my daughter and I'm mad as hell."

"Welcome to the club," said a man who looked like a linebacker in a black suit. "I'm Devlin Michael Novak, Bailey's father. My friends call me Dev."

"And I'm delighted you're on our side," said the blonde in a red power suit and black heels. "You're a super attorney. I'm Priscilla Lindell. My husband, Gifford, is away on business, but he's as outraged as I am by this attack on our daughter, Palmer."

"On all our daughters," Josie reminded her.

A midsized woman in a sensible dark green suit stood at the doorway to the inner office and announced, "Miss Apple will see you. Please keep in mind that you do not have an appointment and our head of school's time is limited."

The four parents brushed past her. Miss Apple's office was designed to impress major donors. Tall, round-topped windows overlooked the Barrington campus. Josie thought the Chippendale furniture might be real.

Josie and Dev took the two chairs in front of Miss Apple's desk. Dev's Chippendale chair creaked ominously. Priscilla stood behind Josie, her scarlet-tipped fingers gripping the top of the chair. Sam paced on the blue Oriental carpet. Josie had heard that the tanned, fit Sam retired at forty. He looked like he played a lot of golf.

Miss Apple was somewhere south of fifty, with frown lines stamped on her face. Her makeup was impeccable and Josie recognized her navy suit as a genuine Chanel.

The head of school tried to take control of the meeting. "I've reviewed the Facebook Web site," she said. "Naturally, I'm as shocked as you are. Unfortunately there's little the school can do. The photos do not seem to have been taken at Barrington.

"Our lawyers have convinced Facebook to take down the Web site. Facebook has been very cooperative. But unless we can prove a Barrington student took the photos, we can't take any action."

"What!" the four parents yelled.

"That's the law," Miss Apple said. "I'm sorry." She didn't sound the least bit regretful.

"Are you conducting an investigation?" Priscilla asked.

"We already have," Miss Apple said. "I was apprised of this reprehensible Web site at ten o'clock when Emerson reported it to me. Our investigation was thorough. There is no connection to Barrington except the use of our name."

"My daughter says Barrington students were involved," Josie said. "The ringleader is Zoe, a known troublemaker."

"And my daughter says Oakley Fallon, the new girl, was in on it, too," Dev said.

"And that little snot Jace Parkington." Priscilla spat out the name.

"There's no need for name-calling, Mrs. Lindell," Miss Apple said.

"If we're talking name-calling," Josie said, "those three little bullies have been tormenting my daughter, making derogatory statements about me."

"All our students have the right to a safe, healthy school environment," Miss Apple said. "If your daughter felt she was being bullied, she should have reported it to me or our staff. We provide staff-development training on this issue and discuss bullying with our students in age-appropriate ways. Has she filed a report?"

"Amelia feels you favor Zoe and her friends," Josie said.

"Absolutely not," Miss Apple said. "Any student who engages in bullying is subject to disciplinary action up to and including expulsion. The rules apply to everyone. I promise you, if any Barrington students did this—and I do not believe any of our students are responsible—I will expel them immediately."

The room's temperature had dropped about thirty degrees. "It's unfair to blame Zoe Delgado," the head of school said.

Delgado? Josie wondered. Did her mother remarry again?

"Zoe had some issues after her sister's tragic death two years ago, but she is now a model student. Oakley and Jace are spirited young women, but they're not behavior problems."

"That's not what my daughter said," Sam said.

"Or mine," Dev said.

"Girls do have their little disagreements, but learning to handle them is part of growing up," Miss Apple said. "I must say I am proud of my students, especially the one who reported the site to me. They've acted in a very mature way."

"Oh yeah?" Josie said. "Then why were they barking at my daughter this afternoon?"

"I didn't notice that behavior," Miss Apple said.

"We certainly did," Priscilla said.

"Amelia was in tears," Josie said.

"I'm sorry that your daughters were upset. But I believe the culprits are students at the Rove School. That, as you know, is the local public school." Miss Apple wrinkled her nose. "Not our caliber, socially or academically. There's a great deal of resentment at Rove toward Barrington students. I don't believe any of our students are behind this."

"Well, I do," Dev said.

"We all do," Priscilla said.

"We'll conduct our own investigation," Josie said.

"And when we find out the Barrington students who did this, we'll sue their overprivileged asses," Dev said.

"Really, Mr. Novak!" Miss Apple said. "There's no need to make threats."

"I don't make threats," Dev said. "I make promises. And I promise whoever hurt my little girl is going to regret it."

Chapter 13

"If you want to catch the creeps who did that page, Amelia, you have to prove the photos were taken at the school by a Barrington student," Ted said. "This roast chicken with lemon is incredible."

"I like how the skin sort of puffs up," Josie said.

Dinner was late that night—nearly eight o'clock. Josie knew it was the first of many late meals until the Chris crisis was solved.

Amelia had insisted on trying her out her new chicken recipe and Josie was grateful her daughter had that distraction. She'd had a wrenching day.

"The chicken's easy," Amelia said. "You just roast it with the lemons inside. I didn't need butter or oil or anything.

"I don't think Miss Apple did any kind of investigation, Ted. I know for sure those photos were taken at school. That picture of me was taken the day I dropped pizza on my blouse at lunch. You can see the big red stain. Mom drove me straight home after school because I didn't want anyone else to see it. Now the whole world knows."

Well, Amelia's whole world, Josie thought.

"We'll examine the photos after dinner," Ted said.

"I thought the page was taken down," Josie said, clearing the dinner plates. "That's what Miss Apple said."

"I made a copy," Amelia said. "Everybody did. Doesn't make any difference if the school took it down or not. Everybody can still see it and laugh at me. I can still see it."

"You don't have to look," Josie said.

"But I know it's there," Amelia said. "It won't go away. Ever."

Her girl was hurting. This was not the time to say that eventually the pain would go away.

"Technology has changed the bully business," Josie said. "Do you want coffee, Ted? More milk, Amelia?"

Amelia nodded. "Make mine decaf," Ted said. "I've got to be at the clinic early tomorrow. It's in chaos with Chris in jail. What's technology got to do with bullies?"

Josie started the decaf brewing. "When I was Amelia's age," she said, "I was bullied by Bonnie. Skinny girl with straggly hair. Bonnie was a year older and a whole lot bigger than me. She didn't like that I used what she called 'big words.' Bonnie would wait for me about two blocks from school, and punch me in the gut. I started taking the long way home to avoid her."

"Did you tell Grandma?" Amelia asked.

"No. Bonnie said her father was in the Mafia and he'd kill her."

Amelia giggled. "You believed that?"

"Yeah, I was stupid," Josie said. "Bonnie had a German last name. I don't even know if she knew any Italians, but she had me shaking in my shoes.

"Here's the difference between me and Amelia. Once I was home, I was safe. Bonnie wouldn't come to my house and nobody else knew about it. Online bullying is there twenty-four/seven."

Josie set a plate of brownies on the table, poured decaf for Ted and her and more milk for Amelia.

"Well, this cyberbullying is going to stop," Ted said. "Amelia, would it spoil your dessert if you brought your laptop here so we could see the page?"

"I'll get it now," she said.

Josie winced when she looked at the photos again. She was furious that her daughter was ridiculed.

Amelia studied them as if they were a school assignment. "They don't look so bad with you here," she said. "See that splotch on my shirt? That's the pizza."

"That's our proof," Josie said. "I picked you up at school and no one else but a Barrington student could have taken that photo."

"Won't work," Ted said. "They could say someone standing across the street snapped it."

Josie pointed to the picture of the red-haired Palmer walking past a chain-link fence. "Is there a construction fence on campus?"

"I think that's the fence around the new library in the back," Amelia said. "You can't see it from the driveway."

"Emma's near a parking lot," Josie said. "That could have been shot anywhere."

"Emma and I think her photo was taken by the teachers' lot," she said. "We're going to push the brightness of the picture so we can pull extra information from the darker areas alongside her." Amelia tried to hide a yawn.

"Is that Photoshopping?" Josie asked.

"No. Photoshop is too expensive," Amelia said. "It's, like, a couple hundred dollars. The computer lab has it, but we don't want to do this at school. There's a couple of free ways to get a Web-based photo editor. Emma says we can use aviary-dot-com. Nothing to download or install. Just go to the Web site, upload a picture, and start editing. She's going to talk me through using it."

"Not tonight," Josie said. "It's nine o'clock and you've had a hard day."

"But I'll sleep better knowing I've started work on this," Amelia said.

"Tomorrow," Josie said, firmly. "Ted and I will do the dishes."

Amelia gave up the fight. Dishes were one of her least favorite chores. Josie waited until she heard the shower, then kissed Ted. "How was the rest of the day?" she asked. She was rinsing the dishes and stacking them in the dishwasher.

"Hectic," he said. "Renzo agreed to represent Chris. She's taking out a home-equity loan to pay him. She's being arraigned tomorrow, but Renzo says there's almost no chance of bail with a murder case." Ted carried over the last dessert plates, then wiped down the table.

"Are you going to the arraignment?" Josie asked.

"No, she wants me to run the clinic," he said. Josie watched him scrub down the stove top and sighed happily. What a man.

"Chris asked you to stay away, too," he said, "and she told her sister to go home to Cincinnati. Susan wanted to stay, but she has to go back to work at the doctor's office."

"So Chris will be all alone," Josie said. "I'm going to help her, Ted. I'm going to find out who really killed Rain."

"Renzo has detectives to do that," Ted said.

"And they'll cost Chris how much an hour?" Josie asked. "I'll do it for free. The neighbors will say more to me than they will to a private detective. We mystery shoppers are good at looking harmless and blending in. And I've had a little success." She closed the dishwasher and turned it on.

"More than a little," Ted said. He wrapped his arms around her and kissed her. "Just be careful. You mean too much to me. Let's sit in the living room."

"More coffee?" Josie asked.

"And more you," he said.

Ted carried the two cups into the living room and Josie snuggled next to him on the couch. He put his arm around her. His brown hair had curled after his shower, and Josie ran her fingers through it.

"That's how Chris wants things, at least for now," Ted said. "She says I'm the face of the clinic and shouldn't be associated with a murder trial. Renzo said I should follow her wishes. We can attend the trial.

"Her sister Susan wanted Renzo to fight for custody of the kids, but Renzo said the trial's more important. He thinks that issue will resolve itself—after a few weeks of being a bachelor father, Rodney may be happy to give up custody."

"Three kids in a cramped apartment will test his fatherly feelings," Josie said.

"I wish I'd been there today to help with Amelia," Ted said. "She looks shaken."

"She is," Josie said. "She's putting on a good show, but those mean girls hurt her. If I ever get my hands on them . . ." She stopped. Everything she wanted to do was definitely illegal.

"I'm glad she and Emma are going to hunt them down," she said. "That gives her something to focus on. I'll keep her busy planning her new room at the house."

"Speaking of our house," Ted said, "want to see the ideas I've sketched for the new deck?"

He picked a manila folder off the coffee table and showed her a sketch. "The deck will join the back porch there," he said. "That porch is about four feet off the ground. The deck is twelve feet wide and runs the full length of the back of the house."

"Good," Josie said. Ted's plan would completely obliterate the gazebo grave.

"It should have concrete footings," he said. "Then I'm thinking a poured concrete pad under the deck."

"Even better," Josie said. Concrete would cover up the site forever.

"We could enclose that lower half and use most of it for storage," he said. "One end would be a doghouse for Festus."

"But Festus sleeps inside," Josie said. "In fact, he usually sleeps in Amelia's room."

"But he does go outside, and when it's hot or cold, he'd have his own shelter."

"Sounds good to me," Josie said.

"Do we want a fire pit?" he asked. "Built-in seating? A small water feature, like a waterfall?"

Josie saw them sitting out by the fire pit on chilly nights after work, holding hands and sipping cocktails, and Festus sticking his big muddy paws in the water feature.

"Yes to the fire pit," she said. "The built-in seating will be nice for parties. No to the water feature. If we want one, we can put it in the yard later."

"About the wood," Ted said as Josie traced her finger down the side of his face. "Do you want cedar, pressure-treated, or composite?"

"Haven't the foggiest," Josie said, kissing his soft ear.

"There are pros and cons for all three," Ted said as Josie trailed her finger lightly down his neck.

"I'm thinking cedar, if we get a premium grade," he said. "It's more maintenance, but cedar is sturdy and solid."

Ted's shoulders are solid muscle, Josie thought. "Nice," she said.

"I agree," Ted said. "Bud Vey, the deck contractor, is coming to see the yard tomorrow. Can you show him these plans? Bud wants to get started. He'll tell us if we'll need an architect."

"Anything else?" Josie asked, kissing his neck.

"Yes," Ted said. "I'm going to be neglecting my beautiful wife, working long hours at the clinic." He gave her a light, teasing kiss.

"That's terrible," Josie said, and kissed him back, a serious kiss.

"I thought so, too," Ted said. "I think I need to spend some quality time with her."

"Right now," Josie said.

Chapter 14

"Josie, dear, why didn't you tell me Ted's clinic partner was a murderer?" Lenore said.

Ted's mother didn't even say good morning, Josie thought. "Chris is no killer," she said, and glanced at the kitchen clock. Nine twenty-five. She had to meet Bud the deck contractor at ten.

"She killed her own sister," Lenore said. "I had to hear about it on the national news. Again."

"She's accused of killing her sister," Josie said. "Chris is innocent until proven guilty."

"No smoke without fire," Lenore said, blithely ignoring her own troubles with the law before Ted and Josie's wedding. "When I met that woman at your wedding, I knew she was strange. She was Ted's best man!"

"His attendant," Josie said.

"Ted refused to ask his own brother to be his best man," Lenore said.

For good reason, Josie thought.

"My son never had these problems before you," Lenore said. "None of his other girls got him mixed up in murder."

I'm not "his girl," Josie thought. I'm his wife. Should I remind her? No, I've won that battle.

"Lenore, I had nothing to do with Rain's murder."

"You picked that house with the body in the back-yard," Lenore said. "With his clinic partner in jail, Ted needs his mother. I'm booking a room at the Ritz-Carl-ton so I can be near him."

"No!" Josie said, then realized she was shouting. "I mean, thank you, Lenore, but there's no reason to put yourself out. I know you like the Ritz, but last time you were here, you had to fly home to have your hair done."

"St. Louis doesn't have the same sophisticated stan-dards of care I'm used to," Lenore said.

"Why subject yourself to more hardship?" Josie said. "Ted's hired a new veterinarian to help at the clinic. I'm making sure he eats well and gets plenty of rest."

Except for last night, she thought. Well, he did go to bed early.

"Then I'll stay home and take care of my husband," Lenore said. "But if I see one more story on the news about this murder, I'm flying straight to St. Louis on Whit's plane."

The last time she had done that, her mother-in-law brought her pearl-handled pistol and that led to more trouble.

Josie's heart dropped at Lenore's threat. My life is al-ready complicated, she thought. My husband's fighting to save his clinic, my daughter's harassed by mean girls, and I'm in charge of remodeling and moving into the new house. Now my gun-toting mother-in-law is threat-ening to help.

If I ever want to see my hunky husband, I'll have to prove the police have arrested the wrong person.

On the way over to Fresno Court, Josie decided she'd question her neighbors—and she'd do a better job than Detective Stevenski. I'll take a closer look at Betty and Cordelia.

Josie saw Bud's construction van was parked in her drive. He waved and climbed out. A square-built man with an open sunburned face, Bud looked a bit like his red-brown dog, a big friendly mutt who jumped out to greet Josie.

"Ranger!" Bud said. "Don't jump on the nice lady. Sit."

Ranger sat, tail wagging. Josie scratched his ears while Bud introduced himself. He and his dog followed Josie to the backyard. "Nice place you got here," he said. "Heard you had a little problem when you tore down the gazebo."

A recent rain softened the grave so it didn't look so raw. "It was a shock," Josie said.

She showed him Ted's sketch of the proposed deck. "Will we need an architect?"

"It's doable," Bud said. "I'll have to put in twenty-four-inch concrete footings for the deck and then pour the concrete pad. You won't need an architect."

They discussed materials. "I'm glad you went with cedar," he said. "It tends to lie flat and straight. You can figure on fifteen to twenty years for cedar deck boards."

Bud gave her his references, a firm price, a time frame, and a payment schedule, then promised, "I'll handle the permits."

"Good," Josie said. Many second-rate contractors tried to foist the permits on the homeowner. She signed the contract, they shook hands, and Bud said he'd start right away.

The yapping Jack Russells reminded Josie she needed to meet Betty.

On the outside, Betty's house looked like Josie's, though the wooden trim was a soft yellow and there were no flowers. Josie rang the doorbell and set off another chorus of barks.

Betty wore a pale green suit with a white waterfall of ruffles on her chest. Her dark hair was sprayed into submission.

"You're my new neighbor, Josie Marcus," she said, talking over the yaps. "I've wanted to meet you. Quiet, Jack Dandy!" The little terrier trotted off toward the kitchen.

"You're all dressed up," Josie said. "Are you going out?"

"No, no," Betty said. "I just got back from a breakfast meeting. Come in. Would you mind coffee in the kitchen?"

"Not at all," Josie said. She recognized Betty's plush pale blue couch from the TV interview. The living room was the same shade from the ceiling to the carpet. It was like being inside a jewelry box. The room felt like it should have been guarded by velvet museum ropes.

Josie followed Betty into the sunny yellow kitchen, where Jack Dandy slurped water from a bowl on the floor. That room was clearly the heart of the house.

"That business in your backyard was terrible. Just terrible," Betty said. "I'm so sorry it happened to you. These are fresh-baked sugar cookies." She put a plateful on the table, turned on the coffeemaker, and set small blue plates, cups, and linen napkins on the yellow tablecloth, then poured them both coffee.

"It's so sad that Rain was murdered," she said, "but not totally unexpected."

Josie watched her put four spoons of sugar in her coffee.

"What do you mean?" she asked.

"She had a lot of boyfriends. A pretty young woman should go out, but some of Rain's men seemed . . . well, unsuitable. I'm a little older than Rain. I'm a widow and my ideas about dating might be old-fashioned. But Rain dated some rather rough-looking men."

Josie crunched a cookie. It was sweetly old-fashioned. "What were they like?" she asked.

"One was Donny Freedman, a bartender and beer can collector," Betty said.

"He drank too much. I'm a little wiser about men, and my late father drank, so I know the signs. The first time Rain introduced me to Donny, I could tell he emptied more beer cans than he collected. And he's not in a good job for someone who has a weakness for alcohol. He tends bar at Judson's Tavern."

"Where's that?" Josie asked.

"A nice person like you wouldn't know about that place," Betty said, sipping her coffee. "I'm addicted to the police reports in the paper, so I know Judson's is a disreputable bar on Manchester. The police are there every other night. Donny and Rain were dating for several months when they had a loud fight on her front porch. That's when I called the police. I felt bad about that, but I had no choice."

Betty stopped talking, then said, "Do you think I did the right thing?"

"The police are supposed to prevent domestic violence," Josie said. "It's their job. What if you hadn't called and she'd been hurt?"

"Oh, she was," Betty said. "He hit her. Hard. I could hear her cry out."

"He could have sent her to the hospital," Josie said, "maybe even killed her."

"That's what I tell myself," Betty said. "But Cordelia— she lives next to you on the other side—said I was a busybody."

"I haven't met Cordelia yet," Josie said, and tried to guide the conversation back to Rain. "What happened after Rain and Donny split?"

"For the next few months she dated a lot of young men. Played the field, as we used to say. These men were very different from Donny—kind of hippielike, with long hair. One rode a bicycle. He looked very fit. Another had a guitar. But they were never at her house more than once or twice.

"Then she took up with Harley Scranton, the Coca-Cola collector. He's a handsome devil and so charming. He seemed crazy in love with her, until Rain made a big mistake. She ruined a priceless Coca-Cola calendar. Spilled tea on it or something, and then put it back like nothing had happened. When he finally found it, he was furious. They had a huge fight outside in that gazebo. I tried not to listen, but I could hear every word."

Betty poured them both more coffee.

"Did he hit her, too?" Josie asked.

"No," Betty said, "but I was afraid he would. I didn't want to call the police again. I knew Cordelia would disapprove—she says too many police reports are bad for property values—but I couldn't have a murder on our street."

She gave a sad laugh. "Well, it happened anyway, didn't it? Murder. But not that night. Poor Rain couldn't see the bad in any man.

"Well, I called and the police came and calmed Harley down, then walked him to his car. I never saw him here again, though I still run into him sometimes. He works at Scranton Hardware in Richmond Heights.

"The next day I called Christine and said I was concerned about Rain's choice of men friends, and I thought she was letting the property go to seed. I guess I didn't say it right. Christine came here after lunch and was quite snippy. But I thought she had to know. One bad apple can ruin a good street.

"She talked to Cordelia. The professor admitted the property looked a little run-down, but said she wasn't upset. After Chris left, Cordelia roared over here. She called me an interfering old bat and said my dogs barked too much. The next day, Cordelia called the police and complained about my dogs. We haven't spoken since.

"To her credit, even though Christine was annoyed with me, she did talk to her sister. I think Rain could be a very provoking person. That discussion turned into a fight. They were outside in the gazebo. I've never heard such a bitter argument—from sisters! Next thing I knew, Christine said Rain had gone to an ashram in California. Sounded like something she'd do."

Josie listened intently, looking for signs of malice. She thought Betty simply wanted to do the right thing.

"I never questioned what Christine said about Rain. Her sister was always meditating in that gazebo, and she never complained about my dogs. In fact, she liked them.

"I was grateful that Christine and her son cleaned up the property after Rain was gone. I'm just so glad that she sold the house to a nice young couple like you and Ted. I hope your husband understands why I don't go to his clinic. I go to a vet who specializes in show dogs, but I've heard nothing but good things about your Ted."

"That's okay," Josie said. "Right now he's got more business than he can handle."

Betty scratched Jack's forehead. "Could I ask a favor? Would you help me with my Jack? He's nearly a year old and he's already won some major points towards his championship at the AKC shows in Gray Summit."

"Sure," Josie said.

"I'm training him for the show ring," Betty said. "I started when he was a newborn, gently handling him and exposing him for a few seconds to a different surface. They say this creates a more intelligent dog.

"At eight weeks, I started clicker training. I use this clicker." She held up a blue rectangle the size of a key ring.

"I wait until Jack does something right, like when I see him stand and look alert at his littermates. Then I quickly click and feed him. I'm hoping he will learn that standing alert makes me feed him. He's beginning to understand that *click* means *food*. Soon he will learn when

I don't feed him immediately, that *click* means *food is coming*. It works well for Parson Russells. They're very bright."

"I thought he was a Jack Russell terrier," Josie said.

"Parson Russell is what the AKC calls his breed," Betty said. "He stands so pretty. A show dog has to stand in a certain way. I trained Jack in stages. First, he learned to stand with his front paws on a step and stay there. It's important that he learns to stand still. He's a fast learner. Soon he was standing all on his own, foursquare–front feet side by side and facing forward. Same with his back feet.

"I've kept three dogs from this last litter, but Jack Dandy is the best one. From the day he was born, I knew he had the makings of a champion. Jack Dandy will stand and stay steady for about two minutes now and I can even walk around him. I'm so proud of him. Terriers are little bundles of energy."

"So I hear. I mean, heard," Josie said. "From other dog lovers."

"I have to check his bite," she said, "so he's used to it."

She lifted the dog's lips to show his teeth in the front and sides. Jack stood patiently while she poked her fingers in his mouth. Betty then clicked and rewarded Jack with a treat.

"Now you do it," Betty said.

"Me?" Josie said. Ew, she thought.

"It only takes five seconds," Betty said. "It's important. If Jack won't let a judge look in his mouth, he can be thrown out of the ring. He has to get used to being touched by strangers. He's good, but I want him exposed to more people he doesn't know."

Josie eyed the small sharp terrier teeth. "Well . . ."

Maybe I can get her to talk more about Chris and Rain, she thought. She pictured her disapproving mother-in-law on her doorstep and decided to brave the dog slobber.

Jack stood alert. Josie gingerly lifted Jack Dandy's lips so his teeth showed. He wagged his tail. Betty clicked and had Josie give him a treat.

"Good dog," Betty said.

"Where's your restroom?" Josie asked, relieved the ordeal was over.

"Next to the stairs," Betty said. "But don't worry about washing your hands. A dog's mouth is cleaner than a human's."

Right, Josie thought. She'd seen Festus lick some personal places.

Josie washed her hands in the pale green bathroom.

When she returned, Betty was at the table with a fat photo album. "I'm not a well-known professional breeder," she said. "But I'm determined. I'm getting on the circuit. Soon Jack and I will be on the road from Wednesday through Monday, every week. We'll campaign like the other pros. I have some money from my late husband. That will go to hiring a good stripper."

Josie blinked. "A what?"

Betty laughed. "Not that kind of stripper. Jack has a rough coat, and the hair needs to be groomed by a professional stripper. Those people are artists, and I have an introduction to a good one. Usually people turn their show dogs over to a professional handler and they show and handle them. But this dog is my life. We're going to work together and be a team. Look at my little champion."

She pointed to a photo.

Josie agreed that Jack Dandy was an adorable pup.

"Even as a baby he had great conformation," Betty said. "See his chest and the set of his tail?"

"I love the way that one ear sticks up straight while the other folds down," Josie said.

"He outgrew that," Betty said, quickly shutting the album. "Now both ears are perfect."

"Button ears, right?" Josie said, scratching them. "He sure is cute."

"Good-natured, too," Betty said. "He likes people and he's patient. That's important.

"It takes hundreds of thousands of dollars to get a show dog ready for Westminster. Usually poodles get the attention, but they're fakes, all primped and puffed. Those white coats? Bleached. Those dogs are whiter than a Klan rally. And the black coats? Dye jobs, most of them! My Jack is a natural. Now that you live next door, you'll love him, too."

"Did Rain like Jack Dandy?" Josie asked.

"She did, but she thought dog shows were cruel. She didn't understand they promote the best characteristics of a breed. My Jack hasn't been neutered. I'll use him at stud when he becomes a champion, so he'll breed more prizewinning pups."

"Who do you think killed Rain?"

"Her sister, of course," Betty said. "I like Christine and I wish it wasn't true. But if you'd heard that argument, you'd have no doubt."

"What about Rain's boyfriend, Harley, the Coke collector?" Josie said. "Or Donny? He has a drinking problem and both men were so violent you called the cops."

"They would have killed her during the fight," Betty said. "After the police talked to them, I never saw them again. It's not like they stalked her or anything. Christine's fight with her sister was different. She argued with Rain, then there was a loud silence, and next she was digging around the gazebo, planting shrubs and hammering on the stairs. That's where she hid the body."

"Yes, I know," Josie said.

"How silly of me," Betty said. "Of course you do. I

feel sorry for Christine. I truly do. I'm sure Rain drove that poor woman to distraction and she snapped. Besides, she poisoned Rain with some kind of vet medicine. Where would Rain's boyfriends get that?

"I wish it wasn't true," Betty said, "but there's not the slightest doubt that Christine killed her sister."

Chapter 15

Josie waited a tense fifteen minutes until Miss Apple called her daughter's name. Finally she heard the head of school's well-bred lockjaw enunciation:

"Amelia Marcus.

"Bailey Marie Novak.

"Palmer Lindell.

"Emma Kleeban."

The four girls branded the Bitches of Barrington strolled out of the sun-splashed redbrick main building, heads high. Black-haired Bailey and Amelia were giggling together. Emma and Palmer were texting, possibly to each other.

Josie sat alert in her car, ears straining over the idling engines for the smallest yelp, yap, or bark. One yip out of any Barrington kid, and Josie would charge into Miss Apple's office and rip off her head.

Josie watched her daughter carefully. Amelia was neither running nor trudging in discouragement. She dressed as well as any girl on campus, and better than some. She wore her new ombre denim shirt, black jeggings, and cute blue flats.

But was Amelia okay, or simply putting on a brave front? She tossed her backpack in the back and dropped into the front seat. Josie wouldn't dare kiss her in public anymore.

"How was your day?" she asked. She wouldn't leave the school until she knew.

Amelia shrugged.

"Did those girls give you any problems?" Josie asked.

"No. Can we go now, Mom?"

Josie decided it was safe to leave. "I need to run by the new house and take some window measurements for curtains," she said. "I think I'll have valances over the bedroom shades. Do you want shades or curtains for your room?"

"Curtains! Can I have purple, please?"

"Is there any other color?" Josie asked, but she was secretly pleased her daughter wanted something besides predictable princess pink.

"Mom, can we not spend too much time there? Emma and I want to work on the photos."

Josie had a quick internal debate, then said, "I'm going to trust you at home alone. But I expect to find you working when I return."

This was a huge step forward. The last time Josie had left Amelia alone, she was ten and had gotten into serious trouble. For that unauthorized adventure, she'd forfeited her freedom until today.

Amelia didn't say thanks, but Josie saw her face flush slightly and knew she was pleased. She went inside with her to fetch a tape measure, a box of coffee fixings, and her home remodeling notebook, which had replaced her wedding notebook. She enjoyed planning their new home more than the wedding.

And this project will last longer than a day, she thought. She couldn't help smiling when she remembered her wedding. That day was perfect, and she had the photos to prove it.

Josie stopped by Amelia's room on her way out. Her daughter was texting on her bed, laptop at her side and Harry the cat curled next to her. "If you need me, I'm five minutes away," Josie said. "Just call. Don't make dinner until we hear if Ted's working late again."

"Bye, Mom," Amelia said, not looking up.

Four minutes later, Josie parked in the drive at Fresno Court. She sat for a moment, admiring their new home. She thought it had the best landscaping on the circle.

A curtain twitched at Betty's house. Oh Lordy, Josie thought. Mrs. Mueller, my mom's neighbor, does that. What if Betty really is the neighborhood busybody? But she doesn't seem to have Mrs. M's sense of entitlement or outraged righteousness.

She hurried inside, feeling a little uneasy. Cordelia and Betty don't get along. I'll have to be careful, Josie thought, so I don't get drawn into their feud. The last thing I want is the ugly fights I had with my mom's neighbor. We got off on the wrong foot—literally—when I put that burning bag of dog doo on her front porch.

But I was just a kid and she'd snitched me out to Mom for smoking by the garage. Now that I'm older, I can handle difficult people better—I think.

Josie unpacked the coffee fixings, made a pot, then poured herself a cup. She needed to be alert while she measured all the windows. She started upstairs, then worked her way down to the living room. She was finishing the last window when Ted called.

"I'll be working late again tonight," he said. "Laura and I are swamped. I should be home about eight. Chris didn't get bail at her arraignment, but Renzo said we should expect that."

"Dinner will be waiting," Josie said. "This extra work has to be hard on you. Any cancellations because of the publicity about Rain's murder?"

"Two," Ted said. "But they weren't regulars, so it's no big loss. Laura's working nonstop. But we definitely need Chris. How's Amelia?"

"She's okay, I think," Josie said. "I didn't hear any barking when I picked her up, but she won't talk to me about it. Maybe you can pry some information out of her."

"I'll try," he said. "I love you."

"I love you, too," Josie said. "And I miss you."

She hung up, wondering when they'd be able to spend another evening together.

The doorbell chimed. Josie angled herself by the front door's art glass window so she could check who was on the porch without being seen. A woman, smaller and thinner than Betty, was holding something flat and fairly heavy.

Josie opened the door and smiled. "Hi, I'm your neighbor Cordelia Madison," the woman said.

Josie was struck by her beauty. Cordelia had a narrow face, almond-shaped eyes, and tawny red-brown skin. Her dark hair was buzzed close to her perfectly shaped head. Stylish and practical, she thought.

"I brought you a chicken pot pie," Cordelia said. "I know when I moved, I didn't have time to cook."

"That's so thoughtful," Josie said. "I just made coffee. Have a cup, will you?"

"I'd love one. I drink it black," Cordelia said.

Josie poured them both a cup and they sat at the dining table with the chicken pot pie as a fragrant centerpiece. "This smells incredible," she said.

"The chicken's poached in white wine," Cordelia said. "There are chanterelle mushrooms, pearl onions, carrots, peas, and fingerling potatoes, and it's seasoned with sage, thyme, and rosemary."

"I hope I have the willpower to take it home to my family without eating the whole thing in the car," Josie said.

Cordelia wore black pants and a distinctive kente cloth top in a black-and-white weave with what looked like stylized gold butterflies.

"You're Dr. Madison, correct? Chris says you're a college professor," Josie said.

"I have a doctorate in English literature," Cordelia said. "But I'm of the school that believes only medical doctors should use their titles full time. I teach Victorian lit at City University downtown. Call me Cordelia, please. My husband is Wil Madison. He's a salesman and he's on the road a lot. Your husband, Ted, is Ted Scottsmeyer, Christine's partner at the clinic. Tell me more about your family."

"We just got married in November," Josie said. "I'm a mystery shopper and I have a twelve-year-old daughter who goes to the Barrington School."

"I hope you're still moving in after . . ." Cordelia stopped, as if searching for the right word.

Josie took over. "We are. Finding Rain's body was terrible. She was so young. And poor Chris, what a dreadful way to learn she'd lost her sister. But we decided to go ahead. We're remodeling the kitchen and building a new deck. I hope the noise won't disturb you."

"I doubt if I'll hear it. These houses are well insulated," Cordelia said. "I'm glad you've removed that wreck of a gazebo."

"We'll move in when the kitchen is finished, probably before fall."

"I'm so happy a real family will be living in this home. Renters don't put down roots."

"Did you know Rain?" Josie asked.

"Oh yes," Cordelia said. "She was a sweet young woman, generous and trusting. She had some dubious boyfriends, but Rain had a good heart and thought everyone else was good, too—until it was too late. I'm guessing Betty gave you an earful about her."

"Not so much," Josie said.

"She will when she knows you better," Cordelia said. "Take what she says with a grain of salt. No, a boulder. Rain was forthright. She loved animals and told Betty it was cruel to make them into show dogs. Betty said her dogs were like members of the family, but Rain said nobody trained their family to stand still for a long time.

"Rain was horrified when she did some research and found out the painful things some people did to show dogs: cutting off their tails, cropping their ears, even tattooing their noses to make them completely black. She said animals were naturally perfect."

"I can see where that wouldn't sit well with Betty," Josie said. "She thinks she has the next Westminster champion."

"Maybe she does," Cordelia said. "I'm not brave enough to have that conversation with her."

"She asked me to examine her dog's teeth so he'd get used to strangers touching him."

"Disgusting!" Cordelia said.

"It was kind of yucky, but I did it," Josie said.

"Guess I'm lucky Betty's not talking to me," Cordelia said. "I told her exactly what I thought when she complained to Christine about Rain and her boyfriends. She said the yard looked trashy, too. Christine was so upset. She asked me and I told her the truth—the yard needed a little work but it wasn't that bad.

"Betty shouldn't have bothered Christine. She's trying to hold down a full-time job and take care of three children. I said if Betty was so concerned about the yard next door, she could do the neighborly thing and mow it herself. Nasty old bat."

No love lost between those two, Josie thought, and I'm not choosing sides. But Cordelia seems to like Chris as much as I do. She knows Chris is a good person—

unlike that stupid Detective Stevenski, who has already decided Chris is guilty without bothering to investigate.

I have to save Chris. Detective Stevenski sure isn't interested in finding Rain's killer. But if I ask this question, Cordelia might think I'm a busybody, too. Well, here goes.

"Who do you think killed Rain?" Josie asked.

Cordelia didn't hesitate. "One of her boyfriends," she said.

"The Coke collector, the beer can collector, or someone else?" Josie asked.

"I go back and forth between the Coke collector and the beer can man," Cordelia said. "The others didn't make much of an impression on me. But the Coke collector is a fanatic, and when he found out Rain had damaged one of his prizes he went ballistic. I heard him yelling at her. Carrying on over an old calendar like it was a Shakespeare First Folio.

"The beer can collector has a violent temper, especially when he drinks. Betty called the police on both of them. Either man seems capable of murder, but I couldn't tell you which one did it."

"What about Christine?"

"You mean as a killer? Never!" Cordelia said.

"Betty said the sisters had a bitter fight," Josie said.

"They did. I heard it. Do you have a sister, Josie?"

"No, I'm an only child."

"So is Betty," Cordelia said. "It's hard for people who don't have siblings to understand family dynamics. My younger sister, Cassandra, and I have had some real knock-down, drag-outs, especially when we were Rain's age. But no matter how much we squabble, we're always there for each other. Betty knows dogs, but I don't think she understands people."

Josie finished the last of her coffee. "More?" she asked.

"No, thanks," Cordelia said. "It's heading toward seven thirty. I've talked your ear off."

"I'm glad you came over," Josie said. "I'll walk out with you." She packed the pie in the same box she'd used for the coffee supplies, and thanked Cordelia again.

I am so lucky to have good neighbors on both sides, she thought. But they dislike each other so much I have a delicate balancing act. I'm caught in the middle.

For real.

Chapter 16

Josie came home to a spice-scented kitchen. This is the smell of success, she thought. My girl has passed the test. She's mature enough to stay home alone for short periods.

Amelia was frosting cupcakes.

"Those smell so good. What flavor?"

"Apple-spice," Amelia said. "I thought I'd throw together some pasta as soon as we know when Ted's coming home."

"He'll be home in about fifteen minutes," Josie said. "No need to cook. Our new neighbor, Cordelia, made us a chicken pot pie." She brought the big red casserole dish out of the box.

"Beautiful crust," Amelia said.

By the time Josie had made a salad and Amelia set the table, a weary, rumpled Ted came home, reeking of dog hair. He was kissed and hugged, then sent to shower. Josie and Amelia made sure all three animals were petted and fed before they sat down to dinner.

"This pie tastes even better than it looks," Ted said. "Did you make it, Amelia?"

"No," Josie said. "But she did make dessert." She told him about her conversation with Cordelia. While they ate the cupcakes, Ted asked, "How's the investigation, Amelia?"

"Emma and I had a breakthrough," Amelia said. "We pushed the brightness of the photos and pulled some information from the dark background. I think we can prove the photos were taken at Barrington. Want to see?"

Josie tried not to smile when Amelia said she "just happened" to have her computer on the extra chair. She slid the cupcake plate aside and set it up in the middle of the table, then pointed to a photo on her screen.

"This picture shows Emma in a parking lot," Amelia said.

The doghouse frame wasn't around this photo. Josie saw Emma was laughing and blurry. Only her upper body was visible. Her skin and white shirt absorbed the flash from the picture. A gray elephant hump was behind her.

Amelia clicked on ADJUSTMENTS and then LEVELS. Josie saw a graph that looked like a mountain range next to the picture. Amelia started dragging the arrows under the "mountain." Emma was disappearing as the background closed around her. Then Amelia dragged the arrows the other way and Emma's face became a ball of white while that gray hump in the background took shape.

"That's Mrs. Grace Edmund's car," Amelia said. "She drives a dark gray RAV4 with Kessinger Toyota dealer plates. And that right there"—she poked the screen—"is a Barrington teacher parking tag."

Ted and Josie applauded.

My girl is brilliant, she thought. I wasn't this smart at twelve. She won't have to scratch for cash like I did when she grows up. She'll finish college and be able to get any job she wants. No slogging through malls like her mystery-shopping mother.

"There's more," Amelia said. She pointed to the photo of the fiery-haired Palmer strolling past a chain-link fence. Part of a blurry red sign seemed drab next to Palmer's flame red ponytail.

"We thought this was the construction company fence around the new library building. We pushed the brightness," Amelia said. "Now look."

Palmer was a nearly white patch, but the fence was sharp and clear, and so was that section of red sign.

"Now you can read the white letters," Amelia said. "It says 'DeSoto' plus 'Building a bet.' DeSoto Construction is the contractor and their sign on our fence says 'Building a better future for Barrington.'"

"Good work," Ted said.

"You've figured out two of the four photos," Josie said.

She nearly burst with pride. My mother, Jane, didn't want Amelia to go to an elite school like Barrington, Josie thought. I've had to scrape together every dollar to keep her there. Even with a scholarship, Barrington isn't free. I pay a thousand dollars a year in tuition, plus books and some hefty fees.

And I work hard so she looks like a Barrington student. I search for the right brands of clothes at yard sales, shop at end-of-season sales, and scour the resale shops so Amelia won't look like a charity child.

I was right to make those sacrifices. This is my payoff. A school where my daughter has sharpened her skills.

"I'm not finished," Amelia said. "Here's that picture of me with the pizza stain on my shirt. See the blue background and that white square? Watch what happens when you push the brightness on this photo."

Amelia's face—and the stain—washed out. Josie could see the blue background was a painted wall and the white blob was a printed poster announcing the April French Club meeting.

"That photo was definitely taken inside the school," Amelia said. "It's the hall by the lockers. This picture of Bailey was inside, too. That hazy gold ball behind her is the school seal."

Bailey's face washed out as the gold seal appeared. Josie saw a giant open book with a flame rising from its pages. Around the seal's edge were these words: "Barrington School for Boys and Girls—Academic Achievement—Ethics—Excellence."

The motto under the book was particularly apt, she thought: "Knowledge Is Power." Her daughter's knowledge of computers gave her the power to track down her tormentors.

"You've got them!" Josie said. "You've proved the photos were taken on school grounds."

"Yeah, but that's not enough," Amelia said. "Miss Apple can say the FedEx guy or the mail carrier shot them, even though we know they didn't. She'll do anything to protect her pets."

My girl's really thought this through. She's been badly hurt, but she didn't lash out, Josie thought. She's calculated the best way to get the justice she deserves.

"I want to prove the three mean girls—Zoe, Jace, and Oakley—did it," Amelia said.

Josie wasn't surprised that Zoe was the ringleader. She'd been a troublemaker even when she was in lower school—wearing makeup to school, bragging about sneaking booze out of her parents' liquor cabinet. When her older sister died of an overdose, she really went off the rails. Josie didn't believe she'd righted herself, either, despite Miss Apple's insistence.

Josie thought Zoe got preferential treatment because she was a double-legacy student. Both her mother and grandmother had gone to Barrington, and her mother met Zoe's father at a dance sponsored by Country Day, a boys' school that was almost as prestigious as Barrington.

She didn't know much about the other two mean girls, except their parents were loaded. Oakley was a new student whose father was a hedge fund manager. She and Amelia had disliked each other from the first day of school. It didn't help that Amelia called her Annie. Josie didn't know anything about the third bully, Jace.

"Miss Apple called an assembly today," Amelia said. "She gave a speech about bullying and said we had a duty to report it."

"A duty!" Hot fury shot through Josie. Trust Miss Apple to blame the victims. Ted squeezed her hand, a signal to let Amelia talk.

"Miss Apple never mentioned names, but everyone knew she meant us. She said if anyone made any inappropriate noises or comments at school, they would be assessed so many points they'd get detention and lose their lunch-hour free time."

These were severe punishments.

"Miss Apple also said that if she had proof any Barrington students were bullying someone, that would result in immediate expulsion."

"That's a tough statement," Josie said. "How did the three mean girls react?"

"They weren't scared at all," Amelia said. "Zoe, Jace, and Oakley sat behind us in assembly. They started whispering 'Bob.' We knew that meant Bitches of Barrington and so did everyone else."

Those weren't three girls, Josie thought. They were a gang. Ted must have sensed her anger. He gave Josie's hand another light squeeze and she let Amelia continue without interruption.

"At lunchtime, Zoe stood in the center of the cafeteria and said, 'Do we want to sit with *Bob*?' She said 'Bob' extra loud, so we'd know she was talking about us.

"Jace said, 'I don't like Bob.'

"Oakley said, 'I never did like Bob,' and looked right at me.

"Everyone in the cafeteria stayed away from our table, except for Emerson. She came over and sat with us. She said the three mean girls were stupid and she was tired of Oakley's sarcasm.

"That's when we got a real break. Emerson said the three mean girls took the photos with their phones and sent them to her cell phone."

"So this girl who decided to sit at your table, this Emerson, will do the right thing and tell Miss Apple?" Josie asked.

"Well, no," Amelia said.

"Is she afraid the mean girls' photos will be traced back to her?" Ted asked.

"Not really," Amelia said. "Zoe took the photo of me first, and sent it to a bunch of kids so they could see what a slob I was. Then they took the other three photos: Bailey because she was fat, Emma because she was fugly . . ."

Josie let that word slide past.

"And Palmer because she doesn't dress cute. Her mom picks out her clothes and they're like old-lady stuff, but that's not Palmer's fault. She can deal with it.

"Then the three mean girls sent the pictures to everyone."

Everyone but you four, Josie thought. And nobody said a word to you about it except this Emerson.

"Zoe was the one who said the four Bitches of Barrington should be in doghouses, so they made that Facebook page."

"Amelia, do you really want to keep going to school with these girls?" Ted asked. "You don't have to. You can transfer. You don't have to put up with their sneaky behavior."

"No, I like Barrington," Amelia said. "Zoe's good at

stirring up trouble, but it will be fine when she's gone. I'm going to get her and her two mean little friends.

"Emerson's e-mailing me all four photos. The e-mailed photos will have the XDIF information attached."

Josie had no idea what an XDIF was. But she understood Amelia's next words: "It will totally nail them as guilty. Then Miss Apple will have to expel them."

Chapter 17

The next morning, Josie switched on the living room TV. Honey Butcher, the blond reporter for Channel Seven, grabbed her by the ear.

"Christine Dillon Cormac, the Rock Road Village veterinarian charged with the first-degree murder of her sister Rain Siobhan Dillon," she said, "was denied bail yesterday at her felony arraignment in St. Louis County."

What? That story didn't make the early news, when Josie was getting dressed to take Amelia to school. She dropped on the living room couch, the coffee in her mug sloshing dangerously. She set it on the coffee table with trembling hands and stared at the video of a shell-shocked Chris being led into court.

This is bad, Josie thought. Ted didn't tell me Chris was charged with first-degree murder. Missouri is a death-penalty state.

A gray-suited man identified as "County Prosecutor Nelson Philippi" was on-screen now. "Due to the heinous nature of this murder, and the premeditation involved, we will demand the death penalty," he said.

The prosecutor was so smooth and emotionless he could have been an animatronic figure. Come to think of it, so could Honey, the blond reporter, Josie decided. Her thoughts skittered away from this frightening update. I'm sure that explains all the look-alike blondes on TV.

Honey Butcher dragged Josie back to harsh reality. "Ms. Cormac pled not guilty," she said. "She is represented by defense attorney Renzo Fischer."

Renzo looked like the only human in this courtroom drama. After the arraignment, the short lawyer with the cowboy hat and tailored navy suit strutted out in blue ostrich-skin boots that added two inches. His turquoise bolo tie looked wildly out of place in suburban St. Louis.

He addressed them outside the courthouse. "I am confident, ladies and gentlemen of the media, that my client, Dr. Christine Cormac, is innocent. We welcome this trial to prove it. Dr. Cormac is a respected veterinarian and mother of three. She's been falsely accused by an inept prosecutor in a mindless rush to what he believes is justice."

A rumpled reporter in khaki pants and a frayed rep tie interrupted. "Mr. Fischer, I wouldn't call the county prosecutor inept," he said. "He has a near-perfect record for convictions."

"So he does, Charlie," Renzo said. "But I have a pretty good record myself. I look forward to matching wits with Mr. Philippi. The best man will win, and that's me."

Josie admired the lawyer's confidence and hoped it was justified. She knew Chris was innocent, and it was up to Josie to prove it. Chris didn't deserve to be railroaded by that arrogant detective. Josie also wanted Ted's partner rescued for very personal (okay, selfish) reasons. Since Chris's arrest, Ted came home exhausted and fell asleep after dinner. That was no life for newlyweds.

As Josie watched Renzo smoothly handle the press, she was slammed with another awful thought. What if Renzo's interview made the national news? He was a quotable character, and the camera loved him. If Lenore saw it, Josie's meddlesome mother-in-law would fly to St.

Louis as soon as she commandeered her husband's plane.

I need to head her off, Josie thought. She quickly called Lenore's cell phone and heard, "I'm not able to take your call now . . ." She whispered a silent prayer to whoever helped new brides, then summoned her cheeriest voice. "Hi, Lenore, it's Josie. Just wanted to let you know that Ted's partner, Chris, was denied bail, but that was expected, so if you see it on the news, don't be concerned. She's innocent and her lawyer is eager to prove it. Nothing to worry about. Bye."

Nothing to worry about indeed, she thought, and sipped her abandoned coffee. Bleh! It had gone cold, but not as cold as Josie. No one had a clue who'd murdered Rain and buried her under the gazebo.

I have to find the killer if I ever want to see my husband again. No, it's more than that. Chris is a friend and a mother like me. She's going to lose her children. She could lose her life. What a horrible development for Todd and his sisters. If Chris goes to death row, their lives will be ruined and they'll have to live with their father.

Josie reheated the cold coffee in the microwave, and thought, What do I know so far?

My neighbor Cordelia thinks one of Rain's boyfriends was the murderer, but she can't decide which one. Both neighbors agree that Donny Freedman, the beer can collector, is a violent drunk. Betty says Donny tends bar at Judson's Tavern, a dive on Manchester Road.

Josie checked the clock. Nine thirty. Would the bar be open so early?

She looked up the number, called it, and heard a man's brusque voice, "Judson's. Donny speaking."

Josie was too surprised to say anything. She heard raucous music and loud voices in the background, then an impatient Donny. "Hey! Anybody there? Speak up!"

Josie collected her thoughts enough to ask, "Uh, how late are you open?"

"Till two a.m." Donny hung up.

Were those customers left over from last night? she wondered. Or was this the night-shift crowd from the local factories stopping by after work?

Even if the bar had a bad reputation, Josie figured it would be safe enough in daylight. She'd get in and out quickly.

She called Alyce next.

"I was hoping you'd call," her friend said. "Ready for a second visit to ReHab? We can take my SUV in case we find those cabinets."

"Definitely," Josie said. "Meet me at my new place at noon. I'm due for some good luck."

That reminded her she might need some backup. "Alyce, I'm going to talk to Donny, Rain's ex-boyfriend, this morning. If I'm not home by noon, call my cell phone. If I don't answer, send the police to Judson's Tavern on Manchester."

"The police!" Alyce said. "What are you doing?"

"It's just a precaution," Josie said. "I'll talk to him while he's working there."

"I'm going with you," Alyce said.

"No, you've got a toddler," Josie said. "Promise you'll call if I'm not home at noon." She hung up before Alyce had a chance to say anything else. Josie thought Donny might not talk if she walked in with an upscale matron like Alyce.

Judson's Tavern was a dingy clapboard building. A dozen battered vehicles were scattered on the gravel lot, along with beer cans—the noncollectible kind. Parked around the side was a new muscle car, a Mustang in "write me a ticket" red.

Josie felt uneasy. Am I making a mistake going in here, even at ten in the morning? she wondered. Well,

I've alerted Alyce. And there's a green Toyota with a crumpled fender and an I ♥ Cats bumper sticker. A cat lover made the place seem safe. But Josie wouldn't linger.

Inside, she nearly choked on the cigarette smoke. Either the bar had an exemption from the local smoking ban, or it wasn't enforced here. Through the blue haze, she could see a long, dark wooden bar with four men in work clothes slouched on red vinyl barstools, and a scattering of tables. An older woman in a cigarette fog sat at a chrome-legged table near the bowling machine. Josie sat down at the table next to her.

"I'm Peg," the woman said, and smiled, showing smoke-yellowed teeth. Josie guessed she was a regular. "There's no waiter. You gotta order at the bar from Donny. Get the eggs and bacon. That's what I had. It's decent."

Josie thought Donny had a seedy handsomeness. He was about six feet tall, with dirty blond hair, blue eyes, and sun-reddened skin. His blue chambray shirt was rolled at the sleeves, showing off muscular arms. A chalkboard announced the breakfast specials.

"Whadaya have?" he asked.

"Eggs, bacon, and black coffee," Josie said.

"I'll bring it to your table," he said, then stepped over to a kitchen pass-through and banged on a bell to alert the cook.

The mirrored back bar featured the second-tier brands of liquor, but the middle shelves were a shrine to long-vanished cone-top beer cans: Altes Lager, Atlantic Ale, and Beverwyck Beer.

One green-and-gold '76 Ale cone top was enshrined in a glass case.

"Are those beer cans from your collection?" Josie asked.

"You bet," he said, slightly slurring his words. "All

cone tops, worth three hundred bucks or more. The one in the case is from the Terre Haute Brewing Company in Indiana. It's an IRTP. That means 'Internal Revenue Tax Paid.' Those are extra rare. It's worth three thousand dollars."

"Wow," Josie said. He seemed to assume that Josie had turned up to see his collection. He leaned so close she could smell beer on his breath and see his bleary eyes.

"Most of my collection is at home," Donny said. "I got more than a thousand cans on specially built shelves, but I loaned this display to Bill, the owner. They're my job insurance. Everybody comes here to see these rare cans. Bill will never fire me. The moment I walk, my beer cans go with me."

"Did you used to date Rain Dillon?" she asked.

He didn't notice the abrupt change of subject. "The hippie?" he said. "Did you know her?"

"I never met her," Josie said. "But my husband and I bought the house where her body was found."

"I heard she was dead," he said. "Too bad." Josie was shocked by his indifference.

"I thought the cops would try to pin it on me," he said, "and I had my alibi and everything. I was working till two a.m. the week she was killed, and a raft of customers will swear I was here every night until closing. But the cops never bothered me."

Why is Donny telling me he has an alibi? Josie wondered.

He turned away from Josie with lightning speed, his voice a whip crack. "Hey! You there! Richie! Are you stealing my ketchup packets? Put 'em back."

Richie, a scrawny rat who had his hand in a box of take-out condiments at the end of the bar, whined, "I don't have anything."

"Don't lie. I see them in your pocket." Donny grabbed

Richie by the collar and dragged him over the bar top until they were eye to eye, then roughly pulled out a handful of ketchup packets from Richie's shirt pocket and threw them back in the box.

Josie retreated to her chair, shaken by his raw anger.

"You've just seen Donny in action," Peg said, puffing on her cigarette. "Man can start a fight in an empty room." She tipped her bottle of Busch to drain the last drop.

"Can I buy you another beer?" Josie asked.

"That's nice of you," Peg said, and smiled. "Bring your purse and come sit at my table."

By the time Josie was settled, Donny arrived balancing a thick white china platter with Josie's breakfast and a coffee mug. She ordered a beer for Peg and he delivered it moments later.

Josie didn't have to ask if Peg was a cat lover. She could see short brown and black hairs on her white T-shirt, which was decorated with dozens of cats and the words CRAZY CAT LADY.

"I heard you say you bought the house where they found Rain," Peg said.

"That poor woman," Josie said. "Did you know her?"

"The little hippie girl? Sweet little thing," Peg said, "but dumb as a post about men. She told me she collected people and treated Donny like some kind of exotic butterfly. Didn't realize she'd caught herself a common barfly. When he popped her one in the face, he knocked some sense into her. She wised up and dropped him. I was sorry to hear she was murdered. She didn't deserve that."

"Do you think Donny killed her?" Josie asked.

Peg shrugged. "You saw how he treated Richie for helping himself to free ketchup. He's mean when he's liquored up, and that's most of the time. Bill, the owner, doesn't keep a gun under the bar, but he has a lead pipe for protection. One Saturday night, Donny nearly beat a lippy drunk half to death before the cops got here to stop it. Guy refused to press charges. Said he tripped and fell.

"Rain didn't spend much time here. She didn't see that side of him until he turned on her. He rarely dates the women here, but why would he? Most are old bags like me who like beer for breakfast."

Peg's raucous laugh turned into a cough, and she soothed it with a sip of beer.

"Is Donny seeing anyone now?"

"Yep, got another girl right after Rain dumped him. Took up with a receptionist at a vet clinic. Another little blonde. Missy. Don't know why that bum attracts such nice women. Maybe she likes animals. I'm praying Missy wises up before he hurts her."

"Do you know the name of the clinic?"

"Sure do," Peg said. "The Best in Show Veterinary Clinic in Brentwood, near the highway. Run by Dr. Arnie Spengler. Specializes in show dogs and cats. That's how I got my Rajah, a genuine Bengal with real papers and everything. He's a retired show cat with a slew of trophies and ribbons. A show-quality Bengal costs thousands, but I got my Rajah for fifteen hundred, thanks to Missy. She knew a lady at the clinic who wanted to sell hers. Donny arranged the deal."

"That's a lot of money for a cat," Josie said.

"Cost me my whole Social Security check, but he's worth every penny. Here, look at him."

Peg dug into a purse the size of a suitcase and pulled out a fat wallet. "That's his picture there. He's a beauty."

Josie thought Rajah looked remarkably like Amelia's striped tabby, Harry, with slightly different markings. "Gorgeous green eyes," she said.

"And the sweetest disposition," Peg said. "Runs to the front door like a puppy when I come home. Those awards didn't go to his head. I told my friend Bernice about Rajah. She lives across the river in Grafton."

"The river" in St. Louis meant the Mississippi, which divides Missouri from Illinois.

"She bought Rajah's brother, Baby Bengal. And Bernice's neighbor Judy was so knocked out by Baby, she bought one, too. Those Bengals have spread through Grafton, Wood River, Collinsville, even Belleville. I bet there's more Bengals in Missouri and Illinois than New York City.

"That's why I can't get too mad at Donny, even when he acts so asinine. He introduced me to Missy, and that's how I got my dream kitty. Missy helped all my friends get their Bengals, and Donny drove the cats all the way to Illinois. Didn't seem to mind at all."

"Does he have the red Mustang?" Josie asked.

"Sure does," Peg said. "Said it was the car for chauffeuring royalty."

"Did Donny really work the week Rain was murdered?" Josie asked. "At the bar here, I mean."

"When was that?" Peg asked. "I didn't hear any dates on television."

"Me, either," Josie said. "But I think she was murdered about six months ago."

"That's about when he got transferred to days," Peg said. "Bill couldn't keep him on nights because he kept showing up late. He missed more nights than he actually worked. He's still coming in late now, but he sure leaves on time when his shift is over at two in the afternoon. I expect he'll be fired soon. Bill will throw him out on his can—or is that cans?"

Peg was still laughing at her own joke when Josie left.

Chapter 18

Josie was encouraged by the construction chaos at her Fresno Court home. She'd escaped Judson's Tavern at eleven thirty that morning. Jeanne's pickup, Bud Vey's truck, a flatbed, and a dented blue van took up most of the circle.

Josie could hear the roar of a Bobcat, a miniexcavator, tearing into her backyard. She raced around to the back, and watched the operator move the sharp-bladed shovel with delicate precision. The rumbling machine swiveled on its base and bit into chunks of green grass and yellowish clay soil, drowning out Betty's barking dogs.

Bud was leaning on a long-handled rake. "Hey, Josie," he said, wiping his sweating forehead with a blue bandanna. "That sun's hot. We're preparing the base for your concrete. See those lines? We've sprayed them where your deck is going to be."

"Looks good already," Josie said. Rain's unmarked grave was now level with the rest of the deck area.

"Where's your sidekick, Ranger?" she asked.

"At home," he said. "I don't bring him on jobs, especially where there's going to be concrete—not after he stuck his big paws in some cement.

"It's gonna be noisy here for a few days. Once the

digging is done, we'll have to compact and level the dirt base with another loud machine, then put down the aggregate—that's crushed rock—and start pouring your deck footings. If you think the Bobcat makes noise, wait till you hear the cement truck."

Bud looked happy as a boy playing with grown-up toys. The Bobcat's racket stopped for a moment and the driver waved him over.

That's when Josie heard an unhappy Jeanne in her kitchen. "Hey, Newt, do I look like an idiot?" she asked. "Of course I mind if that cabinet is installed upside down."

"Aw, Jeanne, you said this lady isn't much of a cook," Newt whined. "Will she even notice?"

"You don't have to cook to know a cabinet door's on backward," Jeanne said. "Fix it right and fix it now."

"All those mothering little screws," he grumbled. "Take forever. If I have to rehang this cabinet, it might mess up my paint job."

"Then you'll have to repaint, won't you?" Jeanne said.

Josie gave a warning knock on the kitchen door, and found a red-faced Jeanne confronting a skinny guy in paint-spotted overalls. Newt looked like a long, skinny reptile with an underslung jaw.

"All right," he said, pulling out his cordless screw-driver. He went back to work on the freshly painted cabinet above the counter.

Josie barely recognized her kitchen. The worn black-and-white-checked floor was gone, replaced by a raw plywood subfloor. Only one white cabinet remained in place next to the stove. Most of the metal and wooden cabinets now leaned against the walls, dirty and rusty.

Will they ever be usable? she wondered.

Jeanne must have read her expression. "They look bad now," she said, "but once Newt works his magic, you'll be amazed. He's the best."

Newt grinned, his grousing forgotten.

"Newt got rid of that broken one," she said, "and he's hauling the rest of these off to his workshop in Maryland Heights today."

"I'm going to need at least six weeks," Newt said, "and that's if the replacement cabinet doesn't need too much work."

"My friend Alyce and I are hunting for it today," Josie said.

"Good," Jeanne said. "As soon as your new tile is delivered, we'll tile under the cabinets, sink, and appliances, then finish the floor when the rest of the kitchen is done. Oh, I almost forgot. Bad news about the wiring."

"Hit me with it," Josie said.

"The electrician says some amateur jerry-rigged the outlets for the stove and dishwasher. He wants to tear out the bad wiring and bring the kitchen up to code. That'll cost at least a thousand dollars."

"Harley strikes again," Josie said. "He's the guy who built that shoddy gazebo."

"Amateur handymen," Jeanne said cheerfully. "If it wasn't for them, I'd be out of work. Sorry you had one here."

Josie didn't feel quite so cheerful, but she reminded herself that's why Chris had given them a break on the price. "Don't skimp on the wiring," she said. "I want it right."

"We'll be on the lookout for more of Harley's home improvements," Jeanne said. "As soon as you get your dishwasher, I'll have a plumber in."

"Give me the dishwater size now," Josie said. "We're going to ReHab at noon."

"That place is a gamble," Jeanne said, "but sometimes I can walk in and get everything I need."

The doorbell chimed and Josie said, "That's Alyce. Do you need anything else?"

"Nope. Happy hunting," Jeanne said.

Twenty minutes later, Josie and Alyce pulled into the

nearly empty ReHab parking lot. "If we finish fast enough," Josie said, "I can see Mom before I pick up Amelia at school."

Eric greeted them at the door to ReHab. "Hi, ladies. Welcome back. What are you looking for today?"

"This is a blitz mission," Josie said. "I want a thirty-six-inch gas stove, a dishwasher, a metal midcentury cabinet, and purple paint."

"Got them all," he said. "I hope they're what you need."

"Cabinets first," Josie said. They followed Eric's bouncing ponytail to another mountain of white metal cabinets, much older than the last batch.

"Look at that one with the cute rounded retro shelves down the side," Josie said. She whipped out her tape measure and checked the size. "It will fit. And there's no rust. How much?"

The price was fifty dollars less than she expected. "I'll take it," she said. "Dishwasher next."

Josie quickly chose a two-year-old dishwasher with a good rating from *Consumer Reports*.

"Now wait till you see the stove," Eric said. "It's amazing."

Josie thought the stove looked nice, as stoves go, but Alyce nearly swooned. "This is a Sub-Zero Wolf stove," she said, her voice soft with awe. "The cooktop can be configured three different ways. It has dual-stacked burners, a convection oven, and an infrared broiler."

Josie had no idea what that meant. She just hoped she could boil water on it.

"I'm not sure I like those red knobs," she said.

"Don't like them!" Alyce shrieked. "Those are the Wolf signature. That's like hating the hood ornament on a Rolls-Royce."

"You get kitchens," Eric said to Alyce. "You, like, totally get it. I'm into cooking, but I don't have fifteen hundred dollars right now or I'd take this home."

"That's a lot of money," Josie said doubtfully.

"This stove sells for six thousand new, and this model looks barely used. Buy it," Alyce commanded, "or I'll get it for myself. Ted and Amelia will adore it."

"Will it fit in your SUV?" Josie asked.

"We can deliver for a small fee," Eric said.

"Sold," Josie said.

"Good," Eric said. "I want it to go to a good home." He patted the stove like a faithful pet.

"For your last request, we just got in some purple paint," he said.

Josie bought paint the color of spring lilacs, then paid for her purchases and arranged for the stove delivery.

By one o'clock, Alyce's SUV was back at Fresno Court, where Newt and Jeanne helped them unload the paint and the cabinet.

"This cabinet's in surprisingly good shape," he said.

"You have a real find," Jeanne said. "I can't believe that stove deal. I'll be here to accept delivery for it."

Josie waved good-bye to Alyce, then called her mother.

"Come over for lunch so we can talk," Jane said. "I have some lovely chicken salad, the kind with the grapes that you like so much, and an apple pie just out of the oven. Be careful where you park. I put a For Rent sign in the window and Mrs. Mueller is on the warpath."

"Uh-oh," Josie said. "I'll be there in ten."

The white paint on the wide porch of Jane's old red-brick flat on Phelan Street gleamed. A rainbow of tulips made a bold show along the walkway.

Josie knocked on her mother's front door. Jane called, "Come on up," and greeted her with a hug at the top of the stairs.

Mom didn't come down the stairs to open the door, Josie thought. Should I be worried? But she's wearing her new green pantsuit and her gray hair is fresh from the beauty shop.

"It's so good to see you, Josie. The house is so quiet without you and Amelia. I miss you."

"I miss you, too, Mom," Josie said, and gave Stuart Little, Jane's shih tzu, an ear scratch. "You didn't come down the stairs. Are you feeling okay?"

"I'm fine, Josie. You can find your own way up the stairs. I've been up and down them six times so far. That's enough exercise for one morning. Now sit down and eat."

Jane's kitchen table was set with pretty plates of chicken salad and homemade bread, and the air was scented with hot coffee.

"Delicious as ever," Josie said after the first bite. "Any good renters?"

"Just one bad one," Jane said. "Mrs. Mueller wants her new friend, Rowena Crum, to live here. Josie, I won't have that—that blue-haired spy living here. She'll report every sneeze to Mrs. Mueller."

"We'll find you someone good, Mom," Josie said. "I'll ask Ted if one of his clinic clients needs a place."

"Thank you," Jane said. "How's my favorite son-in-law holding up after that terrible business with Chris's sister? And how are you?"

It was a relief to tell her mother her worries about Chris and Amelia. Jane listened to her daughter. She didn't used to. Josie also bragged about her husband and then her finds at ReHab.

"A Wolf stove!" Jane said. "I'd give my eyeteeth to cook on one. Would you like some apple pie? I baked it downstairs in your old kitchen. There's another one to take home, too. When you finish, come see what your flat looks like."

Josie was two bites into her pie when she finally asked, "Mom, why did you bake the pies downstairs in my old kitchen?"

"Gets rid of the paint odor," Jane said. "Apple pie smells like home. Ready for the tour?"

Josie followed her mother down the stairs to her former home. Stuart Little pattered behind them, his claws clicking on the freshly waxed floors.

Josie admired the sunlit walls. "The kitchen looks the same, only cleaner," she said, her voice echoing in the empty rooms.

There was a loud knock at the back door. "It's Mrs. M," Josie said.

Jane's neighbor looked like a bad winter day, with slush gray hair and a drab brown housedress buttoned to her neck.

Jane fluffed herself up like an angry hen. "I have nothing further to say to you," she said.

Mrs. M ignored Jane and marched straight over to Josie, jowls wobbling in indignation. "I hope you'll talk some sense into your mother. She has a duty to find a suitable renter for the safety of this neighborhood. I suggested a maiden lady from our church, Rowena Crum. Your mother says she's been too busy to show her the apartment."

"This is my home and I'll rent it to anyone I please," Jane said. She faced Mrs. M, a short, sturdy bulldog in a pantsuit.

"We'll be murdered in our beds," Mrs. Mueller said.

"I'll ask you to leave now," Jane said, and pointed toward the door.

Josie waited until she saw Mrs. Mueller stomping across the yard to her own house, her back rigid with anger. "Bye, Mom. Gotta pick up Amelia," she said. "Thanks for the pie."

Josie had a real murder to worry about.

Chapter 19

Amelia plopped into the car's front seat after school, and Josie was on full Mom alert. She delicately checked her daughter for signs of depression, worry, and fatally wounded feelings. She used her maternal feelers, trying to detect apathy, instability, and lost appetite.

In short, she mightily irritated Amelia.

"I bought some gorgeous paint for your room," Josie said, sounding like an overage cheerleader.

Amelia shrugged.

"It's purple, your fave. The paint's at the new house. Want to see it?"

"Can't you just take me home?" Amelia asked, her voice rising to an annoying whine. "Emma and I want to work on the mean-girl photos. We're getting close, Mom. When Emerson gave us the four photos, that was, like, huge."

"Why?" Josie asked.

"Because iPhone cameras embed information into an image, but Facebook strips it out."

"What kind of information?" Josie asked.

"What type of phone took the photo, the date, and the time, right down to the second."

"Amazing," Josie said. This is the longest conversation we've had in weeks, she thought.

"It is," Amelia said. Josie was pleased her daughter's enthusiasm was reviving.

"We can even find the f-stop settings and ISO speed," Amelia said. "But those aren't so important. The phone, date, and time are. If those photos were taken on a weekend, we can't prove Zoe and her mean friends took them. You see why this is major, Mom?"

Josie did. Her daughter was on a quest. You didn't ask Wonder Woman to pick up a loaf of bread on her way home from saving the nation. Amelia had to solve this mystery and put her world back in order. Then she could worry about purple paint.

"I do," Josie said. "Ted called and said he'll be home about eight o'clock again. Why don't you work on your photos and I'll visit Chris in jail? The next visiting hour is at six o'clock tonight."

"What about dinner?" Amelia asked.

Now that's a normal tween response, Josie thought.

"Ted's doing the cooking tonight," she said. "His coq au vin is defrosting now. I'll heat it up when I get back and make a salad. Grandma gave us an apple pie for dessert. We're all set. You don't have to do anything but investigate. And I have a special surprise for dinner."

"You didn't cook, did you?" Amelia asked, sounding wary.

"No, I bought something you and Ted will love," Josie said. She couldn't wait to spring that stove on her two favorite cooks.

Visits to inmates at the county jail were rationed— only two visitors a week. Josie called Renzo, Chris's lawyer, to make sure she wasn't eliminating someone Chris needed to see.

Renzo took her call right away. She imagined the little lawyer with his cowboy boots propped on his desk.

"Dr. Chris needs a visitor today, Josie," he said. "Her sister Susan's back in Cincinnati and her ex, Rodney, sure as hell won't visit. He won't let her see her children, either. Says they'll be scarred for life if they see their mother in jail." He snorted. "Like he cares about Dr. Chris or his kids.

"I've been blathering on too much. Dr. Chris needs to see a friendly face because she got bad news today."

"How bad?" Josie asked.

"Well, I guess I can tell you," he said. "I know you don't talk. She can't say anything to you because I've warned her not to mention it to anyone. Jailhouse snitches are everywhere, but I don't know how long this news will stay a secret. I'm guessing the prosecution might accidentally on purpose leak it."

"Like what?" Josie said. She was losing patience with Renzo's folksy talk.

"The police confiscated Dr. Chris's laptop and found a bunch of e-mails where she complains to Susan that Rain is a burr under her saddle. The first e-mail says after four months around her sister Chris understands why Susan's husband threw Rain out.

"One of the e-mails says— Wait a minute. Let me find it."

Josie fought back a scream of frustration.

"Here it is," Renzo said, and read: *Every time I look at her, I realize she broke up my marriage. I try not to hate my own flesh and blood, but I can't wipe away that picture in my mind of her and Rodney going at it. I know she wasn't the first woman Rodney screwed, but her own sister's husband? That makes it personal. Then she had the nerve to spout her hippie BS about marriage being patriarchal ownership. You want ownership? It's time she OWNED up to her mistakes.*

"There's a bunch more complaints about her crazy boyfriends, and then Dr. Chris got all fired up about how Rain quit paying rent and let the yard go to wrack and ruin."

Josie groaned.

"It gets worse," Renzo said. "Her last e-mail before Rain was murdered said *I'm at my wits' end, Sis. I wish I could find a way to get rid of Rain permanently. In fact, I'd like a good long drought.*"

"Can it get any worse?" Josie asked.

"Yes, and it does," Renzo said. "Two days later, Dr. Chris writes Susan again: *My prayers are answered!!! She left. Sent me an e-mail saying she's going to an ashram to find herself. Just in time to save my sanity! Typical Rain—didn't bother to say good-bye in person, much less pay her rent. Just packed up her things and walked out. Todd, bless him, is helping me put the house back together. I have to bite my tongue when he talks about his wonderful aunt Rain, but I don't want him to know what a total S–T she is. With any luck, I won't see her for a long time.*"

"So, how damaging are those e-mails?" Josie asked.

"I've pulled slipperier rabbits out my hat," Renzo said, and Josie flashed on a mental picture of the little lawyer struggling to drag a white bunny out of his ten-gallon hat.

"People talk like that all the time," he said. "How many wives say, 'If my husband says he'd rather go fishing than visit my mother one more time, I'll kill him'? If we all acted on those impulses, the planet would be depopulated."

Except Rain really is dead, Josie thought.

Renzo seemed to hear her unspoken objection. "Now, don't you go worrying, Josie. It's my job to make that jury see reason. You help out Chris by keeping up her spirits."

Josie hung up, tiptoed down the hall, and checked on her daughter. Amelia was on her computer and her phone: "So I go there, Emma, and click on what? Wait. There's the link. . . ."

Josie stuck her head in the door, waved good-bye, and

said, "I'll be home in two hours. Remember, I'm trusting you." Amelia nodded and waved, but never stopped her conversation.

Josie fought the rush-hour traffic all the way to the concrete canyons of downtown Clayton. After a ten-minute search on its clogged streets, she found a parking spot, threw money in the meter, and barely made it in time to the county jail.

Josie was shocked by Chris's appearance. Ted's partner was even thinner than she'd been at her arraignment. Her eyes were sunk deep into dark pools and her hair looked greasy and unwashed.

She wanted to hug Chris, but they were separated by a plastic-glass shield. Josie picked up her phone and Chris said, "Josie, I'm so glad you're here." She managed a weak smile, but looked like she might dissolve into tears.

"I talked to Renzo," Josie said. "He says not to be upset by that news. He'll handle it."

"Do you really think he can?" Chris asked.

"That man works miracles," Josie said. "I've seen them."

"He'll have to," Chris said. "I miss my kids, Josie. I'm worried sick about them."

"Do you want me to check on them?"

"You can't," Chris said, her voice hopeless. "Rodney's made sure they're cut off from everyone, even their friends. Todd called my sister from school and said his father has hired a babysitter to watch them until he gets home from work and she has instructions not to let anyone visit. Todd thanked Susan for sending a gift basket with a whole ham, fruit, and other goodies. She also mailed them a big tin of her cookies, so I know they've got good food.

"Susan wants to call Child Protection Services, but Rodney's not doing anything wrong. This is my fault. When he never exercised his custody rights, I should

have had my lawyer change them so I'd have total custody, but I never got around to it.

"Todd promised to call Susan every day on his lunch
hour."

"If he needs someone in St. Louis, he can call Ted or
me," Josie said.

"Thanks, Josie. He knows that. Todd is determined to
tough it out until I'm free."

If you're free, Josie thought. Those words seemed to
hang silently in the air.

"I'm trying to find Rain's killer, Chris," she said. "I
know you're innocent, but there has to be a way to prove
it. I almost never see you wearing earrings. When was the
last time you remember wearing the veterinary earrings
Rain gave you?"

"The day Betty called me and complained about Rain
fighting with her latest boyfriend," Chris said. "The kids
were at school and I had lunch with George, a man I
used to go out with in veterinary school, before I met
Rodney. I don't usually go on dates, but this was just
lunch. I wanted to look extra nice, so I put on my best
suit, wore makeup and jewelry, and we went out for a
long wet lunch in the Central West End.

"George and I were having a good time when Betty
called. Her call broke the mood. Suddenly George had
to catch a plane. I went straight over to the house and
talked to Betty. I was embarrassed that she'd had to call
the police, and I agreed the yard looked raggedy. I asked
Cordelia. She said it wasn't that bad, but I knew she was
trying to be polite.

"I went over to have a chat with my sister and, like I
said, I found her in the gazebo. That's when I blew up
and lost my temper—and my earring. At least, I never
saw it after that."

The missing earring only makes Chris look guiltier,
Josie thought. "Can I ask you a personal question?"

"Go ahead," Chris said.

"Why did you rent your house to Rain, after she'd had an affair with your husband?"

Chris sighed. "Renzo asked me that, too. It looks bad, doesn't it? I knew Rodney had been fooling around on me since Todd was little. I just didn't think about it. But when I surprised my sister and Rodney in our bed going at it like animals, I could no longer ignore it. Rain had stopped by our home overnight on her way to Susan's. Just long enough to wreck my marriage and leave town.

"I tried telling myself she did me a favor when she forced me to face the truth about Rodney."

"What did Rain say when you surprised her with your husband?" Josie asked.

"She got all righteous and spouted her hippie BS about marriage being a patriarchal tool. I was so mad I ordered her out of the house and told Rodney to pack his bags. I didn't see her again for almost two years. That's when Susan's husband kicked her out."

"Did she have an affair with him, too?" Josie asked.

"No! He couldn't stand Rain," Chris said. "I'm surprised he let her live with him and Susan as long as he did. When he finally threw her out, Rain turned up on my doorstep, looking for a place to stay. She didn't give me any warning.

"Her timing was perfect. She waited until Todd was home from school to show up. He was thrilled to see Aunt Rain, and I thought I was over the incident with Rodney. After all, we'd been divorced for more than a year. Plus, Aunt Trudy's house was empty and Rain said she'd pay rent. It wasn't like she was living with me.

"But the longer she stayed in St. Louis, the more I realized it was harder to forgive her than I thought," Chris said. "At least her rent helped pay off my loans. Then Rain quit paying rent. When Betty complained the yard was a mess, I went over there, saw her in the gazebo, and lost it. I screamed at my sister. My last words were so angry and hateful."

A tear slid down Chris's cheek and she struggled to keep from crying.

"I'm so sorry," Josie said. "But you gave Rain a beautiful good-bye. I'm sure she forgives you."

"I hope so," Chris said. She was sobbing now. None of the other prisoners and their visitors seemed to notice. They were used to misery.

Josie sat helplessly while Chris cried herself out. Finally she wiped her damp, tear-reddened eyes with her hands and sniffled.

There must be something I can do to help, Josie thought. "What about your pets?" she asked. "Don't you have dogs and a cat? Do you need us to take care of them?"

"We're down to two dogs," Chris said. "Rodney won't let the kids have their pets at his apartment. Against the rules. My neighbor's looking after the dogs. They like her. Tell me something normal, Josie. How's Amelia? How's the house renovation?"

Josie talked about Amelia and the mean girls and her finds at ReHab, until they heard the announcement that visiting hours were over. Chris looked so lost when Josie stood up to leave, she pressed her palm against the plastic glass. Chris did the same. It was a sad good-bye.

The drive home was much quicker. Amelia was still at work on what looked like the mean-girls investigation, and Josie didn't disturb her. She made a salad, heated the coq au vin, and set the table, all the while brooding on Chris's dilemma.

When she heard Ted's Mustang in the drive, their home came alive. Ted swooped in and kissed her, Amelia and Harry ran out to see him, and the cats and dogs demanded scratches and dinner.

After Ted showered, they sat down to their own meal.

"How's the house renovation going?" Ted asked.

Josie told him about the work on the deck, and her visit to ReHab, saving her surprise for last. "Here's the best part," Josie said. "I found a Wolf stove."

"No way," he said, setting down his fork.

"With lots of good features like a gas convection oven and an infrared broiler. And we can afford it."

"That is so sick," Amelia said. Josie reminded herself that was the ultimate tween compliment. This week, anyway.

Ted got up and gave Josie a hug and kiss. "You are the queen of rehabbers and a master bargain hunter," he said.

"Thank you," Josie said. "And while you're up, bring over Mom's pie and pour us some coffee."

"I wish I could give you a bigger reward," Ted said.

"You can," Josie said. "Do any of your clinic clients need an apartment? Mom still needs a renter."

"I do know one," he said. "Laura, our new vet, says her father is looking for a place. He's seventy and he sold his big old house now that his wife's dead. He needs to find a place and wants to stay in Maplewood. I'll call her now."

Amelia finished her pie. "Mom, can I be excused to go work on my investigation? It's nearly done."

"You go, girl," Josie said. "We'll handle the dishes."

She heard Ted on his cell phone. "Hey there, Laura, how are you? Heck of a day, wasn't it? You got the Levy girls this afternoon? Aren't they cute? Cavalier spaniels are great dogs. Barbara brings them in every year for their wellness checkup. She made sure you listened to their hearts? Twice?"

Ted laughed. "That's Barbara. She knows Cavs are prone to mitral valve disease. Barbara is the original helicopter mom."

He laughed again, showing lots of white teeth. Josie

bristled. Her man sounded awfully familiar with Laura. This new vet was not only ten years younger than Josie, but slender, blond, and single.

"Listen, Laura, is your dad still looking for a place to live?" Ted asked. "Josie's mom has a real nice flat on Phelan Street. Have him call right away. Rentals don't last long in that neighborhood."

Ted recited Jane's number, then said, "Yeah, I miss her, too. I'll be glad when Chris is back."

Then why don't you sound glad? Josie thought, startled by the jealousy that shot through her.

"Mom! Ted! I got it! I got it! Emma and I cracked the case! We can prove that Zoe, Jace, and Oakley took the photos."

Amelia was babbling incomprehensible tech phrases: ". . . Exif . . . GIF . . . MakerNote tag . . . GPS."

"Whoa, whoa," Josie said. "The only thing I recognized was GPS. Tell me in English."

"Short version," Amelia said, breathless with excitement. "We linked the photos to Barrington using the phones' GPS systems. The GPS embeds the location on every picture. The times are right, too. The time stamp on the pictures is accurate to the second. The photos were taken between ten a.m. and two p.m. and the dates are the day that I got pizza on my shirt and the next. The Bitches of Barrington Facebook page went up the day after that.

"Then we tracked the photos to the phones. Oakley has an iPhone5 in a pink rubberized case."

"So do half the girls at Barrington," Josie said.

"Ah, but Emma and I have the phone's ID number. That's embedded in the picture, too. That will cook her," Amelia said. "Jace is the richest and her family travels a lot. She's got a BlackBerry P9981. That's P for Porsche. It costs twenty-two hundred dollars."

"For a kid's cell phone?" Josie said.

"Her father says it's worth it if they're in Singapore or

something," Amelia said. "Zoe only has a Samsung Galaxy SIII. Her dad's a geek and he picked it out. She'd rather have an iPhone5 like Oakley."

"Amazing," Josie said.

"You're a real investigator, just like your mom," Ted said.

Not exactly, Josie thought. I haven't succeeded yet.

Chapter 20

"I can't wait to see Miss Apple when I show her this research," Amelia said. "I want to watch her face when she expels her little pets."

Josie didn't like the gleeful vengeance in her daughter's voice. She'd wanted Amelia to restore order to her world, not turn it upside down.

"I don't think it's a good idea for you to be at the meeting tomorrow morning," Josie said.

"Why? I did the work," Amelia said. "I mean, Emma and me did it together."

"You both did amazing work," Josie said. "But you called the mean girls Miss Apple's little pets, and I think you're right. She seems to favor those girls, and I don't want her turning on you when they're exposed. We parents have to fight this battle."

"Your mom's right," Ted said. "Miss Apple will take it out on you."

"Then how will Miss Apple know what we found?" Amelia said. "You can't explain it, Ted. You don't understand it and neither does Mom."

"I'll tell her we put an investigator on the case," Josie said. "Which is the truth. That's what you are—an investigator."

"Yes, I am." Amelia stood up straighter, as if Josie had pinned a medal on her.

"That way you're not just a middle school student," Ted said. "Investigators get respect."

"I like that," Amelia said. "We've been working on a report. We wanted to put it in writing to show the other kids at school. We have all the tech stuff, step by step, with programs and links and everything. All I have to do is design some supersick stationery, so it looks professional. I've even got a name for us, A&E Investigations. That stands for Amelia and Emma. I can open a Gmail account if Miss Apple decides to e-mail us."

"Brilliant!" Ted said. Josie agreed, but felt a little uneasy. Should her daughter have this calculating streak?

"I don't think it's a good idea to discuss your investigation with the other girls. It could backfire. Promise you'll keep quiet."

"Please?" Ted added.

That clinched it. "Oh, okay," Amelia said. "Are you going to tell the other parents who we are?"

"Emma's parents already know, right?" Josie said. "If Bailey's or Palmer's parents ask for the investigators' names, we'll tell them. But I doubt they will. Now go finish that report so Ted and I can read it. It's almost your bedtime. I'll start calling the parents with your news."

The parents reacted the way Josie expected: shock, outrage, then satisfaction. Red-haired Palmer's mother, Priscilla Lindell, said, "How clever of you to hire an investigator, Ms. Marcus. I wanted to take Palmer to a counselor because of the psychological damage, but she refused. Palmer said she knew which girls did it and they needed counseling, not her. My husband is working tomorrow morning, but I'll meet you in Miss Apple's office right after I drop off Palmer.

"And I agree. We won't make an appointment with

Miss Apple. This confrontation needs the element of surprise."

"Good," Josie said. "I'll e-mail you a copy of the report tonight."

"May I ask you a question?" Priscilla hesitated. "Gifford and I had Palmer later in life, and we're not really 'with it,' as the young people say."

They didn't say that, but Josie kept quiet.

"You're younger and better at communicating with children that age. Palmer made the most curious request after this terrible episode. She asked if she could shop for her own clothes. I always buy her the best. I can't understand why."

Josie knew why. Priscilla bought her daughter dowdy duds.

"That may not be a bad idea," Josie said. "Girls need to learn to handle money and develop their own style. You could give her an allowance and make it clear that skimpy skirts and belly-baring shirts are not acceptable. That would teach her responsibility."

"You're right. It would be a learning experience," Priscilla said. She seemed happy with Josie's explanation.

Josie called Emma's father next. Sam could barely contain his pride. "Our girls are something, huh? Emma's been shut up in her room every night, working on this. They're on the computer now, finishing their report.

"Smart of you to keep our girls out of it. They think their report will nail Miss Apple's ass. I hope they won't be disappointed. Emma told me justice rules. I'm not sure that's true at Barrington. Those who make the money make the rules."

"You have a few bucks of your own," Josie said.

"My money's new," Sam said. "Zoe and her gang have old money and connections, and that's what counts in St. Louis."

"I agree, Sam," she said. "But I haven't said anything about the outcome to Amelia, either."

"Maybe Miss Apple will surprise us both," Sam said.

Dev Novak, father of the black-haired "Fat Bitch" Bailey, had a voice as big as his build. "You beat me to it, Ms. Marcus. I was going to put my firm's investigator on the case, but I've been tied up in court. The jury reached a verdict today, and I won. Now I'll have the free time to help my girl. Unless Miss Apple keeps her word and kicks those three terrors out of school, I'll go after their parents. They'll find out that Bailey's daddy really is the 'biggest lawyer in Clayton.' Those girls are the real Bitches of Barrington. Insulting my daughter! I'd like to—"

Dev stopped and took a deep breath, then said slowly, "I will get them, Ms. Marcus. I promise. They will pay for the pain and suffering they've caused my beautiful little girl. Send me that report ASAP. I'll see you in the head of school's office first thing tomorrow."

Josie collected all the parents' e-mail addresses so they could keep in touch.

She and Ted had finished the dishes and moved to the living room, where Ted put on soft music. They sipped wine and Josie snuggled against Ted's warm, strong shoulder.

"Thanks for telling Amelia that she shouldn't go to Miss Apple's office tomorrow," she said. "She listens to you."

"I'll go with you," Ted said.

"Who'll run the clinic?" Josie asked.

"Laura can take over for two hours," Ted said.

"What about your appointments? You're already shorthanded," Josie said. "What if you have an emergency and a patient is hit by a car? If you're not there to operate immediately, that pet could die. You can't risk that."

"Amelia is important," Ted said. "Besides, what are the chances that will happen?"

"Pretty darn good," Josie said. "Remember the border collie who got hit by a truck when he ran across the street to his lady love? That was two weeks ago. If you hadn't been at the clinic, that beautiful dog would have died.

"I'll be there tomorrow for Amelia. All the girls will have a parent present, and Bailey's father, Dev, is a lawyer."

"Okay, but only if you promise to call afterward," Ted said.

Josie kissed Ted. He kissed her back with skill and enthusiasm. Then Amelia burst out of her room with her report, and they quickly broke apart. Josie was shy around her daughter.

"I printed a copy for both of you," Amelia said, and handed them two pages.

Josie hid behind the report, trying to compose herself.

"Impressive typeface," Ted said. "Looks serious and professional."

"That's what we want," Amelia said. "Emma copied it from her dad's stockbroker's report."

Josie didn't understand most of the language, but the report was terse, businesslike, and tedious. That made it more authentic. "You've built your case step by step and it looks solid," she said. "Let me give it one more read."

This time she noticed the smaller type under the bold A&E INVESTIGATIONS.

It said *We're wicked good.*

"Uh, about that slogan," Josie said.

"You don't like it?" Amelia asked.

"I do," Josie said, "but not for this report. Even the clueless Miss Apple may recognize it as tween slang, and we don't want her suspicious—she knows you and Emma are computer wizards. She has to think we used a top-notch investigator."

"You did," Amelia said.

"Josie means the report has to look like we spent a bundle on an outside investigator," Ted said. "That's how you impress people like Miss Apple. You don't need a slogan. Your work speaks for itself."

"As soon as your report is ready, e-mail it to me," Josie said. "I'll send it to the other parents. And, Amelia, one more thing."

"What?"

"You are incredible," Josie said. She stood up and hugged her daughter. "I'm so proud of you. I know your grandfather will be, too."

Amelia positively glowed as she floated back to her room.

By the time Josie fired up her office computer, Amelia had e-mailed her the final revision. Josie printed a copy for herself and Miss Apple, then wrote an e-mail and sent the report to the other parents.

She was tired, but not too tired to forget that kiss with Ted. She peeked into Amelia's room. Her daughter was asleep under her purple-flowered bedspread, her arm around her cat, Harry. Festus slept on her feet. Josie kissed her daughter lightly on her shining brown hair, then tiptoed out.

It was only ten o'clock, not too late for love with her new husband. Josie heard what sounded like a chain saw cutting through concrete in their bedroom. Ted was asleep.

Josie crawled in beside him and stared at the ceiling, restless and brooding. I have to solve this case, she thought. Tomorrow, after Miss Apple, I'll interview Rain's other boyfriend, Harley Scranton, the Coke collector, at the hardware store where he works.

She rolled over and saw the green letters on the bedside clock: 11:38. Josie's thoughts drifted from her stalled investigation to Amelia's successful one. Even if the parents presented Miss Apple with a detailed report, would justice rule?

She turned again, and Ted murmured in his sleep. Josie tried to keep still, her thoughts whirling like an out-of-control carousel: What if the head of school found out Amelia and Emma had created that report? Would she take it out on them? Would she keep her word and expel the three guilty mean girls? Would she . . .

"Josie, Josie, wake up!" Ted was shaking her.

"Huh?" she said. "What's wrong?" She blinked in the dim light. Ted was dressed for work, his hair still damp from the shower.

"Josie, I'm listening to the six o'clock news while I have my coffee. There's a story coming up about Christine. A bad one. Hurry!"

Josie shook herself awake, grabbed her robe, and followed Ted into the kitchen, where a small TV sat on counter near the coffeepot. Josie stared at a supermarket commercial on the screen, trying to jolt herself awake. By the time Ted poured her a cup of coffee, Honey Butcher, the Channel Seven blonde, was back on. Her frivolous pink suit clashed with her serious tone.

"Channel Seven has an exclusive report on new evidence in the murder of Rain Dillon," Honey said. "The victim's older sister, Christine Cormac, was arrested and charged with first-degree murder.

"Now sources close to the investigation say the police discovered damning e-mails when they confiscated the Rock Road Village veterinarian's laptop. Ms. Cormac had deleted those e-mails, but forensics experts recovered them."

"She makes it sound like a big conspiracy, when Chris was probably clearing out old e-mails," Ted said.

"Renzo suspected this information would be leaked on purpose," Josie said.

The blond reporter oozed, "In the e-mails, Ms. Cormac complains to another sister that she is tired of Miss Dillon living in her rental property in Maplewood and Miss Dillon owes her rent."

File footage of the Fresno Court home flashed on the screen, and Josie groaned. "Aren't they ever going to lose that video?" she asked.

"Sh!" Ted said.

The reporter intoned, "The e-mails also reveal that Ms. Cormac could not forgive her sister for her affair with Ms. Cormac's then husband. She wrote, 'I wish I could find a way to get rid of Rain permanently. In fact, I'd like a good long drought.' "

A blown-up copy of the e-mail flashed on the screen, with Chris's words circled in blood red.

"Sources say Ms. Cormac lied to the police and denied that her sister had had an affair with her husband. They believe Ms. Cormac permitted her estranged sister to live with her so that she could kill her. The medical examiner has determined that Miss Dillon was murdered between two and three days after that e-mail. She was buried in the backyard of the rental property, and Ms. Cormac's distinctive earring, a veterinary caduceus, was found with the body. Toxicology tests also found acepromazine, a common veterinary drug, in the victim's body. The St. Louis County prosecutor has asked for the death penalty in this case.

"Channel Seven's sources say the discovery of these e-mails strengthens Ms. Cormac's motive for her sister's murder."

Chapter 21

The sneak attack on Miss Apple's office began ten minutes after school started. Miss Apple had concluded her morning videocast and retreated to the peace of her posh office.

The parents of the Bitches of Barrington met at the guard's desk at the main entrance. Billy, a beardless Santa in a gray uniform, was on duty and smiled them through the door.

"Hiya, Dev," he said to Bailey's father. Billy enjoyed being on a first-name basis with the powerful lawyer.

"Great day for golfing, huh, Sam?" he said to Emma's dad.

"You got it, Billy," Sam said. "The worst day at golf beats the best day at work."

Billy laughed at Sam's old saw, and gave Josie and Priscilla polite, friendly hellos. He was used to seeing them at the school.

Josie relaxed once they had passed the main hurdle. The four turned the corner and reached Miss Apple's hallway. Dev, the lawyer who looked like a linebacker, led the parents in a flying wedge. They charged past her squawking assistant and invaded the head of school's sanctuary.

She looked up and frowned. "Please!" Miss Apple said. "I'm on the telephone."

"Not now, you aren't," Dev said. His meaty finger punched a button on her phone console and the line went dead. Dev settled his mighty bulk into the delicate Chippendale chair, and it screamed in protest.

Josie, wearing her best black pantsuit like battle armor, sat next to him. Priscilla, Palmer's mother, had chosen a soft flowered chintz chair that complemented her pale blue suit.

Emma's father, Sam, firmly shut the office door on the protesting assistant. "Please hold Miss Apple's calls, Mrs. Purdy," he told her. "We need her undivided attention."

"Miss Apple!" she cried. "Should I call security?"

"No, thank you, Mrs. Purdy," she said. "I'll handle this unwarranted intrusion."

Josie could feel the cold coming off Miss Apple's ice white suit and snowy skin. She assumed an outraged silence and tried to stare them down, but the parents refused to be intimidated. They'd seen their daughters publicly mocked, heard their tears, and felt their pain. They knew their cause was right—and righteous.

The head of school backed down and spoke first. "What is the meaning of this?" she asked, her well-bred diction clipped and haughty.

"You tell us," Dev said. He placed a slim, elegant black report folder on her teak desk. Josie wished Amelia and Emma could see how impressive their report looked in this cover.

"This is for you," he said. "It's a copy of our report on the Bitches of Barrington Facebook page. You claim you had that page investigated and there was no connection to any students at this school."

"That is correct," Miss Apple said. Frost swirled in the air.

"I won't call you a liar," he said. "But if you did have someone check it out, he did a piss-poor job."

"Mr. Novak! There's no need for that kind of language!"

"We need some plain speaking," he said. "We commissioned our own investigation—this one." He held up his report in a similar folder. The other parents got out theirs. The only sound was the rustle of papers and clicking of briefcase locks.

"Our report says that the GPS information embedded in the Bitches of Barrington—I'll call them BOB—photos pinpoints this school. The fourth paragraph gives the GPS latitude and longitude. It's accurate to within ten feet. The BOB photos are encoded with days and times when classes were in session. Our report shows that, too.

"Two of the camera phones have been identified as belonging to your students. One picture was taken on a BlackBerry P9981. Jace is the only student in this school with a two-thousand-dollar Porsche cell phone. Another photo was taken with a Samsung Galaxy SIII. Again, only Oakley has one. Zoe has an iPhone5."

"Many of our students have iPhone5s," Miss Apple said.

"Yes, but our investigator has the ID numbers for each phone," Dev said. "That's in paragraph six. Go ahead, call the girls in here and examine their phones."

"I will not disrupt classes for your ill-timed assault on my schedule," Miss Apple said. Icicles hung from her words.

"Then show us the cell phone IDs in your report," Dev said. "Go ahead. We're waiting."

"That report is confidential," Miss Apple said.

"Right," Dev said, drawing out that word to an insulting length.

"I will question Zoe, Jace, and Oakley at my convenience," Miss Apple said, "when it does not interrupt their schooling. I will not subject those young women to an inquisition by you. Please remember they are minors.

"If your allegations turn out to be true, each girl will personally write a letter of apology to your daughters.

They will also receive a month's detention and lose their lunch-hour free time."

"That's all?" Josie said.

"That's the most severe punishment I've ever given, Ms. Marcus."

"So you won't keep your word and expel those girls?" Sam asked. "You said you would. We all heard you."

The other parents nodded agreement.

"Our lawyers have informed me that I spoke unwisely and made promises I can't keep," Miss Apple said. "As head of school, I can prohibit students from attending school for up to ten days. That is considered a suspension."

"That's a start," Dev said, "but we want them expelled."

"That's a more serious matter," Miss Apple said. "There are legal issues. I'm sure you understand that, Mr. Novak. Our lawyers say students are generally expelled for more serious offenses, such as bringing weapons or drugs to school."

"Bullying is a serious offense, Miss Apple, and should merit expulsion," Dev said. "You said so yourself."

"There are still procedures to be followed," she said. "I'll have to give each student and her parents written notice of the intent to expel and provide the student, her parents, or her representative—that means more lawyers, Mr. Novak—the opportunity to appear before the board of governors to challenge the reasons for the intended expulsion."

"So?" Dev said. "I've no objection to giving my colleagues more work. I'm more than equal to the challenge. I'll represent the interests of these parents, pro bono."

"But you don't understand, Mr. Novak," Miss Apple began.

"I certainly understand," Priscilla said. All eyes turned

toward her. "I believe the real problem is that all three of these mean girls' families are major donors. Zoe is a double-legacy student. Oakley's grandmother contributed most of the money for the new sports center that will be named in her honor. Jacc is a new student. Her family has been out of St. Louis for several years, but her parents have already donated a significant amount for the renovation of the Upper School classrooms and her mother is a Barrington alum.

"You had no intention of investigating or punishing those girls."

"Priscilla nailed it," Sam said.

"If you want legal issues, Miss Apple, you'll get them," Dev said. "You have one week to do a real investigation and take action. BOB parents, let's meet at my office in Clayton. Good day, Miss Apple. You'll be hearing from us soon, I promise."

The parents marched to the parking lot, where Dev gave them his office address. "It's right on Bonhomme in Clayton," he said. "Seventh floor. I'll comp your parking."

Half an hour later, they were sipping coffee in Dev's paneled conference room. The angry lawyer paced the room. "I mean it," he said. "I'm giving that school one week to shape up. Then I'm sending a letter to the mean girls' parents that I'll be filing a four-million-dollar suit— a million bucks for each of our girls—that our children were subjected to public hatred, ridicule, and disgrace and the parents are guilty of negligent supervision. That post on Facebook was defamatory, it's false, it clearly identifies the plaintiffs, and it's damaged their reputations."

"Wow!" Josie said.

"Can we go after Facebook, too?" Sam said. "They've got the real bucks."

"No," Dev said. "Thanks to the Federal Communications Decency Act of 1996, Facebook is protected from liability as a service provider for content posted by others. Besides, they reacted responsibly and took the site down as soon as they were informed."

"How much should we contribute to this cause?" Priscilla asked. "We can afford to help."

"Me, too," Sam said.

"And me." Josie vowed she'd come up with her share, even if she had to pawn her wedding china.

"I don't want a red cent," Dev said. "Like I said, this is pro bono. And it's personal. You don't insult Dev Novak's little girl or her friends."

"Do you want forty percent of any money you recover?" Sam asked.

"No," Dev said. "I want a dollar from each of you to retain me. Then I'll have you sign some paperwork my assistant prepared making me your counsel. Once Miss Apple says she won't do anything—and I expect she will—I'll send a letter to the parents telling them I'm planning to file suit."

"Won't this suit and the publicity embarrass our girls even more?" Josie asked.

"I don't want to see my daughter hurt more," Dev said, "and I'm sure you feel the same way, Josie."

"Why send a warning letter at all?" she said. "Why not go straight to court?"

"I'm hoping this case never goes to court, Josie," Dev said.

"I'm gonna say something here, and I want this information to stay in this room—if we sue, don't expect the court to rule in our favor. There was a big suit over some mean Facebook posts by four girls several years ago. The court dismissed it because the judge said that no reasonable person would believe that those nasty statements were facts. She also said—and I memorized this part because I think it applies to our case—'The entire context and tone of the posts constitute evidence of adolescent insecurities and indulgences, and a vulgar attempt at humor. What they do not contain are statements of fact.' "

Maybe, Josie thought. No one will believe that Amelia is clumsy or Emma is ugly. Palmer's unfashionable clothes are a matter of opinion, and Bailey is just big boned.

"An apology isn't going to cut it," Dev said. "I don't want words. I want money. That case I told you about went on for two years—two expensive years for the mean girls' parents—before it was dismissed."

"If it got tossed, why are we doing this?" Sam asked.

"Because defending a lawsuit is expensive, even for rich people," Dev said. "Those mean girls got two years of bad publicity—worldwide. The parents of Zoe, Jace, and Oakley want their little darlings to get into good colleges. Do you think they'll be accepted at Ivy League schools if they have reputations as mean girls? The media will be licking their chops to do a story about rich mean girls at a snobby school like Barrington.

"I expect the parents to settle out of court before we start a media storm."

Dev smiled. Josie almost felt sorry for the mean girls.

Chapter 22

Scranton Hardware was an old-time neighborhood store pleasantly scented with motor oil, paint thinner, and plywood. Josie liked the orderly jumble of the aisles. Everyday items like showerheads and tile grout were comforting after Barrington's surreal formality.

Buying a few items for my new house is a good excuse to track down Rain's boyfriend, Harley, she decided.

She was greeted by a sixtyish salesman with a pleasantly rumpled face, who directed her to the racks of shelf paper, then helped her pick out a garden hose and spray nozzle.

"Is Harley Scranton working today?" she asked.

"He's at the cash register," he said. "Big guy. You can't miss him."

On impulse, she picked up a purple soap dish for Amelia's bathroom, then carried her purchases to the register, where a dark-haired lumberjack dwarfed the crowded counter. Josie figured he had to be six feet five, with massive arms, broad shoulders, and a narrow waist.

He's handsome enough to distract even a happily married woman, she thought. Is this Rain's Harley? Chris had described him as "rich, hunky, and a rabid collector of Coke memorabilia."

A locked cabinet behind the counter displayed colorful Coca-Cola trays, cans, metal Coca-Cola signs, and more.

"I see you're admiring my Coke collection," he said, and smiled. "I'm Harley Scranton."

"Josie Marcus," she said. "It's nice your boss lets you keep your collection at the store."

"I'm the boss," he said. "My family's owned this store for three generations. I'm Harley the third."

"Oh," Josie said. "I should have realized that." She felt embarrassed.

"Hey, nothing wrong with mistaking me for an employee," he said. "I hire the best. What's your favorite Coke item?"

"That 1892 calendar with the old-fashioned lady," Josie said, hoping that would get him talking about Rain.

"That used to be worth ten thousand dollars," he said. Was that a flicker of anger in his blue eyes? She couldn't tell.

" 'Used to'?" Josie said.

"I showed it to an old girlfriend and she spilled tea on it and then tried to hide the damage. I didn't notice until I took it out for a collectors' show. Now it's worth almost nothing. I should have kept it in its protective case, but I was trying to impress her and I took it out so she could hold it. She didn't even like Coke."

"Was her name Rain Dillon?" Josie asked.

"You knew her?" he asked.

"We bought the house she rented," Josie said.

"I heard she'd died," he said.

She didn't die, Josie thought. She was murdered.

"I did a lot of work around her place," Harley said.

"That's what her sister Chris said," Josie said.

"I was so far gone I even built that woman a gazebo," Harley said.

Where her body was hidden, Josie thought. Does he know that?

"I guess I should forgive her," Harley said. "We broke up a while before she died."

Not a while, Josie thought. Two days before she supposedly took off for that ashram. Right after you discovered she'd ruined your valuable collectible.

"Those eighteen nineties calendars are rare," he said. "Losing a ten-thousand-dollar collectible because she was careless is hard to take. I don't display my really expensive things at the store, but I show the calendar because it's still pretty. Most people think it's that beige color because it's old. Everything else here goes for less than a hundred bucks."

"Even that old glass Coke bottle?" Josie asked.

"That one?" His eyes turned intense as he pointed out its features. "That is a straight-side bottle from the Woonsocket, Rhode Island, bottling plant. I love that name, Woonsocket. It's light green glass. Worth about eighty dollars.

"I like Coke cans, too. That one's a Coca-Cola Polar Bear can from Hungary. Next to it is a Coke can from Germany and . . ."

And I have to get out of here, Josie thought. Ted's supposed to call back to find out about Amelia.

"Can you believe this Coke can?" Harley said. "All the way from Lithuania."

Josie took a step backward and bumped into a silver-haired man in jeans and a polo shirt. Harley gave him a wide smile. "Hey, Doc Clinton, what are you doing here? You ever need a veterinarian, Josie, Doc Clinton Dickson is the best. Takes good care of my dog. The doc's got an even bigger Coke collection than I do. He's my hunting buddy. We look for collectibles on our days off."

"Nice to meet you, Dr. Dickson," Josie said. "Gotta go."

She hurried toward the door, blessing the vet who'd interrupted the Coke monologue. On the drive home, Josie wondered about Rain's ex-boyfriend. He'd seemed both angry and oddly detached when he talked about her. Was he guilty or simply obsessed with his collection? Josie didn't know any other collectors, but Chris said he was a fanatic. Maybe that's what hard-core collectors were like.

Back at home, she brewed a pot of coffee and checked her cell phone. She'd missed Ted's call and one from Alyce. This time, Ted answered his phone and she told him about the showdown in Miss Apple's office.

"Dev Novak is one shrewd lawyer," Ted said. "He's almost as good at publicity as Chris's lawyer, Renzo. Tell Dev I also do pro bono work, if his pets need a vet."

"That's so nice. I love you," Josie said. "And I miss you. I hardly see you anymore." As soon as those last words slipped out, she was sorry. She didn't want Ted to feel guilty. He had enough worries. But a man needed to know he was missed, didn't he?

"I haven't spent nearly enough time with you," Ted said, "but as soon as Chris is back, I'll make up for lost time. Kathy's waving at me to see my next patient. I'll be home late again, probably eight thirty. I love you."

Hearing Ted's voice gave her a warm glow. As soon as Chris's problems were solved, Josie could go back to being a happy bride. She smiled when she heard the first notes of her new ringtone, Rhianna's "We Found Love." Amelia had programmed it. Josie checked the display. Her mother was calling.

"Josie, dear, thank you and Ted so much for sending Frank to see the flat," Jane said.

"Frank?"

"Franklin Hyzy," Jane said. "Laura's father. He loved the place and he's moving in today. It will be nice to have someone living downstairs again."

"Glad we could help, Mom," Josie said. "Maybe Amelia and I can stop by and meet him."

"The movers will be gone after five," Jane said. "Frank's coming upstairs for dinner at five thirty."

"Nice move, Mom," Josie said.

"I'm just being neighborly," Jane said, stiffly. "Moving is very tiring."

"I'm sure," Josie said, and smiled to herself. "I have some of Amelia's brownies in the freezer. We'll stop by for dessert about six thirty and meet your new neighbor."

Josie hung up, brought out the brownies to defrost, then called Alyce.

Her friend peppered Josie with questions: "How's the renovation? How's Amelia coping with the mean girls? What's going on with Chris?"

"I saw her in jail last night," Josie said. "She's not doing well at all. She's worried sick about her three children. Rodney, her ex, has custody and he won't let them see her or talk to their aunt Susan. Todd, her oldest, managed to call his aunt from school."

"That poor woman," Alyce said. "Deprived of her children and on trial for her life. Any good news there?"

"None," Josie said. "Detective Stevenski is hell-bent on sending Chris to prison. I've got my own investigation going. I want another crack at Rain's ex-boyfriend Donny when he gets off work at Judson's Tavern tomorrow. He had a terrible fight with her, and my neighbor Betty called the cops on him."

"And you're going to talk to him alone?" Alyce said. "Josie Marcus, how stupid can you get?"

"He gets off work at two p.m.," Josie said. "I thought I'd talk to him in the parking lot."

"At a low-life tavern?" Alyce said. "Oh no, I'm going with you."

"But he won't talk to both of us," Josie said. "He'll just clam up and walk away."

"Then I'll wait in my car with my cell phone in my hand while you talk to him. If he makes the slightest wrong move, I'm calling nine-one-one. And I won't take no for an answer. What's wrong with you?"

Josie rarely heard her soft-voiced friend sound so angry.

"You've had surprisingly good success with your investigations," Alyce said. "But you're not a trained investigator. Don't get cocky and confront that man on your own. I'll swing by your house at one thirty tomorrow. That should give us plenty of time to get to the bar."

Josie knew she'd deserved that lecture, but she wanted to change the subject. "Mom's finally rented the flat," she said, and updated her.

"Why doesn't your mom move downstairs?" Alyce asked. "Aren't you worried about her going up and down those stairs?"

"Mom says she needs the exercise," Josie said. "She likes her flat and won't abandon her precious wall-to-wall, carefully protected by throw rugs. She doesn't want the expense of a move, either. Even with a son-in-law to help with the heavy lifting, she'd have to get new curtains, carpets, and more. You've seen my kitchen, Alyce. It's okay for a renter, but Mom loves cooking. She won't leave her kitchen. I feel better knowing that Frank is living there now. She'll have someone to keep an eye out for her."

A quick glance at the kitchen clock told Josie it was time to pick up Amelia. As she parked in the Barrington School drive, she waved to Emma's father, but didn't see the other BOB parents. Josie wouldn't put it past Miss Apple to take out her displeasure with the parents on their daughters. But when the head of school called Emma's and Amelia's names, the two girls strolled out chatting and laughing. Josie watched her daughter carefully as she approached the car.

Amelia tossed her backpack into the back and dropped into the passenger seat. Josie didn't ask how her day was. She knew that question would never get an answer.

"Want to go by the new house tonight and check out your paint?" Josie asked.

"Whatever," Amelia said, but today that all-purpose word sounded upbeat.

Traffic was light on the way to Fresno Court. Josie was alarmed to see a Channel Seven news van parked in the circle. "Duck down, Amelia," Josie said. "I'm going to pull all the way up in the driveway to avoid the reporters."

But as Josie got closer she saw TV reporter Honey Butcher was interviewing her neighbor Betty Goffman on her lawn. Betty was slipcovered in pink ruffles, and holding her Jack Russell.

Josie pulled her car alongside her house where it couldn't be seen, turned off the engine, then rolled down her window and motioned Amelia to be silent.

The wind carried part of the conversation Josie's way. "I'm sorry the police found those e-mails about poor Rain in her sister's computer," Betty said. She sounded sad and concerned. "I've been subpoenaed to testify against Christine. I don't want to, but I have no choice.

"I think poor Christine was overburdened. She works such long hours at the clinic. She's raising three children on her own, and Christine is a very good mother. Then she finds out her sister's having loud fights with her boyfriend and letting the property go. Christine is a very conscientious person. She came over to talk to her sister and saw the grass was uncut, the yard littered with trash—and Rain meditating in the gazebo. Meditating! When poor Christine barely had a moment to herself. No wonder she snapped. I'll do my best to make the jury understand the pressure Christine endured.

"Christine needed more time to relax. After my husband died, I devoted my life to raising show dogs like Jack Dandy here." She petted the little terrier and he wagged his tail.

"My baby will be the next Westminster champion.

Get his close-up now, Honey. Then you can say you knew him before he was Best in Show."

Josie rolled up her window and said, "I don't believe it. Chris is facing the death penalty, and that woman is bragging about her stupid dog."

"Chill, Mom. Betty said good things about Chris," Amelia said. "Her dogs are like her kids. She's trying to help Chris by distracting that mean reporter."

"You're right," Josie said. "Let's go in the back door so you can see how the new deck and kitchen are coming along."

Josie was surprised by how much Bud had accomplished. The concrete footings and pad were poured. The supports and thick center beam were up. The backyard smelled of sweet fresh-cut sawdust.

"That deck is legit," Amelia said.

"Wait till you see the kitchen. Ta-da!" Josie said, and opened the door with a flourish.

Amelia stood in the doorway, taking in the missing cabinets, the new subfloor, the one remaining cabinet, and finally the Wolf stove.

"Sick!" she said. "Can I touch it?"

All tween cool was gone. Amelia ran her hands lovingly over the stove top, peered in the oven, checked the dials, then asked, "When can I cook on it?"

"The gas isn't hooked up yet," Josie said. "I still have to clean it."

"It's self-cleaning, Mom."

"It still needs a good scrub on the outside," Josie said. "We don't know where it's been. Don't worry. You'll have many years to cook on that stove."

Amelia pronounced the purple paint legit and asked, "When can we paint?"

"This weekend," Josie said. "It's after six o'clock. We have to stop by your grandmother's flat and meet Frank, her new renter." She herded Amelia to the car.

"Are they, like, dating or something?" Amelia said.

"Grandma says no. It's too soon to mention dating," Josie said. "We don't want to scare him off.

"Uh-oh," she said when they reached Jane's flat. "Look at that blue Lincoln. It's half parked on Mrs. Mueller's property. Wonder how long before she comes raging out her front door."

But Josie and Amelia made it to Jane's porch without any sign of an outraged Mrs. Mueller. Josie knocked on her mother's door.

"Come on up," Jane said. "Frank and I are just finishing dinner."

Woof! said Stuart Little. Jane's dog trotted up to Amelia for a scratch.

Jane was wearing her best pink pantsuit, her hair was newly styled, and she had on a trace of Estée Lauder, her favorite perfume. Her kitchen smelled of roast beef and hot coffee, but there was no sign of the cooking whirlwind that had proceeded dinner. Josie saw the remains of a Caesar salad, oven-roasted potatoes, asparagus, fresh-baked dinner rolls, and a thick prime rib bone on the counter.

A man's dinner, she thought.

Her mother had a vase of tulips on the table, but no candles.

Good for you, Mom, Josie thought. It's too soon for candlelight dinners. She suspected Jane had romance on her mind. And why not? If anyone deserved a good man, it was her mother.

Frank Hyzy had dressed in a blue shirt and striped tie. Josie liked that old-school touch. He was theatrically handsome, with thick white curling hair and chocolate brown eyes. He stood up to greet Josie and gave her a firm handshake.

Amelia presented her brownies.

"Now, isn't that nice?" Frank said. "Homemade, too. The perfect finish to a good meal."

"I'm just pouring the coffee," Jane said. "Sit down and join us for dessert."

"How did your move go, Frank?" Josie asked.

"Surprisingly smooth," he said. "The movers finished on time and didn't break anything. Jane helped me unpack some essentials, so I'll be able to sleep on fresh sheets and fix coffee in the morning. And your neighbor next door brought me a tuna casserole."

"You met Mrs. Mueller?" Josie said.

"I did," Frank said. "She said I could park my car in front of her house. I wasn't sure what that meant. Are there parking restrictions on this street?"

"Only in Mrs. Mueller's mind," Josie said.

"She seems rather, uh, forceful," Frank said.

Amelia snickered.

"I should get some moving tips from you," Josie said. "We'll be moving into our home in Maplewood as soon as the renovations are finished."

"I saw your house on TV," Frank said. "I'm sorry to hear that Chris's sister was found at your home and the trouble Chris is in. She's been so nice to Laura at the clinic. She even stayed late to help my daughter—with all she has to do. You don't find many big-deal partners willing to help a newbie. I don't believe for a minute she killed Rain."

"Who do you think did it?" Josie asked.

"Well, I don't know all the people involved," he said. "Just Chris and Rain's old boyfriend Harley, the Coca-Cola collector. He grew up in my old neighborhood. I hope he didn't do any home-improvement projects at your house."

"He did," Josie said. "We've already torn down his gazebo and an electrician will have to repair the wiring he fixed. I hope there are no more improvements."

"Me, too. That boy thought because his family owned a hardware store he was a born handyman. He's hopeless, but nobody has the nerve to tell him."

"I was at his store today," Josie said. "He seemed nice."

"Be careful," Frank said. "He's calmed down a lot now that he's out of prison."

"Prison?" Josie said.

"You know he served time for beating his wife?"

"How long ago was that?" Josie asked.

"Winter of 2007," Frank said. "Maybe January. He married a nice little girl from Washington, Missouri. Ashley, I believe her name was. Yes, Ashley. Tiny little thing and quiet as a mouse. They moved in next door to us.

"I saw Ashley around wearing sunglasses on a gloomy winter day and asked her if she wanted to be at the beach. Ashley broke down and cried, right in front of me, then took off the sunglasses. They were hiding a great big black eye. She'd tried covering it with makeup and sunglasses, but that only made it worse. Harley had punched her. I wanted to punch him back, but figured he'd just take it out on her.

"My wife was still alive and I went home and told her. Martha knew Ashley better than I did. She took her out for lunch and they talked, the way women do. Martha told her if she needed help she should call us. She also gave Ashley the name of a women's shelter and a good counselor. Martha could do that without causing offense. She was a motherly soul."

Frank paused for a moment, and Josie wondered if he was thinking about his late wife.

"Anyway, about a month later," he said, "Martha and I heard screaming next door at three in the morning. Harley was beating her. Broke her arm and her jaw. Martha called 911 and I ran over there. Ashley had escaped out the back door, her nightgown nearly ripped off. I carried her to our house to wait for the ambulance. Harley was arrested for domestic assault and served three years in the state prison. He got off lightly, you ask me. Ashley spent two months in the hospital.

"He's a handsome man and I guess he could be very persuasive. They got back together for a month or so after he got out of prison, but then she dumped him for good.

"I held my breath when I found out he was dating Chris's sister. I didn't know Rain, but I was getting up the nerve to say something to Chris when Laura told me that Rain took off to live in an ashram in California. My first thought was 'Good. That girl's safe.' But she wasn't, was she?"

Chapter 23

"Can I cook dinner, Mom?" Amelia asked when they were back home from Jane's house. "I want to try something special."

"How special?" Josie asked.

Amelia's last "special" experiment without Ted's supervision resulted in fifteen bucks' worth of ruined roast. She'd forgotten the meat was in the oven while she texted Emma.

"I want to make teriyaki salmon packets," Amelia said. "We already have the salmon and the parchment paper. I'll put on the timer so it won't burn. I also want to bake some chocolate-hazelnut thumbprints. It's a new cookie recipe. You'll be right here, Mom, if anything goes wrong—but it won't, I promise."

"Okay," Josie said, "but only if you bake an extra batch for our neighbor Cordelia. I want to take her something when I return her casserole dish. Do you have time to make the salmon before Ted gets home? He'll be here in forty-five minutes."

"Oh yeah. Parchment pouches cook fast and the cookies take half an hour, total."

"Go for it," Josie said.

Amelia was assembling her ingredients and kitchen tools when the phone rang. Josie recognized that burly voice, even before he introduced himself. "It's Dev Novak, Bailey's father. I hope I'm not interrupting dinner."

"Haven't even started," Josie said.

"Good. I've got news. I heard from Barrington faster than I expected. Miss Apple said she called a special meeting of the school's board of governors and they support her punishment of the three mean girls as, quote, 'just and fair.'"

"It is not!" Josie said.

"I agree, and so do the other BOB parents. The fact that Zoe's mother's cousin is on the board and Oakley's father is a golfing buddy of another board member might have something to do with their decision. I need your consent to send that letter to the parents of Zoe, Oakley, and Jace by registered mail tomorrow. I'll give them a week to decide, but I'm guessing we'll hear back sooner."

"Of course I agree," Josie said. "So much for Barrington's zero tolerance for bullying."

"I could go after the school," Dev said, "but I'm hoping to keep this suit out of the courts and away from the press. The parents are more likely to settle than the school."

"Go get 'em," Josie said.

She hung up. "What's going on, Mom?" Amelia asked.

"I'll tell you, but you have to promise to keep this quiet."

After Amelia mimed crossing her heart and locking her lips, Josie told her about Dev's call.

"I knew it," Amelia said. "I knew Miss Apple wouldn't let anyone punish her little favorites."

Josie didn't remind her daughter that she'd believed the mean girls would be expelled. No point rubbing salt in that wound.

"We're going to wallop them in the wallet," Josie said. "Money is the only punishment those people understand. Why are you cutting that parchment paper into hearts? Are you making a giant valentine?"

"This is a different way to make parchment pouches. It's easier to seal a folded heart than a square," Amelia said.

Josie watched her daughter carefully arrange the salmon on one half of the heart, then expertly fold it together and pleat the edges. She twisted the tip and tucked it under.

"Amazing," Josie said.

"Best part, there's almost zero cleanup," Amelia said.

Twenty minutes later, she had the finished salmon packets out of the oven. She slid in the first cookie sheet of thumbprint cookies. In the center of each round cookie was a generous dollop of Nutella chocolate-hazelnut spread.

"This dinner will be fabulous," Josie said.

Two batches of cookies were cooling on wire racks when Josie heard Ted's car in the drive. Festus and Marmalade burst through the door, eager for Amelia's pats and scratches.

Ted moved much slower. "My poor guy," Josie said. "You look like you've spent the day on the bottom of a dog cage."

"Probably smell like it, too," Ted said. She tried to hug him, but he kept her at arm's length. "I've been peed on by a puppy and scratched by an angry tabby. Let me kiss your cheek, then head straight for the shower."

"Dinner's ready whenever you are," Josie said.

Even after a shower, Ted looked weary. Josie smoothed his wet hair off his forehead and rubbed his aching shoulders. "Don't stop," he said, and groaned. "That feels good."

"You're so tense," she said. "I can feel just how bad this day has been."

She kneaded the tight muscles until Amelia said, "Mom, dinner's getting cold."

"Wait till you see what our chef's made," Josie said.

Ted wasn't too tired to eat—or praise the food. He demolished Josie's salad, then made short work of the salmon, asking Amelia about the seasoning and admiring the perfection of her jasmine rice.

Amelia interrupted his compliments. "I saw the new kitchen and the deck today after school," she said. "That stove is wicked."

"When's it going to be hooked up?" Ted asked.

"The gas company comes out the day after tomorrow," Josie said. "I promised Amelia I'd paint her room this weekend. I'll tape the woodwork so we can start right in on Saturday."

"Yay!" Amelia said. "You aren't going to paint the pink bathroom downstairs, are you?"

"I've thought about it," Josie said. "Pink-and-black bathrooms are so old-fashioned."

"No, Mom, they're retro, like the kitchen," Amelia said. "Do you know there's a Web site called Save the Pink Bathrooms?"

"There's a Web site for everything," Josie said.

"It says Mamie Eisenhower made pink bathrooms popular."

An old photo of the nineteen fifties First Lady flashed in Josie's mind. "You're not convincing me," she said. "I've seen the pictures of Mamie. She was a good woman, but no fashion icon. She also wore flat hats, shapeless coats, and fur stoles with the animal's head biting its own tail."

"Ew," Amelia said. "Fur is just wrong. But she loved pink. She painted all the private parts of the White House pink."

"'Private quarters' is a better word choice," Josie said.

Amelia turned her own shade of deep pink. "You know what I mean, Mom."

Josie was ashamed. "Yes, I do," she said. "I apologize for embarrassing you."

"Save the Pink Bathrooms says we're tearing out part of our home-design heritage."

"We can't have that, can we?" Josie said.

"There are lots of reasons to keep it," Amelia said. "Pink bathrooms make you look younger because the pink light reflects off your skin." Her impassioned pro-pink speech skidded to a stop. "Not that you need to look younger, Mom."

"Okay, enough with the soft soap," Josie said. "We'll leave our historic pink bathroom alone."

"Will you take the pledge?" Amelia asked.

"What pledge?"

"The Web site wants a gazillion people to promise to preserve vintage pink bathrooms."

"Don't press your luck," Josie said. "I'll save our pink bathroom, but I'm not ready to put it in writing."

She saw Ted trying to hide a yawn when she set Amelia's cookies on the table.

"Well, this is a nice surprise. Haven't seen these before, Amelia," he said. He looked so tired Josie was afraid he'd fall face-forward into the cookie plate.

Amelia proudly described her latest cookie recipe. "These are so easy," she said. "Twenty minutes to fix and ten to bake."

"This recipe is a keeper," Josie said, after she ate the first one. "I'm glad you made some for Cordelia, too."

"Cordelia," Ted said. "Where did I hear that name before?"

"She's our neighbor. She made us the chicken pie. You know, the college professor."

"No, I heard that name before we moved in. Is her husband Wil—Wilner—Madison?"

"I think so," Josie said. "Do you know him?"

"Sure, he's a veterinary supply salesman. Our clinic is in his territory. Good guy."

"I wonder why she didn't say something to me," Josie

said. "We had a nice long chat at our house. I really like her and Betty, our other neighbor. Except Betty's a bit crazy about her dogs."

"You haven't spent serious time with dog lovers," he said. "You don't brag about Amelia half as much as they do."

"Channel Seven interviewed Betty again about Chris," Josie said. "She managed to turn the interview into a commercial for her show dog."

"Stage moms look modest compared to show dog trainers," Ted said. "I heard about that interview at the clinic. It was on the six o'clock news."

"I figured it would be," Josie said. "I didn't watch it."

"You should have," Ted said. "Kathy, my office manager, said Betty was very sympathetic to Chris. Kathy hopes the prosecutor doesn't strike her from the witness list. She was so pro-Chris her interview could have been planted by Renzo."

Josie looked over and saw Amelia's head was nodding. Josie shook her gently and said, "Bedtime, Chef. I'll handle the dishes."

"See, that's the other reason I like to cook," Amelia said. "No dishes."

She allowed Josie to give her a hug, hugged Ted good night, and did a sleepy stroll to her room. Ted started to clear the table, but Josie said, "Sit down. You're tired. Enjoy your dessert and let me tell you the latest installment in the BOB fight."

Josie had wiped down the counter and hung the dishcloth on the drying rack. Done! And so was her story.

"I guess I should have expected Miss Apple to dodge the issue," she said, "but Dev Novak is definitely on the case, Ted. Ted?"

No answer. Josie saw him slumped in his chair, sound asleep.

That's two people I've put asleep tonight, she thought, and kissed Ted awake.

"Huh? Josie? I fell asleep, didn't I? I'm so sorry. It's just that—"

"You don't have to explain," she said. "Go to bed."

She locked the doors and checked on Amelia, then crawled into bed. Ted was so deeply asleep he didn't stir.

I have to find Rain's killer, she thought as she studied Ted's chiseled profile. Ted's dead tired. Chris is worn-out with worry for her children and tormented with guilt because her last words to her sister were so angry. Her family life is destroyed and I no longer have a husband.

Ted rolled over in bed and put his arm around her, still unconscious.

This is worse than being single, Josie thought. When I wasn't married, I got used to life without love.

Now I'm in bed with an outrageously attractive man—and he's asleep.

Chapter 24

Josie saw another outrageously attractive man at ten the next morning. She went back to Scranton Hardware. This time, she was after more than a soap dish and a garden hose. She wanted information. When was the last time that Harley had been in the Fresno Court house?

Josie had to know.

She'd borrowed an expensive black-and-yellow cordless hammer-drill from Bud Vey, the deck contractor. The fierce device looked like an oversized mechanical bumblebee. Josie picked up six energy-saving spiral lightbulbs, then waited until Harley was alone behind the counter, polishing the glass case for his Coke collection. She watched him clean the glass with wide, loving strokes.

Now that she knew his past, she studied Harley more carefully. He was still built like a superhero, with broad shoulders and bulging biceps. His hair was so black it had a blue sheen. Josie wondered if his heart was just as dark.

He'd gone to prison because the hands that were so tenderly polishing his Coca-Cola shrine had broken his wife's bones, she thought. Will he attack me if he finds out why I'm asking these questions?

Josie tried not to think about that. She'd make sure

she kept the counter between them. She eyed the heavy wooden-handled rake hanging on the garden supply display behind her. If things went wrong, she'd grab the rake and aim for his eyes. That would stop him.

It was time. She made sure the hammer-drill landed on the counter with a loud thud.

Harley stopped wiping the glass, turned, and smiled. "Josie," he said. "Glad to see you back. How's that new house?"

"Coming along nicely," she said. "I need some help."

"That's why I'm here," he said.

"I can tell you did a lot of work on our place," she said.

"It's that obvious?" He looked pleased.

"It certainly is," Josie said, truthfully. "I know you put in the gazebo and worked on the plumbing and the kitchen wiring, but it would help if I knew what else you did."

Harley smiled. Even his teeth looked strong.

"Let's see," he said. "I rewired the kitchen and fixed the toilet in the pink bathroom. I didn't do anything in the basement rec room and I know I didn't work upstairs."

Thank goodness, Josie thought. "That's good to know," she said.

Now comes the hard part. "I found this hammer-drill in the basement and wondered if it was yours," she said. "It looks like something a professional would use."

She shamelessly slathered on the flattery to get the answers she needed.

"Say, that's a beauty," he said. "But it's not mine. I have one almost like it. I kept a bunch of tools at Rain's house—I love fixing things—and when we broke up I left them there."

Harley didn't mention that the police had escorted him off the property because he'd fought with Rain.

"Two days later, when I'd cooled down, I remembered my tools were at her place," he said. "I tried to call her, but she never answered her phone."

Because she was dead, Josie thought. But if her cell phone ever turns up, you'll have those calls for your alibi.

"I waited until I got off work and drove to her house," Harley said. "Rain wasn't home, so I just let myself in and got my tools."

"How did you get in?" Josie asked.

"She gave me a key," he said. "In fact, I think I've still got it." He pulled a massive metal ring with maybe twenty keys off his belt loop. "It's that gold one there. Do you want it?"

"No, that's okay," Josie said. "We changed the locks when we bought the house."

But if I can prove you're the killer, that key is evidence, she thought. Just keep it on that ring.

To distract him, she shoved the lightbulbs across the counter. "I'll take these."

After Harley rang up her purchase, Josie called AAAAA Locksmith & Keys from the store parking lot. The company had made keys for her mother, and Josie was amused by its efforts to stay at the top of the locksmith listings. It had added two more A's to its name in the last twenty years.

"I need all the locks changed," she said. "We've just moved into our house."

They promised to send a locksmith to Fresno Court as soon as possible.

Josie drove to her new home and sat in the drive, admiring her yard. Yellow and purple iris made a brave show along the walkway. The tall white dogwood was in full bloom, a long-stemmed bouquet. Each dogwood flower had four porcelain petals with dark pink notches.

When Josie was younger than Amelia, her grandmother had told her the legend of the dogwood. She was still small enough to sit on Grandma Marcus's lap. Grandma had white dogwoods in her yard, and every spring, a graceful dogwood branch was the centerpiece on her kitchen table. Josie was snacking on milk and chocolate chip cookies.

"See how the flowers look like a cross?" Grandma asked, showing her the branch.

Josie had nodded.

"When Jesus was crucified," her grandmother said, "dogwoods were as tall and strong as oak trees. That's why his cross was made out of dogwood. The poor dogwood was heartbroken that it had been made into a cross, and Jesus knew this. He could feel it when he was on the cross. He promised the dogwood, 'Because you feel my suffering, I'll make sure that dogwoods will never again be used for crosses. You will grow small, bent, and twisted.

" 'Your flowers will be shaped like this cross, and the edge of each petal will have the print of my nails and the stains of my blood. In the center of each flower will be my crown of thorns, so that all who see it will remember my promise.' "

Later, Josie realized this was only a pretty story, but she still loved dogwoods and saw them as symbols of hope and renewal.

There was plenty of renewal at her home this spring. Fresno Court was cluttered with panel trucks and pickups, more signs that the rehab was progressing. Next door, Betty was pulling dandelions in her front yard while Jack Dandy frolicked in the new grass. Josie waved at her neighbor and Betty gave her a friendly greeting.

She went around back to examine the work on the new deck. The frame was up and Bud Vey's crew was hammering in the cedar flooring.

"Now you're starting to see real progress," Bud said.

She saw more progress in the kitchen. A harried

Jeanne stopped work on the bead board paneling long
enough to say, "Newt has about half your cabinets refin-
ished at his shop. Won't be long now. I've made some
coffee. Help yourself."

A few dusty red curls escaped her ball cap.

Josie poured herself a cup, rustled through the thin
plastic barrier that didn't keep out the drifting construction dust, and wiped the grit off the dining table. She
settled in to wait for the locksmith. It was only eleven
thirty. She had time to work on the next phase of her
plan.

Josie called the clinic owned by Dr. Arnie Spengler,
the show animal vet. Peg, the cat lady at Judson's Tavern,
said that Donny the bartender's new girlfriend worked
at the clinic and had helped her buy a Bengal cat. Josie
wanted to talk to Missy about Rain's ex-boyfriend. "Best
in Show Clinic. Missy speaking. How may I help you?"
the receptionist asked.

Jackpot, Josie thought. Missy sounded young and educated. What did she see in the drunken bartender?

"I have a new cat!" Josie said, her voice unnaturally
high and hyperfast. "I got him at the Humane Society,
but I have a real find—a genuine Bengal! You know,
those domestic cats bred from real tigers."

"Leopards," Missy said.

"Oh, I get them mixed up," Josie said.

"We're familiar with the breed," Missy said. "Did your
cat come with papers? Some Humane Society pets do."

"No!" Josie said "I've always wanted a real Bengal,
but they cost thousands. I looked up Bengals on the Internet and my cat has all the right markings and I know
he's the real thing."

"That's exciting," Missy said. "But why do you need
to see Dr. Spengler? Is your cat sick?"

"No, Harry's fine," Josie said. "But Dr. Spengler specializes in show animals. I'd like an expert to say I have

the real thing. I just know this cat can make me lots of money. You have to see him! He's extraordinary. Please, please, can the doctor see him right away?"

"Dr. Spengler is very popular," Missy said. "We don't have an opening until May."

"Oh." Josie didn't have to fake her disappointment.

"Wait," Missy said. "I see we have a cancellation for three thirty this afternoon."

"I'll take it," Josie said. "This is perfect." I can talk to Donny's girlfriend and the crooked vet, she thought. Maybe I can learn something about my neighbor Betty while I'm there.

She called Jane next. "Mom, would you have time to pick up Amelia at school again?"

"I always have time for my granddaughter," Jane said. "We enjoy each other's company. She still talks to me."

"Right," Josie said, trying not to feel hurt. She remembered the long conversations she'd had with her grandmother. She and Jane were often at odds when Josie was a teen, but Grandma Marcus would always listen.

"Amelia wants to experiment with chicken basil bruschetta," Jane said. "We'll make extra for you and Ted. All you'll need for your dinner is a salad. I'll bring Amelia home about eight, unless you expect Ted home earlier."

"He's still working those brutal hours, Mom," Josie said.

Jane hesitated, then said, "Josie, I don't want you getting hurt, but you do have a knack for solving crimes. Have you looked into Chris's problem?"

"I'm working on it, Mom," Josie said.

And if my daughter finds out what I'm doing this afternoon, she'll never speak to me again.

Chapter 25

"You're very wise to change the locks, Ms. Marcus," said Guillermo with AAAAA Locksmith & Keys. "Many people forget to do that, especially if they live in a good neighborhood."

Guillermo, a slender, dark-haired Latino, was so handsome he was almost beautiful. Josie envied his long eyelashes, high cheekbones, and thick dark hair. Despite his impossible good looks, he had an air of complete trustworthiness.

She watched him change the front door lock with thin, sure fingers.

"This is a quiet neighborhood," Josie said. "But this house was a rental property and you never know who had keys to it."

Like a drunken bartender and a jailbird, she thought.

"So right," Guillermo said. "Do you have a home security system?"

"Yes," Josie said. "A big dog."

Guillermo laughed. "If you'd like one that doesn't eat so much, we install security systems with cameras. They're effective. A burglar can toss a drugged steak over the fence and the next thing you know, your four-legged security is snoozing and your house is cleaned out."

"It's something to think about," Josie said.

Guillermo quickly changed the locks on all three doors, made extra keys, and was finished by one thirty. His truck was backing down the drive when Alyce arrived.

"I'll drive you to Judson's Tavern," Josie's friend said. "It's better if Donny doesn't see your car, since you live nearby."

Alyce looked like spring sunshine with her buttery yellow pantsuit and floaty blond hair.

On the short drive, Josie told her friend about her encounter with Harley at the hardware store. "He has a house key, so I assume Donny does, too. I came straight home and had the locks changed."

"Will you use the same cover story on the bartender that you used on Harley?" Alyce asked.

"No," Josie said. "I don't think Donny ever did any repairs on our house. I have a new one that I think will work better for him."

At 1:45, Judson's potholed parking lot had a scattering of faded cars and dented trucks. Josie didn't see Peg's green Toyota with the I ♥ CATS bumper sticker, but Donny's red Mustang was there, parked away from the other cars. Josie wondered if he was worried about getting dings on the pristine doors.

"That's Donny's muscle car," Josie said.

"A real redneck ride," Alyce said.

"I kind of like it," Josie said. "Ted drives a tangerine Mustang."

"Oh, honey, I didn't mean to insult Ted," Alyce said. "You don't watch trash TV. There's a reality show called *R U Faster Than a Redneck?* A bunch of good old boys in Detroit iron race anything from a Toyota to a Porsche, and the winner gets ten thousand dollars. My little guy Justin loves fast cars. Besides, Ted's Mustang is vintage."

"Guess I missed that show," Josie said, but she felt better.

Alyce parked next to the building near the Dumpster, her shiny Cadillac Escalade pointed toward Manchester Road.

"There," Alyce said. "Now I've got a good view of the side door." Next, she punched in 911 on her cell phone and set it on the console. "If Donny makes a wrong move, all I have to do is hit SEND and the cops will be right here."

This is no time to tell Alyce the police are often here, Josie thought. I'm not sure how fast they'll respond.

Alyce was still plotting their escape. "Leave the door on your side open, Josie, so you can run for my SUV if there's trouble. We'll be out of here in seconds."

As Peg the cat lady predicted, Donny ducked out of work at precisely two o'clock. He had the loose, shambling walk of the perpetual drunk.

"He's not bad-looking, except for the gin-burned skin," Alyce said.

"I think that's beer burnished," Josie said.

Donny wore another blue chambray shirt with the sleeves rolled to his elbows. "The man's built like a prize-fighter," Alyce said, "and he's carrying a six-pack. Looks like he's already well ahead on the day's drinking. You be careful, Josie."

"I will," she said. Josie climbed out of the SUV, heart pounding, and crunched across the gravel to Donny.

"Hi, little lady," he said, flirting with Josie. "I remember you. You were in the other morning admiring my beer can collection. It's something, isn't it?"

In the harsh afternoon light, Josie could see the damage the beer diet had done to Donny's good looks. His features were thickening and red veins were popping out on his nose. She could smell the beer on his breath, even at this distance.

"Sure is," Josie said. "I've never seen cone tops before. Especially one worth three thousand dollars."

"The jewel of my collection," Donny said. He seemed to swell like a bullfrog.

"You told me you used to date Rain Dillon," she said.

Donny was sober enough to look wary. "So?" he said.

"I'm friends with Christine Cormac." Josie watched him carefully for a reaction. Everything depended on his next words.

"Who's that?" he asked.

Safe! Josie thought, but she couldn't let her relief show. "Christine is Rain's older sister."

"Never met her," Donny said. He didn't seem to realize that Christine had been jailed for Rain's murder.

"Christine is short of money after Rain died. She needs help with the funeral and all."

Donny edged toward the red Mustang. "I didn't really know Rain well enough to pay for her funeral," he said.

"Oh, Christine doesn't expect you to pay."

Donny looked relieved. He staggered—or did he stumble over a pothole?—and fumbled for his keys.

Here comes the big bluff, Josie thought. "She just wondered if you'd found a diamond tennis bracelet when you went back to Rain's house after you broke up."

Donny gave a nasty bray. "A hippie with a tennis bracelet? Don't make me laugh."

Josie could hear Alyce race the SUV's engine. Her friend must have heard Donny's ugly laugh. She was anxious to leave. So was Josie, but she had to do this.

"The bracelet belonged to her mother," she said. "Christine wants to sell it to help pay for the funeral. She knows you have a key to the house."

"Oh no," Donny said, backing away. "You're not pinning that on me. I never took nothing that wasn't mine when I went back to Rain's house."

Good, Josie thought. My bluff worked. He admitted going back to Rain's house. Now to find out why.

Donny had his keys out. She heard the beep as he

unlocked the red Mustang. The red door creaked. Josie's mind was racing like Alyce's SUV engine. She remembered her conversation with Guillermo, the locksmith.

"You know Christine owned the house where Rain lived and it had a security camera system," she said.

"You mean that perv taped us in the sack?" Donny was outraged.

"Not in the bedrooms," Josie said. "Just the entrances. The week before Rain died, you were taped carrying a bag out of the house."

"That was my shirt," Donny said. "I left it in the bedroom closet. A good one. A real Ralph Lauren from Marshalls. I wanted to wear it on a date with Missy, because she's classy. But I never took no diamond bracelet." He slammed the door.

"I didn't think so," Josie said. "Gotta run."

And she did. Straight to Alyce's SUV.

Chapter 26

Harry, Amelia's cat, howled mournfully. Josie glanced at the beige plastic pet caddy on the passenger seat and said, "Sorry, old buddy, but I need your help. You have to pose as a purebred Bengal this afternoon."

Harry yowled louder, his plaintive cry dying on a long, sad note.

"You'll be helping Ted and Chris," she said.

Mruphf, Harry said, crouching down in his caddy. His green eyes glared at her.

"And I promise lots of treats when we get home. Wild salmon, your favorite."

Harry's sulky silence seemed louder than his anguished wails. Josie felt guilty, but Amelia's cat was her ticket into Dr. Arnie Spengler's Best in Show Clinic to talk to his assistant, Missy.

She'd see Dr. Spengler today, and if she noticed any sign that he might be Dr. Flimflam, she'd make another appointment and search his records. Ted had heard Dr. Spengler was doing dodgy procedures. What if Chris found out, and the vet wanted to get rid of her? Josie knew she could get Amelia to hack into the clinic computer system, but she wasn't going to drag her daughter into a criminal activity.

Missy was the main reason she was here. Peg, the cat lover she'd met at Judson's Tavern, said Donny had introduced her to Missy, and she'd sold her a genuine Bengal show cat with papers, for "only" fifteen hundred dollars. Then Missy helped Peg's friend Bernice and other cat lovers adopt more Bengals, and Donny drove the cats to Illinois. What was that all about?

Harry had an important part to play. Amelia adored Harry. The gentle tabby was special to her daughter, but Josie knew this ordinary alley cat could help prove Dr. Spengler was a fraud.

She hoped Amelia never found out she'd used her beloved pet as a pawn. Harry hated leaving his home, and it would take Josie some time to calm Harry before Amelia returned from her grandmother's house.

Ted had a client with a Bengal, and he liked to talk about this active, affectionate breed. Josie found out more on the Internet. She learned the Bengal breed was fairly new, developed sometime in the late sixties when Asian leopards, small wildcats, were bred with domestic cats. It took about four generations to develop Bengals.

Now a show-quality Bengal with the distinctive leopard spots, or rosettes, could command three thousand dollars and more.

But expensive Bengals and common tabbies had some features in common. Both had "mascara" lines—dark horizontal striping along the eyes—and dark stripes on their front legs.

Harry was handsome, but he was no show cat. Amelia's cat gave one discouraged howl when they reached Dr. Spengler's Best in Show Clinic. The sign showed a smiling cat and dog with blue ribbons on their collars.

"We're going in, Harry," Josie said. "I'll make this as quick as I can."

The clinic's waiting room was crowded with pets and

their owners, including a magnificent black standard poodle and an odd, hairless Chinese crested dog that looked like it had escaped from a Dr. Seuss book. Both dogs were on leashes. Cats' eyes gleamed from the dark depths of their caddies.

Harry meowed, shifted uneasily, and Josie nearly stumbled.

Missy was seated behind a handsome wooden reception desk, wearing a bright red bandage dress and a bloody slash of lipstick. Her blond hair was up in a chic chignon. The only thing this sleek, showy creature had in common with Rain was her hair color. What was Donny's secret with women?

"I called this morning," Josie said. "I want Dr. Spengler to see my Bengal."

"Right," Missy said. "The doctor will be with you in a minute."

"I believe we have a mutual friend," Josie said. "Donny Freedman."

Missy froze. "How do you know Donny?" she said, her voice cool. Was Missy jealous?

"I've seen his beer can collection at Judson's Tavern," Josie said. "Have you? It's remarkable."

"Oh, I never go to his place of business," she said. "We met here when Donny brought in his mother's toy poodle. Donny's collection is incredible. He keeps most of it at his house."

"He used to date a friend of mine," Josie said. "Rain Dillon."

"That's so over," Missy said.

"Really? Donny went to her house to get his best shirt when he started dating you."

"Dating *me*," Missy said, emphasizing that word. "She was nothing but a dirty hippie. Rain! What kind of name is that? Donny told me all about her. He broke up with her when she complained that he drank too much. Can you believe that? She wanted him to go to AA. Donny likes a drink or two, but that's all."

Missy went out of her way to slam Rain, Josie thought. Had she met Rain, or seen her photo? Surely she didn't think the dead beauty was competition.

Missy handed Josie a clipboard and said, "Please fill out this patient information form and the doctor will see you shortly."

When Josie finished the paperwork, Missy escorted her to an exam room. They passed the file room, located next to the bathrooms. The oak-paneled exam room was much more expensive than the ones in Ted's clinic. Over the exam table was a framed photo of a Bengal cat next to a gold trophy.

Dr. Spengler was as well-groomed as his waiting room patients. His artfully graying dark hair and crisp doctor's coat inspired confidence. Josie suspected his blue shirt and gray slacks were custom-tailored. There wasn't a stray animal hair on his clothes.

He gently lifted Harry out of his carrier and put him on the exam table. Harry squirmed. The vet scratched Harry's forehead, and the cat relaxed.

He's good, Josie thought.

"A fine specimen," Dr. Spengler said. "Look at that long, powerful Bengal body."

Harry didn't try to wriggle free.

"You can see the show cat structure, Ms. Marcus. Note those robust bones. Like all show-quality Bengals, he's muscular. Harry's head is the right shape—slightly small in proportion to his body, but not to an extreme degree. The ears are a little long, but they can be fixed."

"Fixed how?" Josie said, suddenly alert.

"Just a little snip and they'll be the correct rounded shape," Dr. Spengler said. "It's perfectly legal to crop show dog breeds, like Dobermans."

But Harry is a cat, Josie wanted to say.

"Are you worried it will hurt?" the vet asked. "It's an easy operation and this handsome dude will be under anesthesia. He won't feel a thing."

"Well . . . ," Josie said.

"He has the color of a true champion," Dr. Spengler said. "A warm brown base coat under those dark markings."

"I'm concerned he doesn't have the leopard spots that I've seen on some Bengals," she said. "I don't want to invest the money to fix his ears if he doesn't have the right markings."

"The base coat is what's important. The markings can be refined," he said. "A little harmless dye and you'll have a show-quality Bengal. Missy said your cat didn't come with papers."

"No," Josie said.

"We can provide TICA papers," he said. "That's The International Cat Association. I'll stake my reputation that this is a genuine Bengal."

"How much will it cost to fix him?" Josie asked.

"Prep him for showing, Ms. Marcus," the vet corrected her. "It will cost less than a thousand dollars, including the papers."

"A thousand dollars!" Josie said.

"But we have an easy payment plan," he said. "Consider it an investment."

Harry's been neutered. I certainly can't put this so-called show cat out to stud, you fraud, Josie thought. And cat shows don't have big cash prizes.

"If you make an appointment with Missy, she'll explain our payment plan. Then she can set up a time for the ear correction and color refining."

So that's what you call it, she thought.

"I don't know," Josie said, forcing herself to seem doubtful. She couldn't seem too excited. But she definitely wanted to return. "If you really think you can do it."

"Missy!" Dr. Spengler pressed a button on the phone in the room. "How soon can you see Ms. Marcus for financial counseling?"

"I can fit her in at ten o'clock next Friday, Doctor," Missy said. "Ms. Marcus, you can leave Harry at home. We'll set up the show prep appointment as soon as you sign."

Yes! Josie thought. I can check out that file room without having to worry about my cat.

Dr. Spengler took her silence for reluctance.

"Consider it an investment," he said. "You can earn real money with a Bengal who'll walk on the wild side at any cat show."

"Really?" Josie said.

"Trust me," Dr. Spengler said.

Chapter 27

"There," Josie said. "That's the last of it." She felt as wrung out as the yellow sponge she'd used to scrub the Wolf stove. She stood up stiffly and stretched.

The fabulous stove squatted in the center of the retro kitchen, attached by its gas and electric umbilical cords. Josie had cleaned the top and sides on her knees, as if worshipping the metal cube.

The red-haired contractor was tearing rotted paneling off the wall near the door. "You've been cleaning that stove for over an hour," Jeanne said. "Wish my subcontractors were as thorough. They leave a mess when they finish and tell me, 'I'm a painter, not a cleaner.' The truth is men don't like to scrub."

"Neither does this woman," Josie said. "But I had no choice." She stripped off the rubber gloves and set the bottle of spray cleaner on the stove top. "I found puddles of old grease in hidden spots."

"That means the stove was well used," Jeanne said.

"By cooks who were none too clean," Josie said. She heard a loud *crack!* as the contractor pried a stubborn section of wood off the wall. Muscles bulged in her sturdy arms. The paneling gave way and Jeanne tossed it in a huge plastic trash can.

"That's why I insisted on scrubbing this stove myself,"

Josie said. "It's my special gift to Ted and Amelia. Let's take a break and test it. I've brought frozen homemade cinnamon-raisin rolls to warm up in the oven."

She studied the controls. "How does this thing work? It's more complicated than the Space Shuttle."

Jeanne laughed and said, "I'll figure it out while you make us more coffee. Two pans of rolls. Did you think I'd be that hungry?"

"I brought enough for Bud and his deck crew," Josie said.

"Good. We can bribe the boys to help us move this monster back beside that cabinet," Jeanne said. "It's the only one that didn't need any work. A few more weeks and you'll have a real kitchen."

She pulled off her heavy work gloves, then loaded the pans of rolls into the oven. Josie made the coffee, serenaded by the construction noise of Bud's crew.

"Oven's on," Jeanne said. "Let's sit for a minute. You must be beat. You've been working all morning. You taped all the woodwork in Amelia's room plus scrubbed this stove."

Josie wiped the construction dust off the dining room table and they settled in with mugs of coffee. "Painter's tape isn't hard to use," she said. "There's just so much woodwork in that room. The hardest part was getting that soap dish up in her bathroom."

"I could have done that for you," Jeanne said.

"No, I need you to finish the kitchen," Josie said. "Is that a raisin on my clean stove? I can't see it too clearly from here."

"Not unless it's got legs," Jeanne said. "It's running."

"There's dozens of them. What's wrong with my stove? Eeeee-yuckkkkk!" Josie shrieked. "Roaches! Nasty, dirty, little red roaches! My stove is infested."

Reddish brown German roaches scuttled every-where—across the floor, over the new cabinet, even up the wall. They crawled across Josie's newly cleaned burners and rushed down the sides of the freshly scrubbed stove. Josie sprayed them with the cleaner and swatted them with her gloves, but more roaches poured out of the stove, a panicked crowd fleeing a burning building.

"Josie, Josie, stop," Jeanne said. "You can't kill them that way. You need a professional. I'll call an exterminator."

"Roaches! How could I miss them?" Josie said. She was near tears.

"Don't cry," Jeanne said. "Even the cleanest stoves are grease traps. Roaches hide in the splashboard, under the stove, even behind the knobs."

"I'm not crying," Josie said, sniffling. "It's just that I thought it was a raisin and then it was running. . . ."

"Like a scalded roach," Jeanne said.

"At least they're very clean roaches," Josie said. She giggled.

Then the two women were laughing so hard Josie wiped tears from her eyes. Tears of laughter this time.

"You and the gas man worked on the stove," Josie said. "Did you see any bugs?"

"I found a dead one and put down some borax," Jeanne said. "I didn't think much about it. I'm tearing out that old section of paneling and roaches come out from deep inside a house. I'm sorry you did all that cleaning for nothing."

The roaches had disappeared, except for a cluster of corpses on the floor.

"I wonder if these drowned or died from the spray," Josie said. She swept up the dead bugs, then opened the oven and threw out the cinnamon rolls.

"What a waste," Jeanne said. "But we can't tell the roaches from the raisins."

"Sure we can," Josie said. "Raisins don't run."

That sparked another round of giggling.

Then Josie sighed. "I wanted everything to be perfect in our first house," she said. "Now there's a body in the backyard and roaches in the stove. How will I tell Ted and Amelia their precious stove was overrun with roaches?"

"It's not so bad," Jeanne said. "You can't find the spot where the body was, and the roach-infested stove will stay our secret."

"But my family is expecting it to be ready today," Josie said.

"So?" Jeanne said. "Tell them you have a few bugs to get out."

When Josie quit laughing, she said, "I'm glad I left my neighbor's cookies in the dining room. They'll be roach-free."

She looked out her side window and said, "Cordelia's car's in her drive. I'd better clean up before I see her."

"If you want to use the pink bathroom, I put a couple of towels in there," Jeanne said.

Josie used the toilet, washed her face, combed her hair, and freshened her lipstick. There. She looked presentable to visit a neighbor.

"Jeanne," she said, when she finished. "Something's wrong with that toilet. I jiggled the handle and it's still running."

"Probably the flapper valve," Jeanne said. "Let me check."

Jeanne lifted the pink top to the tank and carefully placed it on the floor. "Oh no," she said. "Harley the Hopeless Handyman has struck again. Look! The chain that lifts the flapper valve broke and he fixed it with duct tape."

Josie saw half a broken chain with a square of gray duct tape on one end.

"No wonder it fell apart," she said. "I can't believe this. The man owns a hardware store. I guess you'd better call a plumber as well as an exterminator."

"I could fix this myself," Jeanne said, "but I want a plumber to look at your kitchen sink. It keeps backing up. If Harley fixed that, too, it'll need professional help. You run along next door and I'll line up the repairs."

When Cordelia answered her door, Josie was once again struck by her beauty. Her high cheekbones and long, graceful neck made her face a bronze sculpture rising out of her black T-shirt.

"You caught me at a good time," the professor said. "I wanted a break from grading student papers. Let's have some coffee and sample those cookies."

Cordelia's living room was painted an earthy orange and lined with bookcases. She and Josie sat on the brown velvet sofa.

"Our husbands know each other," Josie said.

"That's what Wil told me," Cordelia said. "He speaks highly of Ted."

If he speaks highly of Ted, why didn't you mention it last time? Josie wondered. Are you hiding something?

"How is Dr. Christine?" Cordelia asked. "I saw our neighbor on TV again, bragging about her dog. Really! That woman is impossible!"

Josie was not about to start backstabbing Betty. "Ted said people thought that interview helped Chris. It made her seem more sympathetic. Maybe too sympathetic. We don't want the prosecutor striking Betty from the witness list."

"Oh, really?" Cordelia said. "And does the prosecutor know that Betty used to take her dogs to Dr. Christine? Then they had some kind of disagreement and Betty went to another vet. That Honey Butcher sure didn't know.

"I got so mad listening to her puff piece about Betty's show dog that I called that reporter and told her that she's letting herself be used. Ms. Butcher just brushed me off."

I'm not surprised, Josie thought. You sound like you have a grudge against Betty.

"Do you know why Betty switched vets?" Josie asked.

"You'll have to ask Dr. Christine," Cordelia said. "But I doubt she did anything wrong. Wil says she's a good, kind vet, like your husband. Not all of them are, you know. Wil says there's one on his route who doesn't care about animals."

"I didn't know that," Josie said. "What's his name?"

"Arnie Spengler," Cordelia said. "My Wil says Dr. Spengler likes to say he specializes in show animals, but he wouldn't know a show dog from a showgirl. He tells all the pet owners that their animals are show quality, even the mutts. What he really specializes in is unnecessary surgeries to 'improve'"—Cordelia made air quotes—"the show animal's appearance."

"I've heard about those," Josie said.

"My Wil says they're incredibly cruel. Can you imagine tattooing a poor boxer's nose to make sure it's perfectly black? Or docking dogs' tails when they aren't even broken? Don't get me started on the subject. But if you ask me, that's why Betty switched vets."

"I'll ask Chris why Betty doesn't go to her anymore," Josie said.

"You can ask," Cordelia said. "But she may not be able to tell you. Wil says veterinary records are confidential in Missouri."

Cordelia glanced at her watch, a not too subtle hint that it was time for Josie to leave. But Josie was suspicious of her neighbor. Under that beautiful surface was a deep vein of anger. Josie decided to risk a quick search.

"May I use your bathroom?" she asked.

"Of course," Cordelia said. "I'll make a quick phone call."

Josie waited till she heard Cordelia talking on her cell phone. Then she bypassed the downstairs bathroom and tiptoed upstairs. The house's layout was the same as hers. Josie was heading for the master bedroom when she passed the small middle room that looked like Wil's office.

Josie saw a cluttered desk, stacks of pamphlets, and boxes labeled CLOSEOUT SUTURES, METZENBAUM SCISSORS 5.75 IN. CURVED, DISPOSABLE ANESTHESIA BREATHING BAG, .5 LTR.

Shelves were loaded with medicines in alphabetical order. Josie scanned them quickly: ACEPROMAZINE, 10. 25 MG, ADVANTAGE II FLEA PREVENTATIVE, AMOXICILLIN 250 MG, 500 MG CAPSULES.

Whoa! she thought. Back up there. Why does acepromazine sound familiar?

Josie felt like a flare went off in her head. Acepromazine was the drug that killed Rain. Angry Cordelia had it right here in her home.

"Ms. Marcus!" Cordelia said.

Josie jumped.

"What the hell are you doing in my husband's office? And don't tell me you were on the way to the bathroom. You know good and well the guest bathroom is right next to the kitchen."

"I—" Josie said.

"Please," Cordelia said. "Don't bother to lie. Just leave."

Josie left. She couldn't look Cordelia in the eye.

I've lost a neighbor, she thought. But I may have found a killer. All I need is a motive.

Chapter 28

Josie's face burned hot with embarrassment. Even Cordelia's ice daggers didn't cool her mortification. Josie hoped it was worth the effort. She finally had some useful information.

Cordelia had the murder weapon. But why would she want to kill Rain? Chris might know.

Josie checked her watch. She could make the next visiting hour at the county jail, if Chris's lawyer agreed.

Renzo quickly okayed the visit. "She looks like death on toast, Josie," he said. "See what you can do to cheer her up."

Josie called Jane next. "Of course I'll pick up my grandbaby," her mother said. "We'll make beef stew and have extra for you to take home to Ted. I gather he's still working those long hours."

"I see him less now that we're married than when we were dating," Josie said.

"Josie Marcus, don't whine. I'm sure he'd rather be home, too."

Josie found a message from Ted on her cell phone. "I'm so sorry, Josie," he said. "A lot of spays and neuters today and I'm way behind. I'll be home about nine, if I'm lucky. Love you madly."

Another lonely night, she thought. On the short drive

to the county jail, Josie tried to figure out who had killed Rain. Was it Harley the not so handy man? Rain had ruined a ten-thousand-dollar Coke calendar and Harley was a fanatical collector. He'd been in prison for beating his wife and he could get veterinary drugs through his good buddy Doc Clinton. He'd broken up with Rain two days before she disappeared. His anger would still be deadly hot.

Donny, the beer can collector and bartender, could get them, too. He was dating that cute veterinary receptionist. He could get acepromazine from her. The man had a hair-trigger temper. Josie'd watched him drag a customer over the bar for taking free ketchup packets. He'd had a bitter fight with Rain, and the police had to intervene. Did he wait, brood, and then one drunken night go back and kill her?

Cordelia could get veterinary drugs through her husband, Wil. Josie had seen her anger when she caught Josie snooping in her husband's office. Maybe Chris knew more about her.

Inside the jail, Josie had only a short wait to see Chris. She was glad Renzo had prepared her. Chris's face looked like a skin-covered skull. Her lifeless brown hair was scraped back. When she reached for the phone receiver to talk, Josie could count the bones in her wrist and hand. Chris attempted a smile and looked so much like a grinning skeleton Josie suppressed a shudder.

"You haven't forgotten me," Chris said.

"Of course not," Josie said. "We're doing everything we can to help. I've been talking to the people the police should have interviewed, to see if I can find the real killer. I've got doubts about both your neighbors. Why did Betty quit taking her dogs to you at the clinic?"

"You know veterinary records are protected under state law," Chris said. "Our clinic won't do surgeries we consider cruel, including cropping ears, docking tails, altering the dogs' vocal cords so they can't bark, or cosmetic surgery on show dogs, like fixing their ears or the set of their tail.

"Some good vets will crop ears because they say it's more humane to have them cut by a professional than sliced by a breeder in a dog show parking lot."

Josie winced.

"It happens," Chris said. "But we don't perform operations unless they are medically necessary. All I can tell you is Betty wanted an unnecessary surgery for a show dog and I refused. She went off in a huff. Renzo's subpoenaed the clinic records for the trial to use against her, just in case she comes off as a hostile witness."

"She hasn't so far," Josie said.

"That's what Renzo said."

"Does this 'no unnecessary surgery' policy cost you business?" Josie asked.

"Some," Chris said. "But we put our patients' interests first. I wasn't surprised that Betty quit the clinic. My sister had been giving her a hard time. Rain thought dog shows were cruel and told Betty that all the time.

"After . . ." Chris stopped, and gulped back tears. "After Rain was gone and I cleaned the house, I saw Betty's show dog again in her yard. Jack looked fine. He didn't need the surgery after all."

What surgery? Josie wanted to scream, but Chris had strong principles. She would keep silent and let Renzo handle this.

"Betty's husband died four years ago, and now she lives for those dogs," Chris said. "He left her some money and she quit her job to train and show her Jack Russells full-time. I felt guilty selling the house, knowing you and Ted were going to live next to her."

"Don't," Josie said. "She's fine. I've put up with Mom's neighbor Mrs. Mueller for years. Betty isn't in her league."

"I felt better knowing you have Wil and Cordelia on the other side. They're good neighbors."

"Cordelia brought us a lovely chicken pot pie," Josie said.

And then I snooped through her husband's office and ruined any chance for a friendship.

"Rain liked Cordelia," Chris said. "One thing bothers me about her, though."

"Something bad?" Josie said.

"Depends on how you look at it," Chris said. "Rain went digging around on the Net and found out something. Cordelia went to an Ivy League school and she was arrested for demonstrating at a protest against a big chemical company polluter along with twenty other students."

"But that's a badge of honor," Josie said.

"That's what Rain said. She wouldn't shut up about it. Finally Cordelia asked her to please stop talking about it. She was quite angry. She told Rain that she was up for tenure at City University. They're very conservative. They wouldn't appreciate a professor who'd been a student protestor, no matter how noble the cause."

"Did Rain shut up?" Josie asked.

"Well, yes," Chris said. "But this happened right before she was murdered."

Chapter 29

"Amelia, you are not wearing that skirt to school," Josie said. "Your cheeks are hanging out."

"Mom, that's gross!" Amelia said.

"Not as gross as that skirt." Josie had bought Amelia that hot pink bubble skirt, and she knew it wasn't that short. Had her daughter hemmed it?

"You know it doesn't meet the dress code. Go change. Now. We have to leave for school."

"Don't have to change," Amelia said. She tugged on the hem and the length was suddenly acceptable. Josie worked hard to hide a smile. She used to roll up her skirts at the waist and Jane would make her take them down before she left home.

"If you roll up that skirt at school," Josie said, "Miss Apple will go after you. You want to stay off her radar right now. The BOB parents trapped her with your report and she's like an angry wasp."

In fact, she is an angry WASP, Josie thought. She's the poster child for that power-loving species, but I won't have her sting my daughter.

"Miss Apple doesn't know Emma and I are A&E Investigations," Amelia said. "None of the other girls have talked."

"Good," Josie said. "Let's keep it that way. You know

Bailey's father, Dev, has stepped up the campaign against the mean girls. Miss Apple will find any excuse to make your life misery. You promise you won't roll up that skirt?"

"Mom, I just said—"

"Pinkie-swear," Josie said. That was the unbreakable promise.

"Mom, we're gonna be late," Amelia said.

"Yes, we are," Josie said. "We're not leaving until you pinkie-swear."

"Okay." Amelia reluctantly locked her little finger with her mother's.

"Thank you," Josie said. "Let's go."

Amelia rode to school in surly silence while Josie fought the morning congestion and worried.

I should never have involved Amelia in the mean-girl investigation, she thought. Emma's father and I should have hired an investigator instead of using our daughters. Playing amateur investigator is a dangerous game. Now all I can do is hope she doesn't get hurt.

Josie quit berating herself at the stoplight before Barrington. Negotiating the school traffic took all her concentration. After nearly getting sideswiped by a Land Rover driver talking on her cell phone, Josie safely dropped off her daughter. Amelia slammed the car door hard and left without a good-bye.

Back at home, Josie sank into the sofa and put her feet up. She needed some time before her day turned hectic. A cup of coffee. A good mystery.

She'd barely read a page before her cell phone broke the quiet. "Josie, it's Dev, Bailey's father," he said, but Josie had already recognized his distinctive voice. She liked how the powerful lawyer identified himself.

"I've heard from a lawyer representing the families of the mean girls," he said.

"That was fast," Josie said. Her heart was pounding. Would Amelia get any money?

"Our bluff worked. They're eager to settle before a suit's filed," he said. "Each family has agreed to chip in a hundred fifty thousand. That's not much, I know, but . . ."

"It's a lot for me," Josie said. She was too shaky to do the math, but her daughter was due six fat figures.

"It's not enough when you consider what our girls suffered," he said. "A million bucks wouldn't be enough. But it's a moral victory. I tried to push them for a little more. Amelia will only get a hundred and twelve thousand five hundred dollars."

"'Only'?" Josie said. She set her cup on the coffee table with trembling hands.

"Well, one BOB parent is disappointed," he said.

"Not this one," Josie said. "I'm thrilled."

"That person didn't expect the full million, but thought I could squeeze at least five hundred thousand out of them. I can't, Josie. I've pushed as far as I can. This could unravel quickly."

"You're right, Dev. Let's quit while we're ahead. You've given Amelia a nice college nest egg," Josie said. "I'm grateful."

"There are conditions," he said. "Amelia has to promise not to mention the episode again. That means she can't discuss it, write about it, blog about it, or put it on any social media, from Facebook to YouTube to forms that aren't even invented yet. She can't use the BOB photos in any way. If she does, she'll have to return the money."

"Fine with me," Josie said. "I'm sure Amelia would like this to be over, too. But that won't keep the incident quiet. Miss Apple has demanded a written apology and detention for the mean girls. Word will leak out at school."

"That's not our problem," Dev said. "Like I figured, their families are worried a bullying scandal could hurt their daughters' chances of getting into a good school."

"What's the next step?" Josie asked.

"It will take a few days to finalize the paperwork," he said. "You'll have to come in and sign it and then I'll transfer the money to your account. I'll need that number, too."

Josie hung up the phone. She couldn't wait to tell Ted, but before she could call, her cell phone rang.

"Josie, it's me," he said. "I've had two cancellations this afternoon. I'll be home early at five. I thought I could meet you and Amelia at the new house and see how the work is going."

"Wonderful," Josie said. "I have good news, too." She told him about her call from Dev.

"You're kidding," he said. "Amelia is an heiress."

"No, she's a girl with a healthy college fund," Josie said.

"We need to celebrate," Ted said. "What should I cook?"

"Why not take the night off and we'll order pizza at the new house?" Josie said. "Do you want beer or wine?"

"I'll pick up a bottle of Chianti on the way home," Ted said. "We'll toast our girl detective."

"Look, Ted, I'm worried about this celebration."

"Why?"

"I don't want Amelia to start thinking she can do more investigating on her own. Don't get me wrong. We should celebrate, but if she talks about being a detective, let's steer her back to school."

"Last I heard, she still wants to be a veterinarian," Ted said.

"That's a good goal," Josie said.

"What if she wants to spend some of that money on herself?" Ted asked.

"It's for college," Josie said.

"Oh, come on," Ted said. "She earned it. She's entitled to something. Don't be harsh. Let her buy herself a present and then put the rest in a CD where it will be safe."

"You're right," Josie said. "I love you. I'm looking forward to our family pizza night."

"Not as much as I am," Ted said. "I won't fall asleep right after dinner, either. Tonight, we'll make up for lost time."

"I miss you so much," Josie said. "I love you."

She called her mother next and told her about the settlement.

"Oh, Josie, that's wonderful," Jane said. "Amelia's college is taken care of! And our clever girl earned it herself."

"Yes, she did," Josie said. "But I'm a little worried she's going to do more detecting. How do I stop her?"

Jane laughed. This was not a maternal chuckle. It was harsh and raucous.

"You're asking me? Josie Marcus, you get yourself into one scary situation after another. I've never been able to stop you. Why do you think I can stop Amelia?"

"Mom, didn't you ask me to help Chris?"

"Yes, but you can take care of yourself," Jane said.

"Well, I'm not sure your granddaughter can," Josie said. "I don't want her hurt and neither do you. If she tells you she wants to do another investigation, please remind her she needs to finish college."

"I can," Jane said. "But that didn't work with you, either. You quit before you got your degree."

"Mom!" Josie said. "What's wrong with you?"

"Nothing," Jane said. "It's just that mothers rarely get paybacks, and this is a double one: you're asking me for advice after you ignored mine—twice.

"I promise I won't indulge Amelia's detective fantasies. But to put your mind at ease, yesterday she told me how much she wants to be a vet and work at Ted's clinic."

"Good," Josie said. "That makes me feel a little better."

Even Jane's snarky remarks couldn't dull her delight

in the news and the prospect of a night with Ted. Josie flew through the household chores, threw in a load of laundry, then spent two hours getting ready for Ted.

She showed up at Barrington with her hair and manicure perfect, wearing Ted's favorite white blouse, her good black pants, and sexy red heels.

Amelia's moods changed like the St. Louis weather—sunny one moment, stormy the next. This afternoon, she flashed Josie a bright smile, waved an extravagant good-bye to Emma, then said, "Can we go to the new house?"

"I was planning on it," Josie said. "Ted wants to meet us there at five o'clock. We'll have pizza and he'll check out the rehab progress."

"Yay!" Amelia said.

"And I have news for you. The BOB case is settled. The mean girls' parents want to pay rather than go to court."

"How much?" Amelia asked, suddenly serious. Josie marveled at how she switched from carefree kid to thoughtful adult in seconds.

"More than a hundred thousand dollars," Josie said. "That's for each of you."

"Wicked," Amelia said. "I'm a hundred-thousand-aire. I can buy anything I want."

"I'd like you to put the money away for college," Josie said.

"Mom!" Amelia said. "I earned it! It's my money."

"You can get through veterinary school at Mizzou without taking out student loans. You don't want to start your career burdened with debt. Ted is still paying off his school loans."

Amelia's unhappy silence lasted for a whole stoplight.

"But before we put it safely away," Josie said, "you need to give yourself a nice treat."

"An iPad!" Amelia said. "Please, Mom, that would be so sick."

Sick? Once again, Josie remembered that was a compliment.

Amelia was still talking. "An iPad and a screen protector and a folding stand and headphones—you'll want me to have headphones."

"You can start picking them out when we get home," Josie said.

She turned into Fresno Court. The redbud's frothy purple flowers were almost gone, replaced by new lime green leaves. The big dogwood was in full bloom, its milky petals tinged with a delicate pink. The grass was emerald. That is one gorgeous house, she thought.

"Can I go next door and see Betty's dogs until Ted shows up?" Amelia asked.

"Well . . . ," Josie said.

"Can't I go see them, please? I'll be home by five o'clock," Amelia said. She gave her mother a sly smile. "Besides, learning about show dogs will be good training if I'm going to be a vet.

"I'll be right next door. It's not like there's any danger."

Chapter 30

"Mom! Ted! I got to play with Jack Dandy!" Amelia burst through the front door of the Fresno Court house, brown hair flying, dark eyes flashing with excitement.

She ran into the dining room, where the freshly delivered pizzas were piled on the table. "I got to play with a real champion," she said.

"Oh? Are champions different from ordinary dogs?" Josie asked. She heard the slight edge in her voice and regretted it. Her daughter was happy, interested, and no longer brooding about the mean girls. That's what I wanted, she thought.

"Festus! Stop!" Ted said. "What are you doing?"

The black Lab, front paws on the table, was sniffing the pizza boxes. Josie was glad she'd kept them closed.

"I'll tell you how champions are different," Ted said. "They obey orders and don't try to sneak pizza. You know better, boy. Outside!"

Festus, tail between his legs, was banished to the backyard. Ted held back the plastic sheets that divided the kitchen construction from the rest of the house, and Festus trotted past, leaving a trail of dusty paw prints to the back door. He turned to stare at Amelia with sad eyes.

"Oh, Ted, can't he stay?" she asked.

"He has to learn, Amelia," Ted said, and opened the

back door. Marmalade, the clinic cat, tried to follow her pal. "Not you," Ted said. "You stay here. You're not an outdoor cat."

Amelia quickly changed the subject. "Jack Dandy can do tricks," she said. "He can sit and he can shake."

"Shake what?" Josie asked.

"Hands," Amelia said.

She saw Josie's raised eyebrow and said, "Paws, whatever. He can jump, speak, and lie down, too."

"Festus is good at that last trick," Josie said.

"Hey, no fair," Ted said. "Festus and Marmalade work. They donate blood for my patients. Festus just needs to practice our 'stay' command when there's pizza on the table."

"Jack Dandy doesn't need to do tricks for the show ring," Amelia said. "But he's smart and easy to train. He can stand still for nearly two minutes. I like all Betty's dogs, but Jack's my favorite. We also looked at a gazillion photos, mostly of Jack. We even saw him nursing with his brothers and sisters. Betty's been keeping a diary for a video and a book she's going to call *The Making of a Champion*."

Josie was relieved to see Amelia so talkative again. She'd feared her daughter would retreat into the silent safety of her computer after the mean girls' attack.

"Betty started taking photos and videos when Jack Dandy was just a baby pup," Amelia said. "He could fit in the palm of her hand. I saw the photo. She has pictures of his brothers and sisters, too, but not so many. Betty says she could tell right away that Jack was a champion, even if he did have one ear down and one straight up.

"I said his ears looked cute that way, but Betty said he couldn't be a winner unless he had what they call button ears. That's both ears folded down, like the collar on a button-down shirt.

"Jack's ears are perfect buttons. The ear fixed itself.

Betty says that happens sometimes as the pups grow up, and it's another sign that he was meant to be a champion. What would happen if his ear couldn't be fixed, Ted?"

"He'd be a family pet instead of a show dog," Ted said. "You know one way to fix a crick-eared dog? Crush the ear cartilage in an emasculator."

Josie winced. "But that's so mean!" Amelia said.

"And painful," Ted said. "No ethical vet will perform it, and if the show judges find out, the dog's disqualified."

"What's an emasculator?" Amelia asked.

"It's a scary-looking tool used to castrate livestock," Ted said. "We get asked to perform illegal or unethical procedures on show dogs all the time. I've been asked to remove a third eyelid and correct the position—the set—of a tail by cutting a nerve that controls the tail. Our clinic won't do any unnecessary surgery on healthy animals, but we think there's at least one local vet who does."

"Can't you report him?" Josie asked.

"No proof," Ted said. "Don't get me started on the subject. Let's talk about something happier. I want to see this Wolf stove."

"It's wicked good," Amelia said.

They trooped into the dusty kitchen, where the stove sat in the middle of the floor, tethered by the gas and electrical hookups.

"It will go in that spot there," Josie said. "Right next to that cabinet. Most of the others have been hauled to Newt's shop for restoration."

"I can't wait till this kitchen is done," Amelia said. "It's going to be so sick."

Once again, Josie had to remind herself that "sick" was good. Living with Amelia at this stage was like learning a new language—every day.

If she and Ted didn't have plans for later that evening,

Josie would have been jealous of the way he fondled the stove's red knobs and ran his hands over its smooth skin.

"It's hot but I'm hotter," she whispered in his ear. He winked at her.

She held her breath when Ted opened the oven and examined the interior, but there were no roaches, live or dead. Whatever the exterminator did, it worked. But she had to distract Ted. If he found a bug, it could ruin his delight in that stove.

"The pizza's getting cold," she said. "Shouldn't we sit down and eat?"

She herded them back into the dining room, where Amelia finally noticed the beribboned vase with graceful iris and glamorous globes of hydrangeas.

"Wicked purple flowers, Mom," Amelia said. "Did Ted give them to you?"

"No," Josie said. "He gave them to you—to celebrate the settlement."

Amelia hugged Ted. "I even like the ribbons," she said.

"I also brought a bottle of sparkling grape juice," Ted said. "It's white, so you can pretend it's champagne."

"That's okay," Amelia said. "I had champagne at your wedding. It's sour." She wrinkled her freckled nose.

Ted poured Chianti for himself and Josie, and Amelia's pretend champagne into plastic cups.

"A toast to the brilliant investigator, Amelia Marcus," he said, lifting his drink.

A wide smile split her face.

"A woman so smart she earns her own money for college," Ted said.

Amelia's smile dimmed slightly.

"After she buys herself an iPad and accessories worthy of her detecting skills," he finished.

The smile was back, brighter than ever. Josie caught a glimpse of the woman her daughter would soon be—tall, slender, with runway-worthy cheekbones, a determined chin, and a sprinkling of freckles future boyfriends would adore.

While they ate their pizza, Amelia described the iPad and its accessories in such detail Josie struggled to follow the technical jargon.

She rhapsodized over a "dual-core processor that makes the iPad faster for CPU functions" and bragged that her iPad would have cameras. "One camera will support 720p video capture."

Josie gathered that was good.

"Another camera is video chat ready," Amelia said, "and I'm getting a Smart Cover, so I won't need a viewing stand."

"Any apps?" Ted asked.

"A bunch, starting with GarageBand, Photo Booth, and iMovie," Amelia said.

She was finishing the last of the pizza when Ted said, "I don't want to rain on your celebration, but don't forget you can't mention anything about the mean girls if you want to keep your money and your iPad."

Josie smiled her thanks to her husband. She didn't want to deliver this Debbie Downer reminder.

"Zoe and her friends are so over," Amelia said. "Everybody at school knows what they did, anyway. No one will sit at their table at lunch. There's, like, this big poison zone around them. Emerson spilled chili on Zoe's shirt and said it was an accident, but it wasn't. I watched her.

"Emerson thought it was funny, but I told her, 'I don't like Zoe, Oakley, or Jace, and they're never going to like me. But we're as bad as they are if we start acting like them.'"

Josie stared at her daughter.

"What? Did I say something wrong?" Amelia said.

"You said everything right," Josie said, her voice

husky with tears. "Everything. I'm just trying to find some new and different way to say I'm proud of you."

"Then let's have another toast to the amazing Amelia Marcus," Ted said.

"Hear, hear!" Josie said.

They clinked plastic and drank. Then Amelia stood up and headed for the pink bathroom. "That john's broken," Josie said. "Harley got us again. You'll have to use the one upstairs. The plumber's coming tomorrow."

When Amelia was upstairs out of earshot, Josie asked, "How's Chris? Any word?"

"More bad news," Ted said. "The prosecution subpoenaed our office for the names and addresses of all our employees and interns past and present, since our partnership started."

"But Chris gets along with everyone," Josie said.

"Not everyone," Ted said. "She fired Dagmar, one of our interns, when she caught her hitting an old basset hound who got sick in his cage. Dagmar said the poor animal was nasty and smelly and should have been euthanized, except Americans cared more about dogs than people.

"Dagmar claimed she hit the dog because she was stressed, but Chris said she had no business being a veterinarian and taking it out on her patients. She got her kicked out of vet school and then her student visa was pulled. Dagmar was shipped back to Denmark and never forgave Chris."

"But can she do any damage in Scandinavia?" Josie asked.

"Kathy, our office manager, thinks so. Dagmar was here when Rain lived in Chris's house and the sisters were fighting. Chris asked Dagmar if she had any sisters. The intern said no, but she wished she did.

"'I've got one you can have,' Chris told her. 'In fact, you can take my younger sister back with you and keep her. I'll be happy if I never see her again.' Kathy heard her say it."

"Everyone says something like that," Josie said.

"That's what her lawyer, Renzo, will tell the jury," Ted said. "But now he has to use that lame argument twice—once for her damning e-mails and now this."

"Oh, come on," Josie said. "Is the prosecution going to chase down a witness in Denmark?"

"This is a major case, Josie, with tons of media attention. Nelson Philippi will go to the ends of the earth to win it."

Chapter 31

"But Chris gets along with everyone," Josie had told Ted last night.

This morning, she knew that wasn't true. Chris loved animals and cared about people. When she'd had to put down a cat dying of kidney failure, Chris had comforted the elderly owners as tenderly as a daughter. She'd taken the couple into her office, given them coffee and a shoulder to cry on.

Chris tried to educate people. When she talked a man out of cropping his Doberman's ears, she congratulated him with a free bag of dog food and celebrated her victory.

But Chris could be brutal to those who mistreated animals. She'd had a puppy owner prosecuted for cruelty when he beat his ten-pound golden retriever pup for piddling on the carpet. The judge had dismissed the case, but when Chris saw the man in a Home Depot parking lot, she threatened to beat him if he ever hurt another dog.

Josie paced her living room and sipped her third cup of coffee. She should be content after her hot night with Ted. She'd had an easy morning driving Amelia to school. But until Chris was free, she wouldn't have her family life back, and neither would Ted's partner.

Ted told me lots of stories about his partner's kindness—and her anger at animal abusers, Josie thought. And I saw her fury when a scruffy man brought a dying black Labrador to the clinic. I won't forget that sight for a long time: the dog on the exam table was so thin I could see his ribs. Wyatt, his owner, was a lowlife with a straggly goatee and a camo cap.

I was hurrying to Ted's office when Wyatt stared at me with those dead eyes. The clinic walls were so thin I could hear Chris in the exam room next door and the Lab's labored breathing.

"This poor dog is in the last stages of heartworm infestation, Wyatt," Chris said, her voice icy as an Arctic morn. "I can't save him. It's too late."

"What do you mean, you can't save Buster?" Wyatt drawled. "He's only six."

"Heartworm is preventable, if you'd given him his medication the way I told you. But you were too cheap."

"I'm going through hard times," Wyatt said.

"Hard times," Chris snorted. "Hard times at the poker table is more like it. If you'd brought Buster in earlier, he would have had a chance. Couldn't you see the signs? You must have noticed he couldn't exercise."

"So? Labs are bone lazy," Wyatt said.

"You're the lazy one," Chris said, her white-hot anger slashing through his lame excuses. "You didn't hear Buster's labored breathing? The constant coughing?"

"I thought it was kennel cough," Wyatt said.

"Then you should have had that treated!"

"You don't have to shout," Wyatt said.

"Yes, I do," Chris screeched. "It's the only way to get through to you."

"I brought him in when he quit eating," Wyatt whined. "Guess there's nothing left to do but take him home and put him out of his misery."

"You are not shooting this dog," Chris said, her voice

shaking with rage. "He will be euthanized humanely—by me. Your credit card is on file and if you dispute this charge I swear all your hunting buddies will know you're too stupid to give a good dog heartworm pills."

Wyatt wasn't the only client Chris had tongue-lashed, Josie thought. Ted told me how she'd raged at a mall princess who'd left her poodle locked in a hot car until it stroked out from heat exhaustion.

Ted's proud of his forthright partner, and I'm proud he supports her. She's cost the clinic clients, but as Ted says, "Only the clients we don't want anyway."

My husband is right. The clinic still has more business than it can handle, even after hiring Laura, the third vet. But there's no denying Chris left behind some hurt feelings. Once the prosecution finds that fired intern, it will start an avalanche of criticism. People will line up to testify against her.

And what will worrying get me, except an ulcer? Josie wondered. But she still felt restless and uneasy. She knew the answer was right in front of her. What wasn't she seeing?

Time to do something productive. Josie dusted the living room, then vacuumed it. Harry fled in terror from the noisy vacuum, convinced it was a cat-killing device. When she finished, the room smelled of lemon polish, but something was still off in her house.

She smiled when she saw the love-rumpled sheets in the bedroom. Nothing wrong here, she thought. Nothing at all. She carried last night's wineglasses and the empty bottle of red to the spotless kitchen, then stripped the sheets off the bed and dumped them in the dirty-clothes hamper in the hall closet.

That's when she smelled the problem. It was under her nose. Josie dropped the sheets on the floor. She dug into the hamper to sort a smelly mountain of dirty clothes, her mind racing.

Ted's underwear and a T-shirt went on top of the white sheets.

The prosecution has a staggering amount of evidence against Chris, she thought, tossing Ted's black socks into the darks pile.

Chris's bitter fight with her dead sister in the gazebo could have been hearsay. But Chris never denied she'd argued with Rain.

Ew. Josie picked up Amelia's wet purple washcloth. It was mildewed. She'd found the source of the stink. She tossed it into a pile of colors and went back to sorting and brooding.

The medical examiner found Chris's earring with the veterinary caduceus with Rain's body. That discovery was followed by the damning e-mails Chris wrote to her older sister, Susan, wishing Rain would go away forever.

What was this on Amelia's pink T-shirt? Grape jelly? How many times do I have to tell her to treat it with stain remover? Josie sighed, carried the shirt into the bathroom, and worked on it at the sink. I hope this isn't ruined, she thought.

Renzo, Chris's lawyer, might be able to explain away the sisters' argument and e-mails, even the lost earring. But the toxicology test that proved Rain was poisoned by acepromazine, a veterinary drug, would make his task tougher.

Add Chris's own lie that she hadn't argued about the illicit affair her hippie sister had had with Rodney, and Josie knew why Chris was pining in jail, her children left in the indifferent custody of their father.

I bet Chris would love to be working on grape jelly stains right now, she thought. I wonder if she'll ever be free.

Josie checked the purple stain. It wasn't quite so vivid now. She threw in the first load of laundry, sipped her cold coffee, then nuked it in the microwave. I know Chris is innocent, she thought. So who killed Rain?

Donny, the beer can collector? He could get veterinary drugs through his new girlfriend. The fatally handsome bartender has a violent temper. He made sure to tell me that he had an alibi for the time Rain was killed— even though I never asked him. I watched him turn on a harmless customer. If he reacted that way to someone who swiped free ketchup packets, how would he take being scorned by a lover?

And what was going on with his new girlfriend, Missy, and those pedigreed Bengals?

What about Harley, the curiously cool Coke collector? Another violent man, who showed no more emotion at the mention of Rain's death than he would a stranger's.

Josie found it hard to believe a collector who rhapsodized about a Lithuanian Coke can didn't seem upset by the loss of a rare ten-thousand-dollar calendar. He'd beaten his wife so badly she spent two months in the hospital and he went to prison. He could have gotten the fatal drug from his vet friend, Doc Clinton.

And what about Cordelia, the neighbor I like so much? She has a veterinary connection through her husband, the salesman. And a strong motive. Tenure's hard to get at universities now, especially for an overcrowded field like English.

At conservative City University, a radical past could be a career killer, even if the cause was just. Josie had read about college teachers whose careers were blighted because they'd helped Vietnam War protestors. The damage was hard to prove, but they were never promoted after they had aided the students. Did Cordelia decide Rain's silence was golden?

Josie's thoughts were as soggy as the freshly washed laundry. She threw in a load of colors, including the jelly-stained shirt. The answer is right here, she told herself. Right under my nose.

Just like that mildewed washcloth.

Chapter 32

Amelia's encounter with the mean girls has changed her, Josie decided, as she watched her daughter that afternoon at Barrington. Maybe it was her mother's pride, but Amelia seemed to glide over the green lawn. She definitely held her head higher and stood straighter.

Josie saw no trace of the hurting, hesitating girl who'd run to the car, pursued by jeering barks and mocking yips, nor could Josie take any credit for her daughter's transformation.

Amelia had healed herself. She and Emma had tracked down their tormentors. Thanks to Bailey's father, the BOB girls had gotten justice. They'd been well paid for their pain.

Maybe too well paid, Josie worried. Amelia made more for her few days of clever work than I made in five years of mystery-shopping. But that's why I sent her to a good school. So my girl can work smarter instead of harder.

She hoped Amelia wasn't lured by the easy glamour and big score of her first detecting adventure. But she'd been surprisingly levelheaded after her success. Jane had assured Josie that Amelia was still talking about becoming a vet, not a detective. And Amelia had avoided the temptation of petty revenge on Zoe and her friends.

My girl is definitely growing up, Josie thought. And she'll be a far better woman than me.

"Hi, Mom," Amelia said, and tossed her backpack into the rear seat. Josie tried to hide her surprise. This greeting was effusive by tween standards.

"Are we going to the new house? I can't wait to see the progress on the new kitchen. Is the stove connected yet?"

"Yes, we're heading to the house now," Josie said. "Jeanne called and said the stove was ready to be moved back in place. Maybe you can help us."

"Okay, then I want to run next door and play with Jack Dandy," Amelia said. "He's so much fun. He needs some playtime. Betty's getting him ready for a major show this weekend in Chicago."

"Chicago is the big time," Josie said. "Is he ready for that?"

"Betty says he's already won top honors at the local shows in Gray Summit, Missouri. He's been Top Puppy once, Winner's Dog twice, and Best of Breed once. He was even Best in Group, which is better than Best in Breed, though it wasn't a very big group. She says it's time to take him to the next level."

"But if it's too early—" Josie began.

Amelia steamrollered right over her mother's objection. "Betty says these shows are good for the dogs. Betty says it's like when Ted goes to a veterinarians' convention. It's good to socialize with your own kind."

Josie tried to block a mental picture of show dogs in a hotel bar—or worse, a pack of vets sniffing one another.

"Doesn't Betty belong to some kind of Jack Russell terrier club?" Josie asked.

"No," Amelia said. "There's the JRT Club of America, but it doesn't belong to the AKC. It refused. It got very political and the group split. Betty shows her dog at AKC shows as a Parson Russell terrier—they have longer legs. People who don't know any better call both Parson Russell and Russell terriers Jack Russells. Betty thinks the AKC is the best way to show her dog and he's going to win Best in Show at Westminster because he's the best of the best."

Josie was uneasy with her daughter parroting Betty's opinions. She'd have to ask Ted to give Amelia a more balanced view of show dogs.

"Betty says he's definitely ready for the next step," Amelia said.

"I hope so. Chicago is a long drive," Josie said.

"They're going to fly. Betty doesn't want him stressed-out for the big show. She just gives him a pill in a treat and he goes right to sleep," Amelia said. "Eating treats is part of his show dog training. Once he hears that clicker, he knows he'll get something good."

Amelia spent the rest of the trip prattling about Jack Dandy. At last, they were at the new house. Fresno Court was littered with working vehicles. Josie saw pickups belonging to Bud Vey's construction crew and Jeanne the kitchen contractor. Parked next to them was a blue van with a pipe wrench gripping the words DECKER'S PLUMBING.

"Good," Josie said. "We need that plumbing done." She and Amelia waved to Bud and briefly admired the progress on the deck.

In the kitchen, Jeanne was trying to push the new stove back next to the cabinet. "Is it safe to use?" Josie asked, and cut her eyes toward Amelia.

Jeanne heard her coded question. "I cleaned it for you," she said. "It's all set."

The contractor pushed on the stove until her arms bulged and her face turned almost as red as her hair, but the stove sat there like a cube of lead.

"Let me help," Josie said.

"Me, too," Amelia said.

With three people pushing the stove, it budged slightly. Josie heard the tromp of heavy feet coming down the stairs and a squat man with a dyed black Elvis pompadour stood in the kitchen door. He had a gray toolbox in one hand and a massive pipe wrench in the other.

"Hi, Deck," Jeanne said. "Josie, meet Decker Goldrich, plumber extraordinaire."

Deck took a mock bow and said, "The dishwasher is hooked up, the sink is fixed, and so's the toilet. I checked all the upstairs plumbing. Anything else you want?"

"Yeah," Jeanne said. "Your body. I need you to help shove this stove back in there."

"Looks heavy," Deck said.

"Come on," Jeanne said. "One more shove and we can get that stove in place."

"I'm a plumber, not a heavy hauler."

"Don't be a whiner, Deck," Jeanne said. "You've got three strong women helping you. A little more muscle and we'll have it in the slot."

"Amelia, stand back, please," Josie said. "We need Deck's muscle."

Deck reluctantly set down his toolbox and three-foot-long wrench and put his back into moving the stove. Now they made progress, but they still couldn't get it to fit snugly into its slot.

Josie looked around the stove's edge. "There's something blocking it," she said. "Looks like a piece of wood stuck behind that cabinet Newt didn't take out."

"Pull the stove back out so Josie can get behind there," Jeanne said. "She's the smallest."

"I can get it," Amelia said. "I'm even smaller."

They horsed the stove out about six inches and Amelia slid through and picked up a piece of pale brown wood.

"Is that molding?" Josie asked.

"No, it's an iPhone in an eco-friendly bamboo case," Amelia said. "I bet it's Rain's."

"The police never found her phone," Josie said.

Amelia powered up the phone. "It's got photos," she said. "Photos of Jack Dandy as a baby pup." She touched the screen. "There he is with one ear up and one down. Here he's older and the ear is bandaged."

"What?" Josie said. "Which ear?"

"The up one—Betty calls it the bad ear. He looks so sad. I bet he's hurting. Now look at this photo. The bandages are off and the ear is perfect."

"It's a cute dog," Deck said, "but can we move the stove back? I gotta leave."

"But you don't understand," Amelia said. "Betty had Jack Dandy's ear fixed. She can't enter him in the dog shows. It's illegal."

Now everything was falling into place for Josie.

Rain had the proof, she thought. That's why she was killed. She threatened to blow the whistle on Betty and ruin her chances to win at Westminster.

"Ladies, much as I love standing here with you," the plumber said, "I have to hit the highway."

"Sorry, Deck," Josie said. "Thank you, Amelia. As soon as we get this stove in place, I'll take this to the police." She took the iPhone from her daughter and dropped it in her purse.

"I'd give it to Chris's lawyer," Jeanne said. "From everything I've heard, that Detective Stevenski won't like knowing she screwed up a major case."

"You're right," Josie said.

"Ladies, I'm begging you," Deck said. "Can we put this freaking stove back so I can leave?"

It took maybe five minutes of concentrated pushing and shoving, greased with sweat and light swearing, before the stove was in place.

"Finally," Josie said.

"Took the word right out of my mouth," Deck said. "Now can I go?"

"With my blessing," Jeanne said. "Thank you."

"Double thanks," Josie said, leaning against the stove to catch her breath. "Amelia, we can finally turn on your stove. Amelia?"

Josie turned away from the stove. Deck was washing his hands at the sink, but there was no sign of Amelia.

That's when Josie heard barks and screams from next door. "Help! Help me! Mom! *Help!*"

"Amelia!" Josie shouted. "I'm on my way! Hold on, baby!"

Chapter 33

"Mom, help! Help me!"

Josie heard her daughter's screams, grabbed the plumber's twenty-pound pipe wrench, and sprinted out her front door.

"Hey!" Deck yelled.

"Call nine-one-one!" Josie shouted over her shoulder.

She ran across her yard and up Betty's front steps. She tried to open her neighbor's massive maple door, but it was locked. The thick dark wood and black wrought-iron hinges mocked her efforts.

"Amelia!" she called. "I'm here. Help is on the way!"

"Mom!" Amelia shrieked. "Mom, she's hurting me! Help me!"

Josie felt new strength course through her arms. She walloped the wide door with the wrench. It bounced harmlessly off the wood, leaving an ugly dent.

"Mom!" Amelia screamed.

"Shut up, you stupid brat," Betty snarled. "You ruined my life."

Josie heard a crash. Something heavy, maybe glass, followed by frantic barks.

"You lied!" Amelia said. "You said you've never hurt Jack."

Thud! Crack! The noise seemed to be coming from the back of the house.

"I didn't," Betty said. "I love him. He's my life. He's my baby!"

"You crushed his ear."

Crash! Josie heard light footsteps, followed by heavier ones.

"I didn't touch him," Betty screamed. "The vet made a little change and you made a big deal out of it. Just like that hippie."

Thud!

Josie gave up trying to beat in the massive door. She eyed the big living room window next to it and slammed it with the pipe wrench. The glass shattered, cascading inside the house. She hit the remaining glass with the wrench until only jagged shards spiked up from the frame.

Betty and Amelia didn't seem to hear the breaking glass or Josie's shouts that she would save Amelia. Maybe that was good, Josie thought.

"Jack is perfect," Betty howled. "Perfect! Nobody would have known."

"It was wrong!" Amelia shouted. "They'd find out when Jack sired puppies."

"You're just like that hippie girl. She wouldn't shut up, either," Betty said. "I begged her, but she wouldn't listen. So I shut her up. Permanently."

Clunk! Thud! Thump, thump, rumble!

"You killed Rain!" Amelia said. The terror in her trembling voice spurred Josie to work faster. She reached through the broken window, and a glass icicle sliced her arm. Josie ignored the pain, grabbed a heavy blue living room curtain, and yanked on it with bloody hands.

She heard a shower of plaster fall and the clang of the heavy brass curtain rod as it toppled a lamp. Josie pulled the curtain out through the window with blood-stained hands, quickly draped it over the frame, and crawled through, hauling the monster pipe wrench along with her. She felt a glass spike reach down, rip her shirt, and tear the skin underneath it.

But she was in the living room now, dripping blood on the pale blue carpet, her senses hyperalert. Betty's home had the same floor plan as Josie's. She scanned the living room and saw the overturned table at the entrance.

The coffee table was knocked sideways and a cut-glass candy dish lay cracked on the carpet. An oil painting had fallen off the wall, the gold frame chipped.

"Give me that phone!" Betty shrieked at Amelia.

Phone? Rain's iPhone with the damning evidence. *Amelia must have sneaked it out of my purse,* Josie thought, *and showed it to Betty. That's what triggered this. Where's my daughter?*

The trail of destruction led into the kitchen, but Josie didn't see anyone in there.

"Unlock this door!" Betty commanded. She rattled the handle.

Upstairs! Josie thought. *That's where she is. Amelia ran up the stairs and locked herself in a room or a closet, and Betty followed. Now my girl's trapped.*

Thud! Thud! Thud!

Josie heard what sounded like Betty beating on a wooden door, followed by softer thuds and growls. Was that Jack Dandy throwing himself at the door?

She raced up the waxed stairs, struggling to grip the blood-slippery pipe wrench.

"You can't escape, Amelia," Betty said. "You're trapped."

Two steps. Four steps. Six. Josie was at the landing now. She heard a *screak!*

"You can't jump out the window," Betty said, her voice soft with menace. "It's too high up."

"My mom is coming and she'll get you," Amelia shouted.

I'm here, baby, Josie wanted to say. But she thought silence would give her much-needed cover.

"Yeah, right," Betty sneered. "Your mother the starry-eyed bride is so wrapped up with her new husband she won't even notice you're gone."

"She loves me," Amelia said. "So does Ted."

"But they'll love their own kid more," Betty said.

A red mist swam across Josie's vision. How dare this woman say that? She charged up the last few steps.

"Make it easy on yourself, Amelia. Give me that phone," Betty said.

"And then what?" Amelia asked.

That's right, Josie thought. Keep her talking, baby girl. Distract her until I can save you.

"You can go to Chicago with Jack Dandy and me. You can see the big dog show."

"I don't want to see it," Amelia said. "I don't ever want to see you again. I hope they take Jack away from you."

Thud.

Thud.

Thud.

Each blow was heavy enough to shake the house. That didn't sound like a body hitting a door. That was wood on wood.

Josie was upstairs now in the narrow hall. She couldn't see Amelia or Betty, but she heard them. They were in the smallest bedroom, the one Amelia had chosen for her own room in their house.

Josie roared around the corner and saw Betty hitting the bathroom door with a heavy wooden chair. The back cracked as she slammed it against the solid maple. Jack Dandy barked and howled and threw himself against the bottom panel.

"Stop it," Josie said. "Right now!"

Betty turned, and burned Josie with a crazy-eyed glare. "You!" she shouted. "You're the one I should kill."

Josie didn't say anything. She swung the pipe wrench like a major-league batter. It connected with a satisfying crack.

Betty screamed. "My arm! You broke my arm."

Her arm is dangling at an odd angle, Josie thought. She can't hurt my girl anymore.

"I've just started," Josie said, and started to swing the huge wrench at Betty's head. But a callused hand stopped her.

"No, Josie," a rumbly voice said. She saw Deck's black Elvis pompadour and tattooed arms.

"Don't turn my favorite wrench into a murder weapon. She can't hurt anyone now."

There was a deafening silence, broken by the sound of Betty weeping, then police sirens.

Jack Dandy, the future Westminster Best in Show dog, howled with them.

Chapter 34

"Mom, Mom, you're here. You're okay."

Amelia's tween cool was gone. She smothered Josie with kisses and hugged her so hard Josie cried, "Ouch!"

A dazed Josie sat on Betty's guest room bed, dripping dime-sized spots of blood on the blue ruffled spread. She hardly noticed the stinging pain from the slashing cuts. She felt lighthearted, light-headed, and most of all, relieved.

She'd found Rain's killer. She had her family life back. Chris would go free and Ted would come home on time.

At Josie's cry of pain, Amelia stopped hugging her and finally noticed her mother's injuries.

"You're hurt," she said, her voice soft with concern.

"No, I'm not," Josie said.

"You're bleeding," Amelia said, as if Josie were the stubborn tween. "You've got a bad cut on your back and another one down your arm."

"Just a scratch," Josie said, then realized that sounded like a line from a corny Western. "I had to break a window to get in here."

"Amelia's right. You don't look good," Jeanne said.

Josie finally noticed that the sturdy red-haired kitchen contractor was standing next to the bed, with Deck at her side. The plumber's mile-high pompadour was tilted like a collapsing cake. His blue tattoos looked out of place in Betty's prim flowered paradise.

"I agree with Jeanne," Deck said. "Look in the dresser mirror. You're green around the gills."

"'White as a ghost' is more like it," Jeanne said. "Where the hell is that ambulance?"

"It's coming, ma'am," the uniformed officer said.

Josie recognized his voice—Officer Dimon, the Rock Road Village policeman who Detective Stevenski had condemned to walk endlessly up and down the stairs while her family waited to be questioned.

He still looked tired from hauling around that bass drum belly, but he'd been kind. He'd escorted Josie, Ted, and Amelia to the car and held off the hordes of reporters so they could escape the media.

Josie looked around the tiny bedroom, but saw no sign of Detective Stevenski. She did catch a glimpse of herself in the mirror of the blue-flowered vanity and shuddered. Her brown hair stood up like Josie had stuck her finger in a light socket, her skin was flour white, and her bloodshot eyes nearly drowned in the dark pools around them.

I look like I've escaped from a low-budget horror flick, she thought. Why does my shirt feel so stiff? It's stuck to my skin.

Josie turned slightly and caught a gruesome glimpse: Dried blood had glued her ripped shirt to her back. She looked away and saw more blood oozing from the deep cut in her arm.

"I'm fine," Josie said, though her words wobbled. "Really."

She was. Better than fine. Josie felt euphoric. She had her lovable little girl back, at least for a bit. Amelia, who'd rather kiss a frog than her mother, was once again her sweet daughter.

I know it won't last, she thought, but I'll enjoy the respite, or relapse, or whatever it is.

She'd seen Betty being led away in handcuffs, protesting her innocence. Then an officer with a pink choirboy face tried to question Josie, but tough little Jeanne Rolwing stepped in and declared that she was representing her until Josie's lawyer arrived.

"She doesn't need a lawyer, ma'am, if she's innocent," Officer Choirboy said.

"Miss Marcus is in no condition to speak right now," Jeanne said. "Can't you see she's going to pass out? You can interview her at the hospital."

Josie told her that Renzo's phone number was on her cell phone and Jeanne called him, never letting Josie out of her sight.

Amelia, under the watchful eyes of Jeanne, Deck, and her woozy mother, told the police that Betty had tried to kill her when she showed her the photos of Jack Dandy's bandaged ear.

"It's all my fault," Amelia said, and Josie's heart lifted. Her daughter really did seem contrite.

"I didn't believe Betty would hurt her dog," Amelia said. "She was my friend. I knew Betty wouldn't get a cruel operation on Jack Dandy's ear. But she did. She had it crushed."

"Who's Jack Dandy?" Officer Choirboy looked confused.

"Betty's show dog," Jeanne said. "She wanted to enter it in the big Westminster dog show. You can hear it barking now."

"It's in the basement until Animal Control takes it," Officer Dimon said.

"Continue your story, young lady," Officer Choirboy said. "You said you didn't believe Mrs. Goffman would have the dog's ear operated on."

"It's just so mean," Amelia said. "Betty always said Jack was perfect and the ear fixed itself. I wanted to ask her. So I sneaked Rain's iPhone—she's the dead lady who was buried in our yard—I sneaked her phone out of Mom's purse and went next door to show Betty the photos. I thought she'd say Mom was wrong, but she went postal on my ass."

"Amelia!" Josie was alert enough to remind her daughter to watch her language.

"Sorry, Mom," Amelia said. "Betty went ballistic. She tried to tear the iPhone out of my hands and strangle me with Jack's leash, the one she keeps hanging by the front door, but I knocked over that little table trying to get away from her. Then I fell over the coffee table and she, like, flipped out and tried to smash my head in with the candy dish."

Josie felt sick as she listened. Amelia had come so close to dying.

"I rolled out of the way and she pulled that ugly painting off the wall and tried to hit me with it. Jack Dandy tripped her—"

"On purpose?" Deck asked.

"No," Amelia said. "I think he was confused, too. But I got away and ran into the kitchen and threw stuff at her—the blender, Jack Dandy's dog cookie jar, a big platter—but she kept coming after me. I skidded on a lot of broken sh—"

She looked at her mother and said, "Uh, stuff on the floor and ran up the stairs. Poor Jack was going crazy, barking and trying to bite me."

"He didn't hurt you, did he?" Josie interrupted.

"Not even a nip," Amelia said. "We're still friends. I think.

"I kept screaming for Mom. Betty said she killed Rain because Rain was going to tell and ruin her chances to enter Jack in a majorly big dog show and now she was going to kill me because I didn't shut up. I kept running and screaming."

Amelia flashed her mother a dazzling smile. "I can't

believe you heard me, Mom. I was afraid you couldn't be-cause of the construction, but I yelled as loud as I could."

"Of course Josie heard you," Deck said. "She's got mom ears. A true mom can hear her kid's hiccup six rooms away."

There goes the baby monitor business, Josie thought. Her dazed brain was still wildly scattered.

Deck somehow took over Amelia's interview, and Of-ficer Choirboy let him.

"I couldn't hear you over the hammering and power saws," Deck said, "but little Josie here grabbed my pipe wrench and took off like a bat out of hell. A twenty-pound pipe wrench, and she picked it up like a tooth-pick! I've read how a mother can lift a car to save her baby, but I didn't believe it till I saw Josie in action."

"I'm no baby," Amelia said.

"But you needed saving," Deck said. "If you'd hadda depend on me, you woulda been dead. But there's noth-ing stronger than an angry mom on a mission. Hell, I thought she'd tip the house over and shake it to get you out of there.

"I called the cops like she told me to, then hotfooted it over here with Jeanne, who was still confused about what was going on."

"I was not!" The kitchen contractor was indignant. "I figured it out as soon as I saw those photos of Betty's dog with the bad ear. I was trying to round up Bud's crew for backup, but they'd already packed up and left for the day. Nothing moves faster than a crew at quitting time." She glared at Deck.

"Hey, I stayed, didn't I?" he said. "Give me some credit. I lost time crawling through the broken front win-dow. I'm a little bigger than Josie"—he patted his flabby midsection—"and I had to move careful-like. I was afraid that broken glass would hit an artery. You were smart to put that curtain down over the window frame, Josie.

"At least I got here in time to stop you from bashing Betty's head in with my favorite wrench. You would have killed her for sure if I hadn't stopped you."

"Good," Jeanne said.

"Nope," Deck said. "A nice lady like Josie woulda felt bad if she'd killed Betty, even if she deserved it."

Would I? Josie wondered. If Betty had hurt Amelia, I would have smashed her skull without a second thought.

But Josie was calm enough now to wonder if that was the adrenaline talking. Amelia had been hurt. A rapidly purpling bruise was coming out on her leg. As she studied that injury, hot fury shot through Josie. She wanted to strangle Betty with her bare hands. She grabbed the bedspread and held on, while the room spun.

"Whoa there," Jeanne said. "You're not passing out on us, are you? And don't give me that bull about feeling fine."

"Just a little muzzy," Josie said. Amelia was holding her hand and petting it.

"Amelia's a bit banged up," Deck said. "But she's okay. She'll heal. But you can't come back from the dead. I say let Betty rot in prison. I'm glad I saved Josie."

"And Mom saved me," Amelia said, giving Josie a careful kiss on her forehead.

A second siren tore through the late afternoon. Jeanne looked out the window.

"The paramedics are here," she said. "It's about time. You look lousy, Josie."

"I do feel dizzy," Josie said.

"Up here," Jeanne called to the paramedics.

Josie heard the clatter of the portable stretcher on Betty's polished stairs. Suddenly the small room was crowded with four paramedics. The smallest was six feet tall and they all had necks like tree trunks. They quickly strapped Josie onto the stretcher.

"Where are you taking her?" Jeanne asked.

"Holy Redeemer in Rock Road Village," said the red-wood-sized paramedic.

"Tell Ted," Josie said.

"He's on his way now," Jeanne said. "I told Renzo to call him. Looks like your lawyer's pulling up now. I don't trust the Rock Road Village cops with those photos."

"Officer Dimon is a good man," Josie said, and flashed him a weak smile. "I bet he won't cry any tears if Detective Stevenski gets in trouble for Chris's false arrest."

"You're a perceptive woman, Ms. Marcus," Dimon said. "But the photos are part of a police investigation now."

"That's okay," Amelia said. "I sent copies to my e-mail account, just in case."

In case your mother was right? Josie wondered, but kept silent. She was glad she did.

"I was wrong, Mom," Amelia said.

Such sweet words, Josie thought. And so unexpected.

"You're good with computers," Josie said. "But people are more unpredictable."

"And dangerous," Amelia said. She gave her mother's bloody hand one last squeeze before the paramedics took Josie away.

Epilogue

August 2013

"Harry! Get your paw out of that paint! Amelia Marcus, remove that cat!" Josie commanded.

She was painting over a scuff mark left by the movers in her new retro kitchen when Amelia's cat decided to take a dip. The striped tabby stuck his front paw in the can of Mexicali Turquoise and watched it drip on the floor.

Josie swooped over and collected the cat. He tried to escape and left aqua streaks on her paint clothes.

"A good thing this is washable latex," she said.

Josie gripped the cat tightly and held his paw under the kitchen tap while he squirmed away from the water.

"You're lucky I don't give you a full-body bath," Josie told him. She wrapped the indignant feline in a towel and handed him to Amelia.

"Keep him in your room until after the barbecue tonight," she said.

"Can't he come out and play with the guests?" Amelia said. "He'll be good. He's just excited by the new house."

"After he has some time out, we'll see," Josie said. "Hurry up and change. The housewarming party starts in less than an hour."

Josie surveyed her kitchen with contentment. She was glad she'd gone with Amelia's idea for midcentury modern. The cheery aqua and white colors made it seem like a tropical holiday. Alyce's window shades had survived the renovation and let in just the right amount of light.

Josie thought the stove was overcomplicated, but she'd learned to boil water on it. Amelia and Ted treated it like a magic machine. They spent hours discussing its wonders until Josie's eyes glazed. Personally she'd rather have a hot car than a hot stove, but she'd never tell them that. Besides, the meals were even better with two freshly inspired cooks.

Ted was sweating at the stove now. He'd just checked his special-recipe baked beans in the oven.

"How much longer?" Josie asked.

"Another ten minutes," Ted said. "The potato salad and coleslaw are ready and the pork steaks are marinating on top the fridge, out of reach of the animals."

"Did you use Maull's Barbecue Sauce?" Josie asked.

"I couldn't use anything else in the pork steak capital of America," Ted said, and grinned. "I've doctored it with brown sugar, onions, mustard, and a splash of beer."

"For you or the pork steaks?" Josie asked.

"Both," he said, and kissed her.

"Let's continue that later," she said. Once Chris was free, so was Ted. The honeymoon was back on, and Josie was a contented bride.

"Mm," she said. "I'm so glad you're back."

"Me, too," Ted said. "Business is booming. Laura's turned out to be a good addition."

"And Christine has custody of her kids," Josie said. "How are Todd, Brook, and Cam doing?"

"You can see for yourself this evening," Ted said. "They'll be here. Chris is bringing a green salad."

"Do you think we'll have enough food for everyone?" Josie asked.

"With your mother's pineapple upside-down cake and Amelia's cookies, we'll be able to feed an army," Ted said.

Josie reluctantly slid out of his arms. "I'd better get ready," she said. "They'll be here soon."

Josie showered and slipped into her white clam diggers, new sandals, and a fresh turquoise blouse. She was brushing her hair and Ted was making margaritas in the blender when the house erupted into happy chaos. Chris arrived first with the twins and Todd, followed by Jane. Ted got everyone drinks and Josie led the house tour.

An hour later, they were feasting on the new deck.

"We planned this right," Josie said. "The deck's big enough to hold all our friends."

"And then some," Ted said.

It was dusk by the time the table was cleared. The twins chased Festus around the backyard while Amelia showed Todd the wonders of her new iPad in the rec room downstairs. Harry, released from his prison in Amelia's room, guarded his mistress.

Marmalade, the clinic cat, settled in on Chris's lap for a long ear scratch. Ted poured another round of margaritas while the lightning bugs winked.

"This has turned out better than I expected," Chris said.

Josie wasn't sure exactly what Chris meant—their new house, her release from jail, her return to the clinic—but she agreed.

"How are the kids after your ordeal?" Josie asked.

"They're happy to be home and away from their father," she said. "You know I have full custody now, don't you?"

"No," Josie said. "When did that happen?"

"Shortly before I was released, Rodney fell for a dancer named Bambi. Three kids cramped his style."

"Let me guess. Bambi didn't wear a lot of clothes when she danced," Josie said.

"Not by the end of the dance," Chris said. "She works at what Rodney called a gentlemen's club."

"Which doesn't have any gentlemen," Josie said.

"Well, Rodney is no gentleman—that's for sure. Once I was free, he decided I was a fit mother again. My lawyer got him to sign away his parental rights. He gave them up without a fight."

"He must have been madly in love," Josie said.

"Lust is more like it," Chris said, and lowered her voice. "The kids don't know it, but I gave him a thousand-dollar signing bonus. I also told him he could see them anytime he wanted. So far, he's been too busy."

"That's so sad," Josie said. "They're great kids. How did they take it?"

"Surprisingly well," Chris said. "They were happy to get back to their old routine and see their friends again. Todd was sick of sleeping on his father's sofa. I just wish I could have picked a better father for them."

She took a long drink of her margarita. Even in the failing light, Josie could see the pain in her eyes.

"They're lucky they have one good, responsible parent," Jane said. "So many children don't."

She reached over and patted Chris's hand. "Don't you worry. I raised Josie on my own and look how well she turned out."

Josie held her breath. She wasn't sure she should be the poster child for good parenting.

Jane kept talking. "You've made the right decision, Chris. Your children are safe from any legal hassle now."

"Did Renzo file suit against Rock Road Village for false arrest?" Ted asked.

"He waited until Rodney signed the custody papers," Chris said. "My ex can smell money. Then Renzo filed suit."

A gleeful scream, followed by giggles, split the warm late August evening. "It's getting on toward nine o'clock," Chris said. "I'd better take the kids home. They're getting overtired."

Ted and Josie sent Chris and her family home with enough leftovers for tomorrow's dinner, and lots of hugs.

After they'd walked the family to Chris's car, Josie caught Amelia yawning.

"Time for bed," Josie said. "Give your grandma a good-night kiss."

Amelia protested just enough to maintain her independence, but Josie could tell she really was sleepy. She hoisted Harry on her shoulder, gathered up her precious iPad, and went upstairs to her purple room.

"I don't know much about computers," Jane said. "But that one looks expensive."

"Amelia bought it herself," Josie said. "Ted insisted that she get a bonus for solving the BOB mystery."

"Ted was right," Jane said. Her son-in-law could do no wrong in Jane's eyes.

"Wish you could have been at the check presentation ceremony in Dev's office," Ted said. "But only Josie, me, and Emma's parents could attend, along with the girls. No one else knew their role in bringing down the mean girls."

"Amelia got herself the iPad of her dreams, plus some wicked accessories."

"She also insisted on buying a blue wisteria vine for the backyard fence," Josie said. "She told us that blue wisteria is really purple and you can't have too many purple flowers."

"How's she been since Betty's arrest?" Jane asked.

"She's quit talking about show dogs all the time," Josie said. "That's one blessing. I thought she'd miss playing with Jack Dandy, but she has enough pets to keep her busy. I just hope she never investigates another mystery on her own. She scared me half to death."

"Now you know what it feels like," Jane said smugly.

Then she hugged Josie. "What I told Christine was true. I'm lucky to have such a good daughter. And you have a good daughter, too. It's a Marcus tradition. Don't you forget that, Josie."

Jane hesitated a moment, then said, "Frank has asked me out to dinner. Do you think that's a good idea, Josie?"

"I think it's a splendid idea, Mom. He's perfect for you."

"You don't know that, Josie Marcus. Don't go marrying us off yet. We haven't even had one date."

"Now you know what it feels like," Josie said, and kissed her mother good night.

Betty Goffman was charged with felony murder and attempted murder of a minor. Both were death-penalty offenses. Her lawyer plea-bargained her offenses down to life without possibility of parole. Josie was relieved Amelia wouldn't have to testify in court. Betty put her house up for sale to pay for her legal fees.

The news stories about Betty's dramatic capture and arrest gave Amelia cachet at school, and the mean girls' harsh words were forgotten.

A veterinarian examined Jack Dandy and Betty's two other dogs. The vet said he could feel the ridge of scar tissue in Jack's altered ear and that a careful show judge would have found it. Jack Dandy never could have been a Westminster champion. Josie hoped Chris didn't see that interview on TV. It seemed to underline Rain's pointless death.

All three dogs were declared healthy and adopted.

Jack Dandy, the former future Westminster best in show, became a pet for a family with three active little boys. Jack spends his days running, jumping, playing, and eating lots of treats. Ted became the family's veterinarian. He sees Jack at least once a year. Amelia was relieved to know that Jack was happy in his new home.

The City of Rock Road Village settled out of court with Christine for an undisclosed amount. She told Ted it was enough to pay off her share of the clinic loans, though she still has Renzo's substantial legal bill.

Detective Stevenski was downsized from the Rock Road Village force after the settlement, shortly before Officer Dimon's retirement to Florida.

Josie sent a plate of Amelia's cookies, along with a contrite note to Cordelia, asking if she could explain why she'd been searching Wil's office. Her neighbor agreed to come over to Josie's for coffee.

"You thought I killed Rain?" Cordelia said. "Because of who I am?" She stood up to leave, magnificent in her outrage.

"A college professor?" Josie said. "No, I suspected everyone—both boyfriends and both neighbors. I don't want you to be my enemy. Maybe we can't ever be friends, but I'd like us to at least tolerate each other."

"I'll think about it," Cordelia said, and swept out of Josie's house.

For the next few months, she gave Josie indifferent waves when she saw her in the yard, but that was better than outright hostility. It took most of the fall until Cordelia thawed toward Josie. She now stops by about once a week for coffee or lunch.

Dr. Arnold Spengler, Missy, and Donny Freedman were arrested for multiple counts of grand larceny, fraud, and federal wire fraud for selling counterfeit Bengal cats. "Wire fraud" included any television, radio, telephone, or computer modem. When Missy and Donny expanded the cat business to Illinois, they crossed state lines and the fraudsters committed a federal crime.

Dr. Spengler had "prepped" more than forty ordinary tabby cats to be pedigreed Bengals.

He was sentenced to ten years in a federal prison and ordered to make restitution to his fraud victims. His considerable fortune disappeared down a black hole of lawsuits and legal bills. He also lost his veterinary license.

Donny received four years in federal prison for his part. He was forced to sell his Mustang and his beer can collection to pay his lawyer.

Missy testified against Dr. Spengler and Donny Freedman and received a year's supervised probation. She, too, was ordered to make restitution. Missy sold her house and her car. She now works as a show dog groomer.

Peg recovered thirteen hundred dollars of the fifteen hundred she'd spent to buy her fake Bengal, Rajah. "Hell, I don't have any fancy pedigree, either," she said. "That cat's given me more than two hundred dollars in enjoyment."

Like all the other owners of the counterfeit Bengals, she decided to keep her cat. "His papers are fake, but he's a real good cat," she said.

On their wedding anniversary in November, Ted and Josie dined at Acero, an intimate Italian restaurant in Maplewood. After dinner, it was warm enough to have champagne on their deck. They sat by the fire pit and held hands. The reflected flames danced merrily in their champagne glasses.

"It hasn't been a year since we moved in, but we have been married a year," Ted said. "What do you think? Do you still want to stay here?"

"Absolutely," Josie said. "The gazebo is gone, and so is our neighbor with the yappy dogs. Amelia is right. This is a fairy-tale place.

"Once upon a time there was a handsome prince," she recited.

"Who searched the whole world for the perfect bride," Ted said. "Little did he know she was practically next door. But he found her and married her."

"I like that story," Josie said, snuggling closer. "Then what?"

"They lived happily ever after," Ted said, and kissed her.

Shopping Tips

Tuna-noodle casserole, frozen peas swimming in butter, Jell-O with Reddi-Wip. That food was made in midcentury kitchens, along with lots of red meat. Brown meat, actually. Meat was cooked until it fell off the bone back then, and pasta—excuse me—spaghetti was boiled until you could gum it. *Al Dente* was that nice Italian man down the street, not a cooking instruction.

Foodies may turn up their noses at pillowy Wonder Bread and meat loaf in tomato soup sauce, but many Americans find that food deep down satisfying. Good memories were made in those midcentury kitchens.

Retro kitchens are the hottest thing this side of a pre-heated oven. Blame it on *Mad Men* madness, a new-found appreciation of the midcentury's sleek, clean lines, or all the couples buying midcentury homes. Whatever the reason, midcentury design is getting a fresh look.

These shopping tips will help you go back in time and create your dream kitchen.

Josie's Kitchen Inspiration

The kitchen on the cover of *Fixing to Die* is inspired by a real kitchen renovated by Carrie Welch, in Metamora, Michigan. Her astute planning, crafty bargain hunting, a bit of luck, and a lot of hard work by Carrie and her family created a classic retro kitchen for less than six thousand dollars. You read that right: less than six grand.

Carrie blogged about her kitchen saga at Retro Renovation. Her retro kitchen project took nine months. You can read her story and see the photos that Josie's kitchen is based on here:

http://retrorenovation.com/2011/02/13/create-a-fabulous-retro-kitchen-and-breakfast-room-for-less-than-6000-carrie-did-it/

Retro Renovation Queen

Carrie credits Pam Kueber and her Retro Renovation Web site for helping her create that fabulous kitchen. Retro Renovation is devoted to "remodeling, decor and home improvement for old homes." http://retrorenovation.com

If you're renovating a midcentury home, Retro Renovation says, "We help you remodel and decorate your midcentury home in retro style." The site has useful tips about midcentury kitchen makeovers, bathroom renovation, living rooms, patios, and more. Want to know where to find midcentury tiles? Where to buy midcentury patio furniture? Pam Kueber has written about that and more.

Better yet, no one connected with Retro Renovation sneers, "I tore that old junk out years ago." Retro Renovation is your introduction to "a like-minded community passionate about their old houses." Follow Pam on Facebook at https://www.facebook.com/RetroRenovation?ref=hl

Repair, Restore, Remodel

Greg Wiley publishes *R3 Saint Louis* magazine—Repair, Restore, Remodel. The magazine's Web site—http://www.r3stl.com/—has a library of how-to articles, plus a contractors' list to help readers find reputable St. Louis–area contractors. I recommend *R3 Saint Louis* magazine if you're renovating a home, no matter where you live.

Not Everything from the Good Old Days Is Good

Don't get a "Max Factor" rehab—a pretty surface covering up major problems with plumbing, wiring, and lead-based paint. Renovate safely. Old homes may have asbestos, lead-based paint and other potentially dangerous issues. Be careful if you remove that old paint, wiring or plumbing. If you hire a contractor, make sure that person follows the rules. Check out the EPA regulations on asbestos: http://www2.epa.gov/asbestos.

Get the Lead Out

If your home was built before 1978, it probably has lead-based paint, a danger to you and your children. http://www2.epa.gov/lea.

Greg Wiley, publisher of *R3 Saint Louis*, said, "Forbidden methods of lead paint removal include open-flame burning or torching, machine sanding without a HEPA attachment, abrasive blasting, and power washing without a means to trap water and paint chips.

"A variety of approaches are used to remove lead-based paints, such as wire brushing or wet hand scraping with liquid paint removers. Your contractor may opt to wet-sand surfaces, and must use an electric sander equipped with a high-efficiency particulate air (HEPA) filtered vacuum. Another option is stripping off paint with a low-temperature heat gun and hand scraping."

You may also have to replace the lead-pipe plumbing with safer materials.

Hot Wired

A rehabber friend bought a three-story Victorian home. When he remodeled it, he discovered the third floor had no electrical outlets. The previous owner had been running a fan, a television, and a lamp off an extension cord papered into the wall. An electrical fire can destroy your perfect renovation. http://www.usfa.fema.gov/citizens/home_fire_prev

Renovate Green

ReHab, the store Josie mystery-shops in *Fixing to Die*, is based on ReStore, a chain of nonprofit home improvement stores and donation centers in all fifty states and Canada. ReStore sells donated new and used furniture, household items from chandeliers to doorknobs, building materials, and appliances at amazing prices.

ReStores are run by the local Habitat for Humanity affiliates. The proceeds go toward building homes in your community and around the world. You get to buy green, build green with donated items, and keep them from piling up in landfills.

Green contractors, decorators and home remodelers enjoy ReStore bargain-hunting. Here are three finds from the Habitat for Humanity's ReStore–St. Louis: (1) a vintage African cherrywood entry door, threshold and art-glass sidelights, (2) heavy-duty construction adhesive, (3) granite, stone, tile and grout sealer.

There's usually a good selection of Sheetrock, countertops, recycled cabinets, light fixtures, door hinges and other hardware.

You can paint green, too. Many ReStores sell recycled Amazon Select paint, which is made of reprocessed high-quality waste paints, in twelve colors, including various neutrals, sage green, light blue and merlot. Recycled paint runs about thirty dollars a gallon cheaper than conventional paint.

ReStores are also a good source for home appliances, including dishwashers, stoves and cooktops. You'll find ReStores in all fifty states here: http://www.habitat.org/restore

Retro-renovators have these shopping tips for ReStore:

If you like it, buy it. That retro cabinet or stove may not be there tomorrow.

If you're looking for items from a particular period — Victorian, say, or midcentury modern — you'll score more finds in cities that were prosperous during those periods. Habitat for Humanity's ReStore–St. Louis is especially rich in Victorian and midcentury modern.

Hot and Cold

My grandma had a massive Coldspot fridge with curved corners and shiny pivot handles I had to pull on to open the door. The white fridge loomed over her kitchen like an iceberg.

That vintage look with modern updates is available from Big Chill. This Colorado company makes retro-style fridges, ranges, dishwashers, even microwaves. Okay, microwaves didn't appear in home kitchens until about 1967, but these sure look old. Big Chill appliances come in candy colors like orange, cherry red, pink lemonade and jadite green, as well as black and classic white.

A 20.9-cubic-foot fridge starts at about three thousand dollars. You can also get an ice maker instead of Grandma's metal ice cube trays. (I sure don't miss wrestling with those.) Thirty-inch stoves start at $4,590, and a retro-looking dishwasher is about eighteen hundred dollars, plus shipping and delivery. http://www.bigchill.com

You can also search garage sales, Craigslist, ReStore, and the classifieds for used retro appliances.

I took a different route, and scored a 1940s Magic Chef from a guy selling old stoves out of his alley garage. The price was cheap. Sure, I had to pay extra to have it wrestled upstairs to our second-floor apartment, but that stove came with extras.

Hundreds of them. Running all over the kitchen the first time I turned on the stove. My bargain stove was bug-infested. That incident was the inspiration for the scalded-roach scene in *Fixing to Die*.

Back to the Future

A Moment in Time Retro Design is an Oneida, New York, company that makes 1950s designs from retro furniture to vintage vinyl, metal banding and laminates in old-school designs like cracked ice and boomerang. http://www.heffrons.com/retro/aboutus.html

Sinking into Vintage

Need a vintage drainboard sink—an old-fashioned sink with a wavy porcelain top that directs the dish-drainer water into the sink? Those old sinks are often porcelain-coated cast iron and rust out.

Good places to look for replacement drainboard sinks are local salvage companies or ReStore. Some people have found them online or through classified ads, but don't buy a rust-prone vintage drainboard sight unseen.

Another choice is Nelson's Bathtub Inc. Nelson's makes fiber-reinforced polymer reproductions of the classic drainboard sink. Nelson's says its vintage-look sinks "are molded from original fixtures." http://www.nelsonsbathtubinc.com/reproductions.html

Backsplash

Ever think about the backsplash—the surface above your kitchen counters and stove? Me, either. But the wrong backsplash can ruin the look of your vintage kitchen. You'll want the right flooring, too.

Finding midcentury modern tile for the backsplash and floor is a time-consuming search, and the tiles can be expensive. Here are few shortcuts:

Modwalls: http://www.modwalls.com/kitchen-tile-gallery.aspx

Ann Sachs: http://www.annsachs.com/

Inhabit Living: http://www.inhabitliving.com/

Mosa Tiles: http://www.mosa.nl/en

Or you save your eyeballs and pop over to Retro Renovation, where Pam has done the work for you. Just search her site for kitchen flooring or backsplash and come up with sites like these: http://retrorenovation.com/category/kitchen/flooring/

http://www.retrorenovation.com/2012/02/16/back splash-tile-fantastic-affordable-new-old-stock-vintage -from-world-of-tile/

http://www.oscarandizzy.com/default.asp

Dated Wallpaper

Elegant 1930s leaves. Cabbage roses like Grandma's guest room. Eye-popping pink and orange stripes from the 1970s. You can find them all at Hannah's Treasures Vintage Wallpaper. The Web site sells authentic vintage wallpapers dating from 1900 to 1970 and has more than six hundred patterns.

"Most rolls contain seventy square feet of wallpaper," the site said. "You can expect to cover fifty-five square feet of wall space after matching the pattern. http://www .hannahstreasures.com/servlet/StoreFront

Bradbury & Bradbury also has vintage wallpapers from Art Deco to the Atomic Age and beyond. http://www.bradbury.com/modernism.html.

Getting Trim

Retro trim gets battered over the years. One source is Eagle Mouldings. http://www.eagle-aluminum.com/Retro-Aluminum_ep_43.html

You've Got Pull

Rejuvenation Lighting & House Parts has classic retro cabinet pulls and knobs, including the boomerang, or chevron, pull. http://www.rejuvenation.com/

House Tours

Don't you love house tours? Especially Internet tours—no driving, looking for a parking spot, trying to plan the best time. You can browse at two in the morning, if you want. Search for midcentury house tours on these sites:

Houzz: http://www.houzz.com/
Retro Renovation: www.retrorenovation.com
Dwell: http://www.dwell.com/

I'll stop with Martha Stewart, the last word in home decorating. She has midcentury home tours here: http://www.marthastewart.com/276999/home-tours

Twisted Retro Wit

Whether your kitchen is brand-new or a retro delight, you'll enjoy the witty sayings of Anne Taintor. Snappy dishtowels tell you to "Make your own damn dinner." Napkins confide, "Oops! I spent the grocery money on shoes again." Magnetic notepads show 1950s housewives cooing over a coffeepot and a saucepan: "Sign up for a life of drudgery and receive these free gifts!" Father doesn't know best in Anne Taintor-land. http://www.annetaintor.com/

Industrial-Strength Help

Total breakfast cereal, Carnation Coffee-Matc, Spam, Tang, and Pop-Tarts were found in most midcentury cabinets. But where do you find the cabinets now?

Carrie—the creator of Josie's kitchen—found her cabinets at unconventional places. That's how she saved so much money. Industry buyers and savvy kitchen designers check MacRAE'S Blue Book to find the product or service they need. The amount of information is staggering. The Web site has more than 1.2 million North American industrial companies with more than two million product listings indexed under some fifty thousand product headings. Anything from kitchen counters to kitchen cabinets can be found online at MacRAE's Blue Book.

Http://www.macraesbluebook.com/search/product_company_list.cfm?prod_code=9001244

Designing Your Kitchen

"If you're going to do the work yourself—or not—check out kitchen design software," Karen Maslowski, a former kitchen designer, said. "It's easy to use, a modified version of the more powerful CAD programs kitchen designers use. I created my own kitchen redesign plan on it when we added on to the house in 1999, and my architect used it almost exactly as it was to draw up the blueprints. The programs have come a long way since then. Here's a site that reviews the different design programs: http://kitchen-design-software-review.toptenreviews.com/

"Places like Home Depot and Lowe's that sell cabinets, countertops and appliances will create plans using your measurements," Karen said. "It is easy to make a mistake when you do your own measuring. I once had a plan that was a half inch too long for the space. Not much you can do with that!"

In the Pink

Amelia has been trying to get my attention. Josie's daughter wants me to tell you that your old pink bathroom is no longer an embarrassment. Now it's chic. A Web site called Save the Pink Bathrooms has a mission to save the shade beloved of First Lady Mamie Eisenhower. The site will show you how to find replacement items for vintage pink bathrooms, or create your own pink powder room. Don't forget to sign the pledge. http://www.savethepinkbathrooms.com/

Just like Lucy and Ethel

Remember the aprons and hair wraps BFFs Lucy Ricardo and Ethel Mertz wore in the old TV show *I Love Lucy*? You can get new vintage styles from Bella Pamella. http://www.bellapamella.com/

Hang in There

Modern decorators call them window treatments, but in midcentury kitchens they were curtains. They'll give your kitchen the right feel.

Contempo Curtains: http://www.contempocurtains.com/retrocurtains.html

Artek has kitchen curtains and other retro items from dishtowels to potholders: http://www.artek.fi/products/abc_collection

Don't overlook JCPenney. www.jcpenney.com.

Country Curtains has midcentury curtains from twenty to two hundred dollars.

http://www.countrycurtains.com/search.do?query= kitchen+curtains

Etsey, eBay, and other online sites are sources for authentic midcentury modern curtains.

Midcentury Cooking

Midcentury brides had *Betty Crocker's Picture Cook Book* on their shelves. You can buy first editions online for between ten and forty dollars, or a 1998 reprint. Newer versions are at http://www.bettycrocker.com/

Another classic fifties cookbook is *The Joy of Cooking* by Irma S. Rombauer. Irma slyly tells new cooks to "stand facing the stove." *Joy* is still in print, and I love the story behind it. Here it is, straight from the publisher:

"Seventy-five years ago, a St. Louis widow named Irma Rombauer took her life savings and self-published a book called *The Joy of Cooking*. Her daughter, Marion, tested recipes and made the illustrations, and they sold their mother-daughter project from Irma's apartment. Today, nine revisions later, *The Joy of Cooking*— selected by the New York Public Library as one of the 150 most important and influential books of the twentieth century—has taught tens of millions of people to cook.... Ethan Becker, Marion's son, leads the latest generation of *Joy*."

But what about those women who didn't conform to the midcentury stereotype of joyfully cooking for their families?

They read *The I Hate to Cook Book* by Peg Bracken. You can buy various versions online and in stores.

"There are two kinds of people in this world," Peg wrote, "the ones who don't cook out of and have never cooked out of *The I Hate to Cook Book*, and the other kind. . . .

"The I Hate to Cook people consist mainly of those who find other things more interesting and less fattening, and so they do it as seldom as possible. Today there is an Annual Culinary Olympics, with hundreds of cooks from many countries ardently competing. But we who hate to cook have had our own Olympics for years, seeing who can get out of the kitchen the fastest and stay out the longest."

Bon appétit!

Read on for a sneak peek at the next
Dead-End Job Mystery
by Agatha and Anthony Award–winning author
Elaine Viets,

Catnapped!

Coming in hardcover from
Obsidian in May 2014.

The bedroom phone shrilled at five a.m.

Phil Sagemont squinted at the caller ID through bloodshot eyes. "Uh-oh, it's Nancie Hays," he said. "This can't be good."

Helen Hawthorne groaned, reached for the lamp, and knocked over an empty wineglass. "I don't want to go to work before dawn," she said.

"We don't have a choice," Phil said. "We're the PIs for her firm." He put the phone on speaker and they both winced at the lawyer's clipped, brisk voice.

"Helen, Phil, I need you in my office now," she said. The lawyer was barely five feet tall and a hundred pounds, but she had the authority of a four-star general. "It's a custody case. We think the husband's violated the visitation agreement. We need you to get her back."

"How old is the kid?" Phil said.

"It's not a kid. It's a kitten," Nancie said. "Five months old."

"A kitten!" Phil said. "Call Animal Rescue."

"This isn't any ordinary cat," Nancie said. "It's a pedigreed Chartreux, a show cat owned by Trish Barrymore."

"The socialite married to Smart Mort?" Phil asked.

"That's the one," Nancie said.

Helen could almost see the little lawyer fighting back her impatience. She kept her dark hair short and practical. She'd be wearing a no-nonsense dark suit, even on a stifling September morning in South Florida.

"Trish says the cat's bloodlines go back to prewar France," Nancie said. "Hers go back a lot farther. She's paying and paying well. That cat is her child and she's upset that her baby has been kidnapped by her husband."

"Oh, please," Helen said. Phil snorted.

"If you two want to keep working for this firm," the lawyer said, "you will take her problem seriously. Trish and Mort are in the middle of a bitter divorce. They're fighting over everything: who gets the two mansions, the Mercedes and the Ferrari, even her great-grandfather's cigar case. It's the biggest headache I've ever handled.

"The only thing they've agreed on is the shared custody of their cat, January's Jubilee Justine. Trish keeps her during the week. Mort picks her up Saturday morning and returns her Sunday night. He gets Justine every holiday. Phil, if I hear another snort from you, you're fired.

"Trish is living at their Fort Lauderdale mansion. Mort's at their estate in Peerless Point, about five miles away. Saturday, he picked up Justine at eight o'clock, like he always does, and took her to his place. He was supposed to return her at seven o'clock Sunday night.

"When Mort didn't show by nine, Trish was frantic. She called the Peerless Point police and wanted them to issue an AMBER Alert."

"For a cat?" Helen said.

"That's what the cop said. When he figured out she was talking about a kitten, he laughed at her. Then Trish made it worse and said, 'Do you know who I am?'

" 'Yeah, a crazy cat lady,' the cop told her.

"Trish said, 'I'll have your job.'

" 'You're welcome to it, lady,' the cop said. 'Have fun dealing with nuts like you.'

"Trish called me and I called you last night. You didn't answer your phone. I lost track of how many messages I left." Nancie didn't hide her annoyance. She expected her in-house detectives to be on call around the clock.

"Uh, we unplugged the phone," Phil said. He sounded sheepish.

"Newlyweds!" Nancie said. "You've been married more than a year. Aren't you over that by now?"

"I hope not," Phil said.

Helen felt her face flush hot with embarrassment in the dark bedroom. She slipped on her robe, as if Nancie could see she was naked.

"Why did they agree on custody of the cat, if they fight about everything else?" Helen asked, hoping to distract the lawyer.

"They care about Justine's welfare," Nancie said. "Pet custody is tricky. The court regards pets as property. Some judges won't order visitation for the other pet parent. Get the wrong judge, and it's like asking if you can visit your ex-wife's couch. The judge will think you're crazy."

"I wonder why," Phil said.

"Take this seriously, Phil. Don't you two have a cat?" Nancie asked.

"Thumbs," Phil said. "He's a great cat, but he's not our four-legged son."

Thumbs heard his name and jumped up on the bed, rubbing his head against Phil's hand. The detective absently scratched the cat's ears and said, "Now that your client has destroyed any hope of police cooperation, you want us to rescue the situation?"

"She's *our* client, not *mine*," Nancie said. "Get your clothes on and come straight to my office. Don't bother making coffee. I have a fresh pot and a bag of bagels. Be here before six. I want you to meet Trish, then pick up Justine at Mort's house."

Helen and Phil showered together to save time, but

there was no romance this morning. They dressed quickly, and Helen poured breakfast for their six-toed cat. "At least you get to eat," she told Thumbs.

He ignored her and stuck his head in his food bowl.

Phil quietly shut the jalousie door. No other lights were on at the Coronado Tropic Apartments. The two-story white art moderne building loomed over the palm trees. Window air conditioners rattled in the soft pre-dawn light. Helen and Phil tiptoed past the turquoise pool. The humid air was so sticky-hot, Helen felt like she was swimming to her white PT Cruiser. She was grateful for the Igloo's air-conditioning.

"I can't believe this," Phil said, as he plopped resentfully into the passenger seat. "Coronado Investigations has solved murders and saved lives and now we're rescuing kittens."

"Hey, it pays the rent," Helen said, starting the car.

"A kitten!" Phil said. "Not even a cat—or a dog. WWBD? What would Bogie do?"

"Take the job to pay for his scotch," Helen said.

She admired her husband's chiseled profile and noble nose as she listened to him grouse about the kitten rescue. She thought her man looked like a rock star, with his long silver hair tied back in a ponytail. He'd certainly performed like one last night.

She smiled at the memory, then turned into Nancie's parking lot. The law office was a neat, stripped-down charcoal cube with an imposing wooden door. The lawyer's silver Honda was parked in back, leaving the best spots for visitors. A sleek black Mercedes brooded under a palm tree by the door. Helen parked next to it.

Inside, past the foyer, she saw Nancie at her desk. Like the lawyer, it was plain, white, and strictly business. A pale blonde in a black lace dress sat in the lime green client chair.

"Bogie would definitely approve of our decorative client," Helen whispered, as they headed for the office.

"Helen and Phil, help yourself to coffee in the conference room and join us," Nancie said. "We'll eat after we talk to Mrs. Barrymore. She's anxious to get home in case Mort returns with Justine."

Helen looked longingly at the basket of bagels and bowl of fruit as she poured two black coffees into white china cups. Phil snatched a grape. Nancie introduced them, and the private eyes took the two chairs across from Trish Barrymore.

"Now, tell Helen and Phil what happened this weekend," Nancie said.

"My baby's been missing almost twelve hours," Trish Barrymore said, and dissolved into tears.

Helen Hawthorne watched the woman's well-bred reserve crumble like a hurricane-slammed seawall. She thought Trish was overreacting, but she didn't seem to be faking her distress. Her blond hair straggled out of its chignon and she'd gnawed patches of pale pink polish off her nails.

"You have to find her," Trish said, her voice unsteady. "Nancie said you would." She quit gulping back sobs and unleashed heart-wrenching wails.

"Now, Trish, I said Helen and Phil would *try*," Nancie said, attempting to walk a line between caution and comfort. "Coronado Investigations has had amazing success, but I can only promise that Helen and Phil will do their best."

"Justine needs her mother," Trish said. "She's all alone."

"Trish, you don't know that," Nancie said. "We believe she's with your husband."

"Former husband," Trish said. "Almost former." She discreetly tugged on the hem of her black lace skirt and crossed her legs at the ankles.

"You know Mort would never hurt Justine," Nancie said.

"No, he loves our baby as much as I do," Trish said. "But she's so tiny, he could step on her. He walks around the house without his glasses. What if he accidentally hurts her?"

"Justine is a smart kitten," Nancie said. "She won't let herself get stepped on. If something should happen, Mort would take her straight to the hospital."

"He's not cruel," Trish said, trying to reassure herself.

"You and your husband are going through a difficult divorce," Nancie said. "You've instructed me to fight for everything—even your silver pickle forks."

"Those belonged to my great-grandmother!" Trish's temper flared like a lit match. "That Tiffany pattern was created for her. Both our homes have been in my family since they were built in nineteen twenty-five. The Barrymores have been social leaders for centuries. Mort came from nothing!"

But Smart Mort knew how to make money, Helen thought. And Trish knew how to spend it. Tastefully. The CPA with the boyish curly hair and lopsided grin raked in so much cash that Trish could turn her crumbling family mansions into designer showcases—and there was still more to splash around.

"That's why he married me, you know," Trish said. "For my name."

"Oh, I'm sure he married you for more than that," Nancie said.

Helen was, too. Even burdened by grief, Trish had style. This morning she was mourning her potential loss in a black lace dress that cost as much as a summer vacation.

"You're beautiful," Nancie said. "You're regal. You serve the community. I've lost count of all your civic and charity boards."

"Twenty-three," Trish said. "Mort's last name was

Draco! Like a *Harry Potter* character! What kind of name is that? He used me. He changed his name to Barrymore."

And painted himself with the dull green patina of old money, Helen thought.

"Custody cases are always difficult," Nancie said. "But despite your differences, you and Mort worked out an agreement for Justine."

"We did it for the emotional well-being of our child," Trish said. "Justine has a brilliant future as a show cat. She's a pedigreed Chartreux. They're known for their smoky gray fur and copper eyes.

"Here. See for yourself." She produced a photo from a slim black clutch. The kitten was a fluffy gray cloud with eyes like new pennies.

"That's January's Jubilee Justine," Trish said.

"She's beautiful," Helen said, though she felt disloyal. She knew Thumbs, her big-pawed white-and-gray cat, wouldn't really mind if she admired another cat.

"Big name for a little cat," Phil said.

"She was born in a J year," Trish said. "Chartreux have their own naming system. Their names must start with a particular letter of the alphabet, depending on the year they were born. I'm lucky 2014 is a J year. I would have hated it if she'd been born last year. I don't like the 'I' names nearly as much."

"So Mort didn't return your cat on time," Phil said, steering her back to the story. "Did you call him when he didn't show up?"

"I gave him ten minutes' grace time," Trish said, "in case he was caught in traffic. Then I called his landline and his cell phone. He didn't pick up. I called every ten minutes until nine o'clock. Then I called the police. They were no help at all. That's when I called Nancie and she contacted you."

"Do you think Mort left town with Justine?" Helen asked.

"No," Trish said. "Our baby doesn't like to fly and long car trips upset her tummy."

"How do you transport your cat?" Helen asked. "In a pet caddy?"

"We each have a Baby Bus," she said, producing a soft-sided carrier that looked like a small black school bus with clear mesh windows and jeweled headlights. "I brought it for you. She won't go anywhere unless she's in her bus."

She handed the bejeweled bus to Phil, who handled it like a live snake. Helen hid a smile.

"Continuity is so important to help Justine transition," Trish said. "We each have a Zen Cat Tower for her to relax."

"What's that?" Helen said.

"It's a graceful mahogany tower, six feet tall, with three levels," Trish said, "plus a sisal scratching pad and a hideaway. It has washable suede cushions.

"Justine has the same toys, dishes, and food, so she will always feel at home. We explained that Mommy and Daddy still love her, but they just can't live together anymore. She seems to be coping well.

"We know we're not the only couple in this situation. Britney Spears and K-Fed and Jennifer Love Hewitt and Ross McCall fought over their fur babies."

"So did another Barrymore," Helen said. "I read that Drew Barrymore and Tom Green had a custody dispute over their Labrador."

"Those Barrymores are no relation. They're *actors.*" Trish spit out the word.

"I guess if you don't have children, you have to fight about the pets," Phil said.

"Tell that to Jon and Kate Gosselin," Nancie said. "The reality show stars had eight kids and still fought over their dogs."

"Please, please bring my baby home," Trish said. "And

if it's possible, try to keep our names out of the media. We've already had too much publicity."

"We'll do our best," Helen said.

"Here are the keys and the alarm code to the house where Mort is living," Trish said. "He didn't change them in case I needed to get Justine in an emergency. Nancie and I agreed it would be better if you picked her up."

"The situation is too volatile at this stage in the negotiations," Nancie said.

"May I go home now," Trish said, "in case Mort's there with Justine?"

"Of course," Nancie said. "You can count on Helen and Phil to handle Justine's return discreetly."

"Our divorce has already had too much publicity," Trish said.

The PI pair waited until the front door closed before they attacked the bagels in the conference room, then carried their plates to the table.

"Is this case for real?" Phil asked, then bit into a garlic bagel slathered with onion cream cheese.

"Very real," Nancie said. "I know you'd rather have a nice, clean murder or civil suit. I don't usually take divorces, but Trish and her family are good clients. Pet custody and visitation rights are the hottest area of the law right now."

"But it's ridiculous," Phil said.

"Not to Mort and Trish Barrymore. If you think they're hard to take, you won't believe the Laniers of Tennessee. When they split, the wife said she deserved custody of the dog because she kept it away from 'ill-bred bitches'—her words—and made sure the dog went to a weekly ladies' Bible class."

"Was it a lady dog?" Phil asked.

"I have no idea," Nancie said sharply. "Mrs. Lanier wouldn't let anyone drink around the dog. Mr. Lanier said he deserved custody because he taught the dog how

aviary.com

to ride on the back of his motorcycle and never drank beer around him. The court gave the couple joint custody. Each spouse got the dog six months at a time."

"I would have bought the dog a beer and given him to someone who wasn't so crazy," Phil said.

Helen saw a frown crease Nancie's forehead. She was running out of patience. "Let's go pick up Justine," Helen said. "What's Mort's address?"

"Forty-two Peerless Point," Nancie said. "Mort and his cat are rattling around in eight thousand square feet of prime waterfront real estate. Call me as soon as you get Justine."

Helen and Phil made the trip in twenty minutes, slowed by morning rush hour traffic. Peerless Point was an enclave of historic waterfront homes. Mort's estate was hidden behind a ten-foot white stucco fence. Phil punched in the code and the ornate wrought-iron gates swung open.

"Wow," Helen said. "This looks like a silent screen star's house." The two stucco wings were perfectly balanced by a series of arches: arched windows, an arched portico draped with red bougainvillea, and a white arched door.

The pale rose brick drive wound through a sculpture garden. They drove past time-weathered marble statues of gods and angels.

"Mort's at home," Phil said. "At least his red Ferrari is. It's parked under the arches."

Helen parked behind it and they walked carefully to the front door.

Phil had the door keys out, but Helen tried the massive wrought-iron handle.

"It's open," she said. "What's the dark red puddle on the door step? Paint?"

Phil kneeled down for a closer look, but the coppery smell and clouds of flies gave them their answer.

"It's Mort," he said. "He's dead."